Manifest
An Alice Meriwether Novel

Beth Dolgner

Redglare Press
Atlanta

Redglare Press
1270 Caroline St. Suite D120-303
Atlanta, GA 30316
www.redglarepress.com

ISBN 978-0-9849156-4-4

Nonfiction books by Beth Dolgner
Everyday Voodoo
Georgia Spirits and Specters

The Betty Boo, Ghost Hunter Series
Ghost of a Threat
Ghost of a Whisper
Ghost of a Memory
Ghost of a Hope (August 2012)

For more information, visit bethdolgner.com.

BETH DOLGNER

**For my grandparents,
Estel and Betty Jane Holloway**

Acknowledgments

Thank you to the test readers who indulge my love of steampunk: Hunter, Morgan, and Emily. I also offer my continued gratitude to my mom Ann for her editing skills and to my husband Ed for his unyielding support. Also, thank you to the Atlanta history buffs who will, I am sure, excuse me for rearranging some things in our city's timeline. And finally, I offer a hearty "Kungaloosh!" to Meriwether Pleasure, after whom my heroine is named.

Chapter 1

"He is going to ask for your hand tonight."

"Is he?"

"Certainly. In fact, Colonel Forbes told your father that his son was going to ask you yesterday afternoon at the picnic. It would have been the perfect opportunity if you hadn't disappeared."

"I didn't disappear, Mama. I told Father I was going to the train station."

"Yes, and he assumed you would come right back. My nerves were in quite a state by the time we heard the carriage returning three hours later."

"The train was late, and I wanted to stay and see Dr. McGuffey on his way to Atlanta." Alice saw her mother's lips stretch into a thin line at the mention of Dr. McGuffey and sighed. Her family—and especially her mother—just couldn't understand her fascination with the New Science. Such amazing inventions were being introduced, and Dr. McGuffey was among the elite inventors. The McGuffey Drilling Machine had revolutionized mining, allowing work to be completed faster and safer than ever before. Dr. McGuffey was greeting people at each train station on his way to the International States and Cotton Exposition in Atlanta, and Alice had been thrilled to not only see him, but to actually shake his hand.

Of course, she had been the only person there to greet him. The people in Fairburn, Georgia, just didn't appreciate the New Science. If it wasn't related to farming or the railroad, no one in the little town cared.

Except for Alice Meriwether: she cared very much. Each month she took the carriage out under the pretense of going for a ride through the country, but her first stop was always the post office. She would pick up the new issue of American Science Journal— delivered to the name "J. Verne," though the postmaster knew very well it was for Alice—before driving into the country where she could read without interruption. The new issue had arrived a week before, announcing Dr. McGuffey's train tour, including a stop in Fairburn.

Dr. McGuffey had been everything Alice had hoped: a middle-aged gentleman with polite manners and a rather shy demeanor, as well as a brass stereoscopic monocle swinging elegantly from a chain attached to his waistcoat.

There weren't many passengers getting on or off the train, and Alice had just a few moments to shake Dr. McGuffey's hand and tell him how much she hoped to see his new, still-secret invention at the Exposition. She didn't add that the chances of her family allowing her to attend the Exposition were low, but Dr. McGuffey's words gave her comfort. "Science comes from the mind and the heart," he had told her. "If you love science, you will find it even here in this small town."

Alice had been so encouraged by Dr. McGuffey that even her mother's stern lecture about leaving home for too long had, so far, been unable to dampen her spirits.

Now, though, as Alice sat at her vanity, her mother's firm expression made her quail. Instead of trying to explain how much it had meant to her to see a real scientist with her own eyes, she nodded her head demurely. "I'm sorry, Mama."

"You should be. You could have been an engaged woman by this time." Mrs. Meriwether's back remained ramrod straight, but her tone softened. "Look your best tonight, Alice. You are going to remember this night for the rest of your life."

"Yes, Mama."

As her mother left the bedroom without another word, Alice turned her attention to her reflection in the vanity mirror. Her lavender gown was brand new, but her corset was already digging into the skin around her hips. "I wish one of the New Scientists would invent a gown that doesn't require a corset," she said.

"What science stuff are you mumbling about now?" Alice's sister had entered the room unnoticed. She was three years younger than Alice—only fifteen—but just as pretty. She had the same delicate features as her sister, set off by dark blue eyes. Where Alice had blonde waves, though, Emma had straight auburn hair.

"I was actually mumbling about corsets," Alice answered. "Mine is killing me."

"Yes, but you've got a tinier waist than anyone else in this town."

"And Mama says envious people never get what they want. It's not my fault I'm smaller than you."

Emma shrugged. "I'm not envious, though I do wish I was the one getting proposed to tonight."

"Well, if I say no, you are welcome to him," Alice said.

"Alice, do be serious! Mr. Forbes is the best-looking man in Fairburn, not to mention rich."

Alice's smile dissolved. "Yes, and sometimes I think he's courting me simply because we're the only other rich family in this town." She paused, unsure how much to tell her sister. "I don't know that he really loves me, Emma."

Emma wrapped her arms around Alice's shoulders and met her eyes in the mirror. "Of course he loves you. You're beautiful, and kind, and witty, and rich. By the time the new decade arrives, you'll be married with at least three children running around the house. Knowing you, science will be the first subject they study."

Alice felt her breath catch. "Don't talk that way. I'm not sure I'm ready for all of that."

"But don't you love him, Alice?"

"I'm told that I do."

"What's that supposed to mean?"

"It means that it's what everybody in our family and his wants, regardless of what I think. I should love him: he's always been a gentleman to me, and you're right, he is handsome. Sometimes, though, I think that I don't feel enough for him. I enjoy my time with Mr. Forbes, but I don't feel…" she searched for the right word, "passionate about him."

"But you feel passionate about airships." Emma's tone was dry, and Alice glanced up just in time to see her roll her eyes.

"Yes, I don't see how anyone could *not* be passionate about them. I really did see one on the horizon last week."

"Too busy looking up in the sky to see the wonderful man right in front of you."

"Now you sound just like Mama."

Emma laughed and squeezed Alice's shoulders. "Well, if you don't want him, let me have him, then. I've got to go finish my toilette so I'll look my best when you tell him no."

By the time Julia, the Meriwethers' domestic, had finished brushing, twisting, and pinning Alice's hair into an elaborate bun, the grandfather clock in the hall was chiming six o'clock. Alice stood up and smoothed her dress self-consciously. She briefly considered claiming to be ill in order to avoid the inevitable proposal.

No, Alice thought, I have to go through with it and say yes, just like they all want me to. Alice shook her head at the thought as she gathered her handkerchief and gloves. She wanted to be the ideal daughter, the proper example to her sister that Mama was always reminding her to be, but at what cost? She was embarking on what her mother promised to be a night to remember, yet all Alice felt was trepidation.

At least Mrs. Meriwether was pleased with what she saw when Alice descended the stairs into the foyer. "Oh, my dear, you do look lovely. Julia has achieved perfection with your hair."

"Thank you, Mama."

"I think you look just like that porcelain doll I used to have," said Emma. "The one whose nose I broke on the hearth when I dropped her."

"It's fortunate I'm not made of porcelain, then," replied Alice. Mama raised her eyebrows at Alice's curtness, but the sound of the carriage pulling up to the front porch prevented her from noting that young women hoping to become engaged should always be pleasant.

The carriage ride from the Meriwether estate into downtown Fairburn seemed to take an eternity even though it was less than a mile, and Alice's nerves grew more tense with every turn of the wheels. She fanned herself with the present Ian Forbes had given her on her eighteenth birthday in May, a dainty fan with a pearl-inlaid handle. It looked fragile but held up under Alice's frantic fanning. Beads of sweat formed on her powdered forehead, and when she finally alighted at The Crossroads Inn, she had to grip her father's hand to steady herself.

The Crossroads Inn was currently the home of a traveling medium, and the parlor in her suite of rooms was the staging area for her séances. Alice preferred the New Science—practical inventions that could change the way everyone lived—but the rest of society preferred spiritualism. Every newspaper, every magazine, and every talkative stranger who came through Fairburn was raving about the Spiritualist

Movement. Women who claimed to be mediums conversed with the dead, charging their elite audiences a tidy sum to do so. Mediums went into trances and allowed the departed to speak through them, tables tapped and danced under the command of unseen fingers, and phantom knocks could be heard ricocheting through the room at a séance. Some of these spiritual adepts even claimed to have evidence in the way of ectoplasm, wispy white tendrils of it draped around them. From the engravings she had seen in Harper's Bazaar, Alice thought that ectoplasm looked a lot like cheesecloth.

As the Spiritualist Movement grew, so did its reach. Finally, the movement had come to Fairburn in the form of the traveling medium. Families from all over the county were coming, paying to sit in on the nightly séances. Only eight people were allowed to participate in each séance, making it the exclusive event that every family wanted to attend. The medium had been in town for three days, and tonight the Meriwether and Forbes families would be the envy of Campbell County.

Outside, the shadow of the Crossroads Inn loomed over Alice. It wasn't the séance that was making her feel faint; the prospect of a proposal from Ian was enough to make her wish she had remembered to put smelling salts in her small beaded bag.

Even as she was still clinging to her father's hand, Alice glanced up and saw Ian Forbes standing on the front steps of the inn. His expression was a mixture of surprise and concern—surprise, Alice guessed, that she had shown up, and concern that she might "disappear" as she had from yesterday's picnic—but even that couldn't mar his handsome features. Ian was a portrait of Old South gentility. He wasn't particularly tall, but he held himself regally, his perfectly tailored gray suit flattering his lithe frame. The late-afternoon sun glinted off Ian's dark blonde hair, which swept back off his forehead and fell in soft curls at the nape of his neck. Despite his high cheekbones and defined chin, there was a softness about Ian's tanned face that seemed to reflect his easy upbringing and gentle manners.

Alice's father leaned in and spoke quietly in her ear. "Be on your best manners tonight. This means the world to your Mama and me." Frederick Meriwether released his daughter's hand and gave her a gentle push toward the approaching Ian.

Ian greeted Alice with a slight bow. "Miss Alice," he said gallantly. His next words, though, were tinged with hesitation. "We certainly missed you at the end of the picnic yesterday. You didn't get any dessert."

"Yes, I know. I'm very sorry I wasn't able to return as I had hoped." Not that she was obligated to apologize, Alice thought, but it was what Mama would have told her to do. Besides, she might not love Ian like she should, but she had known him most of her life and had always looked up to him. If she had hurt his feelings by ruining his intended proposal yesterday, she certainly hadn't meant to. "I hope you had a slice of Mrs. Mitchell's apple pie," Alice continued, turning to a lighter subject. "She must have told me three times how hard she worked over it."

"Yes, and I could tell in every scorched bite," Ian answered, lowering his voice so the others wouldn't overhear. He smiled easily at Alice, and she felt relieved. He offered his arm as she turned to greet Colonel and Mrs. Forbes.

"Good evening, Colonel," Alice said courteously, her father's words reminding her to be the embodiment of a well-bred young lady. "Mrs. Forbes, I am very much looking forward to our adventure tonight."

"Well! Let us hope it is not too much of an 'adventure,'" clucked Mrs. Forbes. "I had it from Lorna Weber that Sarah Baxter fainted during their séance."

The thought of Sarah Baxter's plump form

slumping over during a medium's demonstration made Alice want to giggle, but she bit her lip and furrowed her brow into a look of concern. "Oh, dear," was her only reply.

Mrs. Forbes shook her head as if clearing her mind of the same mental image—albeit without the humor—and gave Alice an appraising look. "You look well this evening, though you do perspire."

"The heat in the carriage has affected me, ma'am," said Alice, fanning herself with even more ardor.

"I daresay you will be cool enough inside the inn. Colonel Forbes, let us go inside at once."

Her husband nodded his consent, taking Mrs. Forbes by the arm to lead her into the dining room of The Crossroads Inn. Once again, Ian offered his arm to Alice. His pace was deliberately slow, and in the short distance from the front steps to the lobby of the inn, Alice could sense that they were being left behind. He's going to ask me now, she thought. Oh, not now, just let me get through supper!

With each agonizing step, Alice waited for Ian to speak, but he remained silent. She felt a wave of relief when they stepped inside the dim lobby of the inn, joining the rest of their party. In addition to her family and Ian's parents, Mrs. Forbes's brother Jonathan White was joining them. Jonathan had traveled the world and was generally considered to be the wildest member of the family. After all, he had visited ten different countries, camped with the natives in Ethiopia, and had never married. Whatever his family thought of him, Alice believed he was the most delightful member of the party. Jonathan only visited once a year, but he was always ready to regale Alice with new tales when he arrived.

The party was shown into the dining room, where gas lamps mounted on the walls burned bright. Large wicker fans hanging from the ceiling were attached to ropes, and servants on one side of the dining room pulled the ropes to fan the diners. The long table for the two families was elaborately set.

Alice followed Jonathan, who gladly pulled out the chair next to his for her. Ian followed and seated himself on Alice's other side, knowing that her attention would be on his uncle for the duration of their supper. It wasn't jealousy Ian felt—he knew Alice's attraction to Jonathan wasn't a romantic one— but a sense of shame on his intended's behalf.

"Ladies should not be so eager to hear about a single man's wild exploits," Ian whispered to Alice. He smiled to soften his correction, but was still surprised when Alice returned his smile.

"I haven't even spoken to your uncle about his latest travels," she answered, "though I believe it would be quite rude of me to not make conversation with him during supper."

Ian opened his mouth, but could find no response to counter Alice's logic.

From that point until the time the waiters collected the empty supper plates, Alice's attention belonged to Jonathan White. Alice gladly told herself that she had simply been polite to the middle-aged man, asking him about news of himself. The question had been all the prodding Jonathan needed to narrate the prior six months of his life. His food sat half-eaten while he regaled Alice with tales of getting caught at sea in a hurricane, wandering through a spice bazaar in Morocco, and—in a whisper—booking a room at a Parisian inn only to discover it was a brothel.

Alice was in raptures over the stories, though she blushed as Jonathan described the "ladies" in Paris. "Ruffles down to their ankles, but not a pair of pantaloons in the whole building!" he told her.

In fact, Alice was so absorbed in the companion sitting on one side of her that she didn't notice the one on the other side rising from his chair as the custards were placed on the table. "If I may say a few words," began Ian.

The table grew silent and Alice turned to him, her smile rapidly disappearing.

"First," Ian continued, "I would like to say that I am glad we can all be here together this evening. On behalf of my family, I can assure you that there is no other family we would rather share the experience of a séance with."

He's going to ask me right now, thought Alice. Suddenly her corset felt much too tight against her straining lungs, and her vision blurred. She reached for her glass of water, grasping at it several times before she was able to get a firm grip. She could see it shaking in her hand as she brought it to her lips, and she hoped that everyone's attention was too fixed on Ian to notice.

"Because of the closeness of our families, I think it is safe to share with you some of our personal hopes and wishes."

Alice looked up and caught her mother's eyes, which were shining with tears waiting to be shed.

"As you know, my mother gave birth to a girl, Regina, who died when she was only seven years old. I was just ten when the scarlet fever took her life. It is our hope that the medium will be able to call Regina's spirit to us tonight during the séance. I am sure you will forgive our selfishness in asking for this." Ian stopped and looked at the heads nodding in approval around him. He sat down and sighed, turning to Alice.

"Miss Alice, I have upset you!"

Alice was too shocked to answer immediately. Despite her anxiety and the mounting pressure of the moment, he hadn't proposed after all! Perhaps her mother had been mistaken, or maybe Ian had changed his mind. Either way, Alice felt like her corset was suddenly much too loose instead of achingly tight. Alice took a deep breath. "No, only I am very touched by what you said."

"Then your family will not mind if we try to contact my sister?"

"Of course not. How could we?" Alice was so relieved that she would be willing to sit through a spiritual appearance from every departed Forbes child, grandparent, uncle, and aunt.

Ian's expression smoothed. "Thank you," he said.

"You are most welcome," assured Alice.

Chapter 2

Following supper, the ladies retreated into a corner of the lobby where they settled into red velvet chairs. The men went into another room to smoke their pipes, and Emma was quick to take advantage of their absence. She pulled her chair close to Alice's and leaned in close.

"I thought for sure Mr. Forbes was going to propose to you just now!" she said.

Alice glanced up to make sure her mother and Mrs. Forbes weren't listening, but they were engrossed in their own conversation. "As did I," Alice answered. "I have never been so nervous in my life."

"I was preparing to be very envious of you, but now it seems I don't have to be just yet."

"Do not be envious of me, regardless. If you keep talking about envy so much, I am going to think that you're the one in love with him."

Emma stiffened at the remark. "I am only fifteen. There is no need for me to be in love with anyone right now."

Mrs. Forbes turned toward the two of them at that moment, commenting, "I hope Ian's announcement at dinner didn't startle either of you. Alice, you surely remember playing with my sweet Regina when you were a child."

"A little, ma'am," answered Alice. "I was two years her junior, but I do seem to remember we played often in the old barn behind your estate."

"Yes, running around like a couple of boys. Shocking behavior for girls in the city, but allowable for country girls such as you were."

Mrs. Forbes then introduced the subject of the medium, assuring the other ladies that this particular woman could summon any departed soul. She listed the deceased relations of several of their neighbors, elaborating how they had spoken through the medium's own mouth. Alice found her attention wandering, her eyes straying to the stack of newspapers and magazines sitting on the small table before them. Underneath the local newspaper, the top of a magazine peered out at her, the words "Steam Powered Science" written across the top. Alice's hand darted out and pulled the magazine toward her, turning the cover as she did so to keep the title hidden from view.

The cover of the magazine featured a drawing of a large device constructed mostly from brass pipes and large cones that looked like they came from a phonograph. The caption underneath the drawing read, "Dr. Hofdort's Mobile Voice Amplification Machine."

Just as Alice began to turn the pages to read more about the machine, a shadow fell over her page. She looked up and saw Jonathan White standing over her, the smell of tobacco swirling around him. "Probably not the best reading for such company," he said in an undertone. Alice could see Ian and Colonel Forbes approaching behind him, and she slid the magazine back into place underneath the newspaper.

"Thanks," she mouthed to Jonathan. He responded only with a wink.

With the party gathered once more, the man standing behind the desk in the lobby came out to greet them, announcing that if they were ready, then so

was "the esteemed, world-renowned medium Madame
Beauregard."

"Right this way," he said, waving his arms
dramatically toward the staircase. Mrs. Meriwether
and Mrs. Forbes went first, followed by their husbands
and Jonathan. Ian motioned Alice ahead of him, and
she lifted her skirts carefully as she climbed the grand
mahogany stairs. They were led to the room at the very
end of the long second-floor hallway, and the hotel
clerk knocked quietly.

Alice stood on her toes so she could get her first
glimpse of the medium. The door opened slowly and a
woman of average height stood there dressed all in
black. Other than appearing as if she were in
mourning, the woman looked quite normal. Her brown
hair was shot with gray, and her wide eyes peered out
from wire-rim glasses.

The voice that came from the woman's lips was
altogether a surprise, though. It was rich and deep, and
she enunciated every word, pausing now and then for
dramatic effect. "Good evening," she began. "I am
Madame Beauregard, seer of the spirit world and
doorway to the afterlife!"

Alice felt everyone around her stand a little
straighter, their collective gasp audible. "Oh, good
night," Alice breathed. Her father responded by
glancing sharply at her, the warning clear in his eyes.

"Come in, come in," the medium continued. "The
spirits have long been anxious to speak with each of
you, and they are becoming most impatient." She
stood to the side and waved everyone into the hotel
suite's sitting room.

The suite was probably a bright, sunny room on
most occasions, but heavy black material had been
draped over the windows and the air was hot. The
wallpaper, a dark silver flocked with red roses, took on
an ominous look against the dark wainscoting. Even
the furniture looked gloomy, the rich velvets turned
drab by the faint candlelight flickering throughout the

room.

A round table was set up in the center of the room, with nine chairs set neatly around it. Madame Beauregard's chair was obvious, its tall, carved back standing out among the smaller parlor chairs. Jonathan seated himself on the medium's left side, the grin on his face indicating that this experience would someday provide entertaining supper conversation. A more somber Mrs. Forbes sat on the other side of the medium.

Alice and Ian took chairs next to Jonathan. Once everyone was seated, eight heads turned anxiously to the medium. She slowly pulled a shawl from her chair and draped it around her shoulders before taking a turn about the room, blowing out candles. The only illumination came from a blaze in the fireplace.

After the bright lights of the lobby, Alice couldn't see anything for a moment as her eyes adjusted to the darkness. She heard a click and a hiss, then the sound of the medium settling into her chair. Madame Beauregard's pale face floated in the darkness, her black-clad body fading into the shadows.

"In this room, the veil between the spirit world and the living will be lifted for a time," Madame Beauregard said. "Do not fear, for the spirits cannot harm you. I will keep you safe. Before we begin, is there anyone in particular you would like me to contact?"

Mrs. Forbes spoke up then, her voice unusually quiet. Madame Beauregard nodded her assent to contacting Regina's spirit, then turned to the others. "Now," she said, "it is time. Please, hold hands to complete our circle."

Alice took Jonathan's hand without a second thought, but she hesitated to offer hers to Ian. Their hands had met briefly on many occasions as he handed her into a carriage or took her hand in greeting, but never had the two of them maintained the contact. His hand was warm as it gently took hers.

"Focus your thoughts on bringing the spirits to us. Think especially of your dear departed daughter Regina," she said, addressing the latter to Mrs. Forbes. "Close your eyes and concentrate. Once the spirits have gathered, I will let you know and you may open your eyes once more."

The dramatics seemed unnecessary to Alice, but she complied with the medium's instructions. The entire group sat there in silence, their eyes closed, as Madame Beauregard began to chant slowly:

> Spirits and saints from beyond the gloom,
> We ask you now, come into this room!
> Friends who were lost, return to us here,
> Speak through me to those who were dear.
> Fill my voice with your words to impart,
> We come in love and pureness of heart.

When Madame Beauregard paused, Alice cracked one eye open, but it was still too dark to see much of anything. She could see Mrs. Forbes's face scrunched tight in concentration. The medium's eyes were wide open, staring over their heads into the darkness beyond the reach of the fire.

"Yes, I can feel the spirits approaching," she said, "but they are shy. Keep your eyes closed! They are not ready to be seen yet."

Still feeling unconvinced, Alice bowed her head to resist the temptation to look around her. Instead, she found herself thinking of Ian's hand, and how strong yet soft it was against her own. Perhaps I do love him, thought Alice. Maybe this is what love is supposed to feel like: a little uncertain, but nice all the same. I spoke of passion to Emma, but what is that? Mama and Father don't seem to be passionate about each other.

So engrossed in her thoughts was Alice that she didn't even hear the medium's call for everyone to open their eyes. A gentle nudge from Ian brought her out of her reverie, and she realized the medium was issuing more instructions.

"…the center of the table. See him there with your mind's eye, hovering just above us."

Alice couldn't see anything there, with any sort of eye.

"I am sensing that his name," Madame Beauregard's voice trailed off, and now she was the one whose eyes were shut tight. "It begins with a 'J.' Do any of you know a man whose name was J-, J-, Jo-…."

"Joshua!" Mr. Meriwether spoke up. "My brother, who died of consumption in 1868. Is it him?"

"Joshua, yes," the medium said. "He says he is sorry to have left you so soon. There was…unfinished business."

"My father's estate. There was much work to be done after his death."

"Joshua says he is sorry to have made you do so much, when he could do so little."

"Do not be sorry!" Mr. Meriwether was looking at the center of the table now, addressing his dead brother. "It was not your fault you contracted consumption. I only wish we could have done more to help you. I wish you could have lived!" His voice broke on the last word, and he fell silent.

"'Do not despair on my account,' he says," continued Madame Beauregard. "'It is wonderful here. I am happy and finally healthy.'"

Mr. Meriwether brought his handkerchief to his eyes and dabbed at them hastily.

"He is fading. Joshua has delivered his message and is ready to move on." Madame Beauregard paused, then stiffened with a gasp. "What! Who is this that comes? Can it be Regina?"

Mrs. Forbes cried out, "My little girl!"

"Yes, your little girl. She is a beautiful angel, even prettier than in life."

"What does she say? Is she all right?"

Instead of answering, Madame Beauregard fell silent. Her head drooped to her chest but her eyelids

fluttered rapidly. When she finally looked up once
again, the gaze she turned to Mrs. Forbes was hazy
and unfocused.

"Mother?" she said, her voice higher.

"My darling!" It was apparent that Mrs. Forbes,
her eyes already spilling over with tears, needed no
further proof that her daughter was truly speaking to
her through Madame Beauregard. Everyone else
seated at the table, though, raised their eyebrows in
quiet skepticism.

"Mother, I have missed you," Madame
Beauregard said.

"Oh, my little girl!"

"Do not cry, Mother."

"I can't help it, Regina."

"Would you like to see me do a trick? That might
make you smile." Madame Beauregard shifted ever so
slightly in her chair, and Alice heard the same quiet
click that had interrupted the silence just before the
séance began.

By now, all eyes were pinned on the medium,
whom they all expected to perform Regina's "trick."
Whether she would caper about, demonstrate a magic
trick, or produce some secrets known only to the
family was unclear, but the anticipation in the room
was so high that the very air seemed to vibrate.
Something was going to happen, and soon.

Click. Thump.

One side of the table rose an inch into the air,
landing again with a quiet thump.

Mrs. Meriwether gasped. "Did that...?" she said,
while Colonel Forbes simply said, "Oh!"

Now eight heads collectively turned to the table
itself, Madame Beauregard forgotten for the moment.

Click. Thump, thump.

The same table leg rose and fell twice more, this
time gaining both height and sound as it landed firmly
on the wooden floor. There was a pause.

Hiss. Click.

The table seemed to dance then, the surface rising and falling in short jerks. The loud pounding of the settling legs echoed throughout the stuffy sitting room. Emma screamed and dropped Ian's and her father's hands to cover her ears. Mrs. Forbes fell into hysterics, crying and rocking back in her chair to wail loudly. Her handkerchief waved about in her hand like a flag of surrender.

Alice's parents and Colonel Forbes were all wide-eyed but silent. On her right, Jonathan was laughing, while Ian stared in shock and embarrassment at his mother.

The only person looking at Madame Beauregard was Alice.

Alice stared at the medium for a few moments before she pushed back her chair and pulled up the burgundy tablecloth that draped to the floor. In one quick movement, Alice leaned forward and pushed her head under the table. She knew she would hear from her mother about this; it was difficult to be ladylike when one's rear end was waving in the air.

After taking a long look under the table, Alice stood up, her face flushed. "It's fake," she announced.

Everything stopped at once. The table stilled with a final *click*, Mrs. Forbes sobbed one last time, then stared at Alice, and even Madame Beauregard lost her faraway look.

"Alice," began her mother.

"No, Mama, this is fake. It's not Regina who's moving the table." Alice spoke quietly but firmly.

"You apologize at once to Madame Beauregard," her father said.

"I will not apologize. It is the truth."

Every Forbes and Meriwether at the table began talking then, but the deep voice of Madame Beauregard overrode all of them.

"Please, do not concern yourselves. This young woman suffers from the inability to see the spirit world. Instead of owning her lack of sight, she instead chooses to attack those who do have a gift. You have all witnessed the appearance of departed loved ones tonight, yet this girl remains a skeptic. I have turned thousands into believers, but there are always lost causes."

Alice gripped the tablecloth in her hands but kept her face and voice calm. "I may be skeptical, but I am not against the idea of spirits. Unfortunately, Madame, all that we have witnessed tonight is a show."

Madame Beauregard gave Alice a condescending smile. "Indeed? Please, young lady, do tell me what you think caused this table to move. As you see, I have been sitting in my chair the entire time, so it was through my channeling of the spirits that it rocked."

"You used a Bergfors Device."

"What?" A hint of doubt crossed the medium's face for the first time.

"Steam builds up in copper tubes, each of which is capped with a piston. When enough pressure builds up, the piston pops up. The device was invented for the Swedish Army: they put targets atop each piston and use them for rifle practice. A Bergfors Device was also used in the haunted boat ride at the Paris World's Fair. You put the pistons underneath the table legs, so every time a piston pops up, the table moves. The clicking I heard was you locking the pistons so they wouldn't move until you wanted them to."

"Oh, Alice, not another one of these inventions."

"But, Mama," Alice began, but Madame Beauregard cut her off.

"Our séance has ended. The spirits will not return with so much animosity here," she said, rising and gesturing toward the door.

Mr. Meriwether turned to her. "We are so sorry, Madame. We are most ashamed of our daughter's behavior, and you can be assured that she will be punished."

The party rose and reluctantly turned toward the door, but Alice stood her ground. "Look!" she cried, pushing the table a few inches from its spot. It was surprisingly light—built of a lightweight wood to make it easier to move, Alice thought—and she found what she was looking for without even needing candles. There, in the floor where a table leg had rested, was a hole about an inch in diameter. The top of a copper piston sat just below floor level.

But surely the hotel would not let anyone, medium or otherwise, cut holes in the floor. Perplexed, Alice looked toward the fireplace. Two copper tubes led out of the floor and into one side of the fireplace, exiting on the other side and disappearing under the floor again. On closer inspection, Alice saw that the wooden floor actually sat a few inches higher than the fireplace hearth. In fact, the floor on the sides of the room sat lower, too, and was covered in rugs that sloped gently up to the floor in the center. The dim lighting had prevented anyone from noticing.

"This is a false floor," said Alice. "Look, it is higher than the carpeted areas. These copper tubes run underneath, and they are filled with water, which turns to steam because of the fire's heat." She pointed down. "Come look, you can see the piston!"

"Do not try to defame me!" Madame Beauregard had been shocked into silence, but she had recovered her voice at last. Turning to the others, she spoke again, "Do not listen to the false claims of this girl. Surely she is possessed by an evil spirit."

Ian walked quickly to Alice and took her arm firmly. "Come," he said, then looked down and paused. "She's right." Ian stooped and looked at the exposed piston, his eyes then scanning the rest of the floor and the fireplace. "Alice is right," he said again. "But either way, I agree that it's time to go." He stood and took Alice's arm once again, but this time his touch was much more kind.

The eight of them hurried out, Madame Beauregard's shouts of innocence following them to the stairwell.

Colonel and Mrs. Forbes went ahead of the rest, calling for their carriage as they entered the lobby. Mrs. Forbes had her handkerchief to her face, only her red, swollen eyes visible.

Mrs. Meriwether rounded on her daughter and spoke quietly but sternly. "You have disgraced us tonight. Never in my life did I expect one of my daughters to behave in such an outlandish manner. Mark my words, your punishment will be severe."

"But, Mama, I…" began Alice, but she was interrupted by Ian, who was still close to her side.

"Perhaps Alice and I will go take a turn in the fresh air, ma'am. I'm sure it will do some good," he said.

Alice's heart sank. Disappointing her parents and facing punishment was bad enough, but the last thing she wanted was a lecture from Ian about how proper girls should behave.

Once they were outside the hotel, Ian proceeded down the front steps and walked a short distance down the wooden sidewalk. He finally paused when they were beyond the hearing of the few people—including his parents and uncle—who were waiting outside for their carriages.

Ian's breathing was rapid and his eyes were shining in the dim light from the hotel's windows when he finally turned to Alice.

He's not just going to lecture me, thought Alice, he's going to mortify me. He is terribly angry.

Somehow, knowing that Ian was angry with her hurt even worse than displeasing her parents. He had always been so kind to her, and the thought of not living up to his expectations made Alice wish she had remained silent during the séance.

"Mr. Forbes, please, let me explain," she said, hoping to curb his anger before it burst forth in a vocal tirade. "When I realized what those sounds were and how the table was moving, I just didn't think. I should not have spoken out as I did. But please, Mr. Forbes, I did not want your mother to believe a lie."

"I know." Ian's voice was shaking. Suddenly he stepped forward and took Alice by the waist. "You saved all of us from a charlatan. You have exposed a woman who would have preyed on thousands more if you had not spoken tonight."

Alice stared at Ian, too surprised at his words to make any reply.

"I have loved you for a long time, Alice, but never more than at this moment. Please, consent to be my wife and let me love you for the rest of our lives."

Alice involuntarily took a step backward, out of Ian's reach. His face fell at the reaction, and Alice realized that his expression hadn't been angry, but amorous. Perhaps, if he could feel so strongly for her, then she could learn to feel the same for him.

Besides, Alice reminded herself, it's what Mama and Father want.

Alice took a deep breath, then stepped toward Ian once more, her eyes locked on his. "Yes, Mr. Forbes, I will gladly marry you," she said, keeping her tone as even as possible. Part of her wanted to rejoice—after all, wasn't it always meant to be this way?—but another part of her was screaming that she was giving up her life and her dreams, exchanging them for a husband, a house, and a family.

"Oh, Alice!" Ian said. He leaned in and Alice thought he was actually going to kiss her. At the last moment, though, he seized her hand and kissed the back of it. "Come, let us tell our families. They will be so happy."

"I don't know that we should tell your mother tonight," warned Alice. "She seems terribly upset."

"Nonsense, this will make her feel so much better."

As it turned out, Alice's warning was pointless. As soon as the newly engaged couple turned to walk back to the hotel, Alice saw Colonel and Mrs. Forbes staring at them, Mrs. Forbes's hand still on the coachman's arm as she readied to hoist herself inside the carriage. Ian and Alice's exchange had not been overheard, but their body language was unmistakable. Colonel Forbes walked forward and shook both of their hands jovially, his smile genuine.

Mrs. Forbes was as dramatic in her joy as she had been in her shock during the séance. She bustled over to Alice and enveloped her in a hug, tears streaming down her cheeks. "You are to be my daughter-in-law?"

"Yes, ma'am," said Alice.

"I am happy for you both! You shall be as a daughter to me, and perhaps now I will not feel the loss of my little Regina so much."

Alice balked inwardly at the idea of replacing the woman's dead daughter, but she smiled anyway. "We shall be family as much as those who share the same bloodline," she said.

It was just what Mrs. Forbes wanted to hear. She finally released her, only to take her hand to lead her inside the hotel. "Come, we must tell your parents. Jonathan, what do you think? You shall have a new niece soon!" Alice followed Mrs. Forbes, Ian trailing behind and smiling happily the entire time.

Chapter 3

Although her parents were very happy—and greatly relieved—to have their daughter engaged, Alice did not escape chastisement for her outburst at the séance. It may have been the catalyst that brought about Ian's proposal, but it was yet another display of Alice's unseemly interest in the New Science.

When Alice woke up the next morning, her mother was sitting in the chair beside the canopied bed. As soon as Alice opened her eyes, Mrs. Meriwether spoke. "You are getting married."

"Today?" mumbled Alice, still half-asleep.

"Do not be ridiculous; of course not. But you are engaged, and you are a grown woman now, Alice."

Alice realized that this conversation was going to turn into something she didn't want to hear, and she snuggled further into her covers as if they could protect her from what was coming.

"It is time you gave up this fascination with science for good."

Alice sat up straight. "Mama, no! It's what I love most!"

"More than your sense of duty to your family? More than your Father and me?" Mrs. Meriwether paused, then said, "More than your fiancé?"

"I did not mean I love it more than my own family. And I do not understand why it is so shameful for you to have a daughter who likes to learn about new things."

"Because it is beyond your sphere." Mrs. Meriwether was indignant. "As a well-bred woman, your concern is to your family. You should be learning how to manage a household, how to plan menus for dinner parties, and how to be a good wife."

"You have taught me many things already," answered Alice.

"In that case, you can handle the planning of your engagement party. I shall oversee you, of course, but we will find out just how ready you are for marriage."

Alice wanted to answer that she wasn't at all ready for marriage, but she remained silent.

"Once again, Alice, it is time for you to give up this silly hobby of yours."

Alice paused before she answered, choosing her words with caution. "If I can continue in my scientific study while proving I can manage a household, perhaps I will not have to give up anything." It wound up sounding like a question, and the look on Mrs. Meriwether's face answered it.

"Certainly not," she said. "Your father and I will not tolerate it any longer, and neither, I am sure, will your husband-to-be. You are forbidden to speak of science or to read about science. We know you're learning about it somehow, though you've been secretive enough. That is deceit, Alice, brought about by your ideas of science. From this moment forward, it is no longer a part of your life."

Having made her declaration and not concerned with any of Alice's objections, Mrs. Meriwether stood. "Julia will be in shortly to get you dressed and ready. Ian will be here after breakfast. I know I need not remind you to behave properly, unlike last night.""It was my 'misbehavior' that finally made him propose!"

Mrs. Meriwether stopped, her hand on the

doorknob. "Ian was going to propose to you last night, regardless of your actions. Just because you allow yourself to be ruled by impulse, does not mean that he does. You would be wise to follow his example."

Once her mother was out of the room, Alice slumped down onto her pillows. She knew that Ian's proposal had been a result of her actions at the séance, whatever Mama said. Mama hadn't been there on the sidewalk to see the barely-restrained passion on Ian's face or felt his hands so firmly holding her waist. If the proposal had been pre-planned, it would have been formal and stiff, like most things in Alice's life. She was tired of ceremony and tradition. What was so wrong with a woman studying science? There was, even now, a woman working at Harvard University on a new kind of airship. Alice wondered if anyone ever spoke to her about behaving properly.

That woman probably doesn't even wear a corset, Alice thought. I bet she wears what she wants, swears when she stubs her toe on a stair, and goes out without bothering to don gloves.

Besides, Alice consoled herself, women could be both smart and proper. After all, she was still a proper young woman, all wrapped up in a corset and yards of voluminous gowns. She knew how to act appropriately, whether at a picnic or in church, and the New Science would not change that.

Alice's thoughts were interrupted by Julia, who entered just then with a bowl of hot water so Alice could wash. "Good morning, Miss Alice," said Julia.

"It has not been one so far, but let us hope that changes," Alice answered.

Alice hurried to wash, dress, and allow Julia to arrange her hair in a chignon, anxious to be at the breakfast table early. She would prove to her mother that her manners were just what they ought to be.

In fact, Alice was the first person to enter the dining room. When her father came in after her, he patted her shoulder and offered a sympathetic look.

"Your mother is quite determined," he said quietly. He glanced behind him quickly, then continued, "I know it is a difficult change, but you have a lifetime of happiness with Ian ahead. Giving up your science may seem like a heavy blow now, but soon you will not even think of it."

I suppose this is supposed to make me feel better, thought Alice, but it really does not. Still, at least Father feels for me, and that is better than nothing. "Thank you, Father," she answered, then impulsively gave him a hug.

Mrs. Meriwether and Emma filed in, and the four of them settled into their customary spots at the table. Alice sat straighter than ever; she'd even had Julia lace her corset extra tight to ensure a tiny waist and immaculate posture. She was so constrained that a piece of toast and a cup of coffee were all she could ingest. Mrs. Meriwether eyed Alice all during the meal, pleased with Alice's feminine appetite and relative silence. Alice appeared to be properly chastised and ashamed of her past behavior.

Alice was still acting like a proper young woman when Ian was shown into the parlor an hour later. She was sitting on the edge of a carved chair, her head bent in concentration on a glove that she was mending. Alice was so intent on making perfect little stitches— and still so absorbed in thought about the one thing her mother had forbidden her to enjoy—that she didn't even realize anyone had entered the room until Ian called her name.

"Mr. Forbes, you're here," said Alice, rising hastily and tipping her head toward him. "Forgive me for not rising properly to greet you; as you see, I was quite distracted by my sewing." And obviously, she added to herself, I am capable of doing these household tasks that Mama thinks are so important.

"There is nothing to forgive. And please, call me Ian. We are no longer just friends," he answered, settling onto the settee next to Alice's chair. "I watched you for a moment. It is quite lovely to watch you mending your own glove."

Alice blushed, wondering just how long he had stood there watching her in what, she had thought, was a private moment. Ian sensed her discomfort and began making pleasantries. "It is a lovely day outside," he began.

"Yes," Alice answered.

"Perhaps later we could take a walk. We can enjoy the green leaves on the peach trees before they are gone for the winter."

"I would enjoy that very much." Alice bent her head to her sewing again, not sure why she felt so shy suddenly. Last night during his proposal, both of them hidden in the darkness, Alice had had no trouble looking Ian in the eyes. Today, though, with the morning sun streaming into the parlor and her shoulders hunched over her sewing, Alice felt timid. Emotions had been high the night before, but today Alice could see that she was as she might always be: sitting at home, tending to tasks, and providing Ian with pleasant conversation.

The conversation was of no importance. The two of them had always conversed fairly easily, and Alice knew that with time and even more familiarity, the words would flow effortlessly between them. It was the idea of always having those conversations while seated at the same chair in the parlor or the same spot at the table. No, Alice quickly corrected herself, it would be the same spots in Ian's home.

"Where will we live?" she blurted out.

"Pardon?"

"When we are married. Where will we live?"

Ian's brow furrowed. "I thought you already knew. My father purchased an estate several years ago in preparation for my marriage. It is about four miles from here, on the other side of Fairburn."

"I should like to see it."

Now Ian smiled. "Instead of going for a walk,

perhaps we could ride out there today. The house is still shut up, but we can walk through the grounds."

"What a wonderful idea. If I am going to spend the rest of my life there, I ought to at least know how it looks." And in which parlor I'll spend most of my dreary, science-free hours, Alice thought.

Then Alice had a different idea. Ian, five years older than Alice, had completed law school not long ago. He had gotten his degree in Atlanta and come back to work as a lawyer in Campbell County. He would be in courtrooms many days, leaving Alice to herself. She could continue to pick up the American Science Journal at the post office, and the only people who might catch her reading it would be servants. And they, Alice assured herself, would not tell a soul since their jobs would be at stake. Alice nearly laughed out loud at the thought of balancing household accounts after perusing articles by New Scientists. What an absurd contradiction!

A hint of a smile must have shown on Alice's face, because Ian looked at her quizzically. "You look like someone who is keeping a secret," he said.

"Oh, it is nothing," said Alice. "I am just thinking of how nice it will be to fix up our own house." Alice's stomach flipped at the lie.

"Then we shall go look at once. I came in my carriage; we can take it to the estate."

Alice excused herself to get ready for the journey across town. When she reappeared in the parlor, she had her fan, her lace gloves, and a parasol. Ian escorted her to his carriage, a lightweight, elegant model that made him look like a racing jockey as he navigated all over the county. With just enough room for two people, Alice's left arm and leg were both snug against Ian's as he took the reins and the carriage sailed forward.

The ride to the estate was pleasant. Alice's parasol kept the sun off her face until Ian slapped the reins and urged the horse into a run. With a cry, Alice put down her parasol and hung on to both Ian and the side of the carriage. Clouds of red Georgia clay kicked up behind them, and the lower branches of the pecan trees lining the drive blew in the carriage's wake.

By the time Ian's estate was in sight, Alice was laughing, the breeze on her face invigorating. When Ian began to slow, she realized that the two-story home they were approaching would soon be her own.

Not my own, Alice reminded herself. Ian's.

It was a sprawling farmhouse, and although it was older, the façade had been remade in the latest style. Wooden latticework lined the eaves of the house, and a tower—like something from a fairy tale castle—had been tacked onto the front right corner. The entire house was painted a pale blue with white trim. It was obvious that a great amount of work had already gone into making the place modern. Ian had been planning his marriage for quite some time.

"Oh, it's lovely," said Alice, who realized with some surprise that she actually meant it. The two-story estate was large but not ostentatious, and a pair of magnolia trees flanked the circular drive, their dark green leaves throwing shade over the wide front porch. Behind the house, a fallow field, bordered by pine trees, rolled gently over the landscape.

Ian brought the carriage to a halt in front of the house and jumped down to hand Alice out. She alighted eagerly and instantly went up the front steps. The shutters were closed tight over the front windows, but she pressed her face to a small opening between two of the slats, hoping to get a glimpse inside.

"There is not much to see inside, anyway," said Ian. "You and I can choose furnishings together."

Alice straightened and turned to Ian. "Can we walk around the outside of the house?"

"Of course, but watch your step; the lawn is far from what it should be. There are rocks and holes hiding everywhere."

Alice took Ian's arm and they set off through the

ankle-high grass. They rounded the turret and walked through the side yard, Ian narrating the estate's history while they walked. When they came to the back of the house, Ian led Alice onto the small back porch. He pointed at a sizable two-story building a short distance away. It, too, had obviously been renovated and painted to match the house, but it was a much simpler style.

"The carriages will be kept in the back of that building. The kitchen is in the front," Ian explained.

"You mean the kitchen isn't in the house? What a long way to carry food for every meal! And what if it's raining outside, or cold?"

Ian smiled at Alice's protests. "They are servants; it's what they do. If they must carry the food that distance, then they will."

Alice frowned at Ian's dismissal of the household staff. "Perhaps we can build a kitchen onto the house, or convert one of the existing rooms," she said.

Ian shrugged dismissively. "Perhaps, though I do not see why we should."

"We could get a Goldman Machine to carry food to and from the house." The words were out of Alice's mouth before she could stop herself. She gasped and put a gloved hand to her lips. "I beg your pardon," she mumbled, as if she had said something offensive.

Ian eyed her curiously. "And what is a Goldman Machine?"

Alice blushed and looked down at the hem of her grass-stained gown. "An invention. It's been around for quite some time now, actually."

"Go on."

"A set of rails goes between two places. A little car sits on the rails with a guide wire connected to it. Steam turns a cylinder that either winds or unwinds the wire, making the car go back and forth. It's the same thing they use for the cable cars at that mountain in Tennessee. Steam winds the cylinder, which turns the cable, which ferries the cars up and down the mountain. The Goldman Machine is smaller and ferries things like trays of food."

Ian looked mildly interested, so Alice continued with more enthusiasm. "There is always a fire in the kitchen, so producing steam would be easy. The cook could put food on the car and send it up to the house without having to carry it. We could have a cover made so the food won't get wet when it rains."

"And who would build it? You, I assume?"

"No, of course not. We would have to hire craftsmen for that. But I could probably draw up the designs."

Ian's expression had changed from interest to amusement to concern in the span of just a few seconds.

"I didn't realize you were so skilled."

Alice paused, knowing that what she said next was going to determine her relationship with Ian. She could feign ignorance and let him believe that her interest in the New Science had waned. On the other hand, she could open up to him and hope that he would be understanding.

I should just tell him, Alice thought. He is going to be my husband and there should be no secrets between us.

And, she realized, if I have Ian on my side, then maybe Mama will give in.

Alice took a deep breath, her decision made. "I have never built any of my designs, but I do have drawings. I started out just copying things I found in the American Science Journal. Eventually, though, I began making changes to them, making the inventions even better. At least, I think the changes would work. I hope someday to have some of my designs turned into working machines."

Ian raised his eyebrows. "I had no idea you were such a scholar. Can I see your drawings?"

"You really want to see them?"

"Yes, of course."

Alice smiled and unconsciously reached out for Ian's hands. "Yes, I would be happy to show them to you! I have never shown them to anyone, and I would so like to know your opinion."

"So your parents do not even know of your drawings, then. How do you keep them hidden?"

"They are underneath the old gowns in my red trunk. I will get them out and bring them outside, where no one will see us. We can look through them in the barn behind our house. Oh, Mr....Ian, thank you. I didn't think you would have any interest in my ideas."

"You are to be my wife. I think it is important that I know all about you, Alice."

Chapter 4

The morning had passed quickly, and once Ian and Alice returned to the Meriwether home, he made his excuses and left for the courthouse, where he was expected at one o'clock. Alice spent the rest of the afternoon in an elated mood, though she had little more than her mending to keep her occupied.

During supper, her mother noticed Alice's bright appearance. "You have been in a happy mood today. I thought, after our conversation this morning, that you would not be smiling so."

"I enjoyed my time with Ian this morning, is all," Alice answered. "I am looking forward to helping him fit up the house once we are married."

Mrs. Meriwether didn't answer; she simply raised her eyebrows and looked at Alice narrowly before returning to her bowl of tomato soup. Alice's expression remained unchanged, but inwardly she was frowning at her mother's little faith in her. Being proper was easy; pleasing her Mama was not.

As they were finishing, Mr. Meriwether wiped his chin with his napkin and drained his wine glass in one long sip. "Well, well, I must be off. I am going to have a brandy with Colonel Forbes. We have business to discuss." Her father looked pointedly at Alice. After her mother's lecture that morning and her father's "business" discussions, Alice suddenly felt very much like livestock at auction, every bit of her being scrutinized so the deal making could begin.

Alice excused herself, also, claiming that her outing with Ian had tired her. She bid goodnight to her parents and to Emma, then retired to her room. Once there, Alice quietly opened the red trunk at the foot of her bed and pulled a wide sheet of paper out from underneath a stack of winter gowns. She cleared the perfume bottles and powder boxes from her vanity and spread the paper there, pulling an oil lamp close for more light.

The airship design wasn't her own, but Alice had meticulously copied the drawing from one of her magazines. Whatever Emma said, Alice knew that she'd really seen one, though it had been miles away on the horizon. Now, Alice stared at the drawing and imagined flying somewhere with Ian. A honeymoon, Alice told herself, or a tour of Europe, bounding from one country to another without ever stepping foot on a train.

Alice had added her own touches to the airship drawing. Along the back panel of the airship's cylindrical balloon was the name "mAIRiwether," and pennants sketched at the bottom of the paper announced the ship's first flight.

Before bed, Alice slid the drawing back into the hiding place where her other drawings, plus every American Science Journal issue she'd ever received, were concealed. She fell asleep dreaming of boarding the fictional ship with Ian, while the captain congratulated them on their recent nuptials.

When Alice went down to breakfast the next morning, her father was absent from the table. Her inquiry about it brought only a curt reply from Mama that he was "too tied up to trifle with breakfast." Alice wondered vaguely if he and Colonel Forbes were still locked in a debate over Alice's value as a good to be traded.

As soon as breakfast was over, Mrs. Meriwether turned to her daughters. "Alice, you will proceed to the parlor immediately. Emma, return to your room or go for a walk. We do not require your presence."

Alice started, but rose and proceeded to the parlor while Emma dashed away with a look of relief. Her father and Ian were already there, standing in front of the fireplace and talking in concerned whispers with each other. They stopped talking as soon as Alice entered the room and turned gravely to her.

The look on the faces of the two men was so alarming that Alice felt faint, and she would have turned and run from the room had not her mother followed her in, ushering her forward with a hasty step.

"Alice, have a seat," Mr. Meriwether instructed.

Alice stood for a moment, too nervous to move. She finally sat down stiffly when her mother prompted her with a hand on her shoulder. From her perch on the edge of the settee, Alice's father had never looked so large and ominous. Even Ian, always so slender and gentle, looked threatening.

"Your drawings and your magazines are gone," her father said. "I burned them in your fireplace while you and your mother were at breakfast."

Alice felt the room spin around her, and she put out a hand to steady herself. She opened her mouth to speak, but no words would come.

After a long silence, Ian spoke. "When your father came to our house last night, I told him of your drawings. He and your mother did not know your obsession went so far."

"And when your father told me of them, I insisted that they be burned at once," Mrs. Meriwether added.

"I am sorry, daughter, but it had to be done," Alice's father finished.

Alice's eyes turned from one person to the next, and she felt betrayed by them all. Her beloved drawings! She had spent hours on each, laboring over the intricate lines while listening every moment for the sound of someone approaching her bedroom door.

Finally, Alice's gaze came to rest on Ian's face. His expression was stoic, and she could see no remorse in his eyes for having told her parents about her drawings. If she had been on the verge of loving him before, then her heart was surely breaking now. She had risked everything in telling him her secret, and he had encouraged her to open her heart to him by pretending to be interested in seeing her drawings.

"This is your fault," Alice said quietly. She could feel tears beginning to run down her cheeks.

Ian never dropped his gaze as he replied, "No, Alice, this is your fault. You were forbidden to pursue this abominable hobby of yours, yet you wouldn't listen. The very morning you were told not to speak of science anymore, you came to me with ideas about adding ridiculous inventions to our house!"

Ian's tone made Alice's temper flare and she stood up, her hands clenched in fists at her side. "Not 'our' house, yours!" she shouted. "I will never live there with you."

"Of course you will. Once we are married, it is where we will live," Ian said, as if speaking to a child who refused to see reason.

"There's not going to be a marriage. Not between us." Alice was crying harder now, her grief and her anger vying with each other. She pulled out her handkerchief and wiped her nose hastily. "I trusted you, Ian. You tricked me into telling where my drawings were."

To Alice's satisfaction, Ian finally looked stung by her words. His voice remained calm, though. "Alice, as your husband to be, it is my duty to see that you are a proper woman. Your parents have always been responsible for you, and now they are turning that privilege over to me."

"You are not farmers dealing a cow!" Alice

turned to her father. "You can't just sell me to him like some piece of livestock!"

"That's enough, Alice." Mr. Meriwether's tone was stern and commanding, and Alice had rarely heard him speak so forcefully. She had never shouted at anyone like she was now, and Alice knew she would be dealing with the aftermath for a long time to come. Her mother's horrified expression was to be expected, but the look of disappointment on her father's face was almost unbearable. He had always sympathized with her, always comforted her by a kind look or a quiet word after Mrs. Meriwether's frequent lectures. Letting her father down was worse than any lecture of her mother's.

"I'm sorry, Father," Alice said, "but I cannot marry anyone who would betray me like this."

"Alice, I did this for your own good." Ian reached out his arms as if he would shake sense into Alice. "Do you think any gentleman would want to marry a woman whose head is so full of these ridiculous ideas?"

"You wanted to marry me."

"And I still do."

"Then you must not be a gentleman."

Ian stared at Alice for a long moment. "As a gentleman, I saw it as my duty to help you be a proper gentlewoman. I was prepared for some struggle, but not like this. If this is how you are going to behave, then my affections have been terribly misdirected."

"Then we are agreed: our engagement is over." There was anger in her voice, but once the words had been said, remorse replaced all other feeling. With a sob, Alice turned and fled the room, stumbling up the stairs to her bedroom. She barely heard the cries from her parents and Ian as she ran.

Once she was safely inside her room, Alice flung herself onto her bed and buried her face in her pillow. Her body shook with the force of her sobs, and her lungs burned as she heaved for breath.

Not once did anyone disturb Alice's grieving. There were no footsteps in the hallway, and there was no knock at the door. She had at least expected a furious tirade from her mother, but there was neither a fresh assault nor a flag of truce from any of them. She paced back and forth all afternoon, interrupted only by fits of crying.

Eventually, Alice cried herself to sleep, still fully clothed and lying facedown on her bed. She woke up sometime in the middle of the night, her throat dry but her cheeks still damp. Someone, probably Julia, had been in to light the oil lamp on her vanity, but otherwise there was no sign of visitors.

Alice pulled herself into a sitting position and sighed. She hoped morning might never come: the thought of facing everyone at breakfast was far too intimidating. What would her parents say to her? And how could she ever face Ian again? Even if she tried to avoid him, Alice knew that their paths were bound to cross, when society in a place like Fairburn was so limited.

More to relieve her mind than her physical comfort, Alice busied herself by changing into her nightclothes. It took much longer without Julia there to help, but eventually Alice was free of her gown and corset. With her white linen nightdress on, she sat down in front of her vanity to brush her hair. Most of it had been pulled out of the chignon during her crying fit, and she winced as she dragged the brush through tangles.

Finally, Alice gave up and pushed the brush away from her. She cupped her chin in her hands and gazed at her reflection in the mirror. The flicker of the lamp's flame only served to highlight the shadows beneath her swollen eyes.

Knowing that sleep was nowhere near, Alice opened the bottom drawer of her vanity where she kept all of her drawing and writing papers. It was empty! Every sheet of paper, even the fine stationery she had gotten for Christmas, was gone. Her pens and pencils had been taken, too. When her father and Ian had burned her drawings, they obviously wanted to ensure that she didn't replace them with new ones.

The realization brought on a fresh flood of tears. Alice put her head down on the vanity and remained there until dawn. As the new day began to brighten the room, Alice rose and returned to bed. The tomorrow she had been hoping to put off had come after all.

Chapter 5

Alice lay in bed and watched as the rising sun moved the shadows throughout her room. Julia never came in to get her dressed, so Alice stayed where she was. Too exhausted to rise and too wretched to sleep, she continued to stare blankly at the walls of her bedroom. She felt as if all of her emotion had been spent, the anger and grief replaced by a depressed lethargy.

Sometime after the grandfather clock in the hall struck nine, there was a firm knock on her door. Without waiting for an answer, Mrs. Meriwether entered. She appraised Alice's appearance with a stern eye before speaking curtly. "You were not at breakfast this morning."

"I don't think I shall ever eat again," answered Alice.

"You will, but for now perhaps your time is better spent here, where you can meditate on your behavior."

"I feel ill."

"You begin to feel how deeply you have disgraced yourself and this family."

Alice wanted to answer that she felt ill because she had spent the entire night crying, and that she was not the disgrace, Ian was. Her fiancé had betrayed her and driven her to tears! How could it be that a man whose company she had so enjoyed one morning could turn into such a villain by the next? Alice knew that her mother would never sympathize with her, though, so she simply replied, "Yes."

"Good. I will have some tea brought to you, and something to eat. You may not think you want it, but you will be hungry soon enough." Without so much as a kind word of encouragement, Mrs. Meriwether left Alice alone again.

As promised, Julia came in soon after with a tray of tea and a few slices of bread. Alice still refused to eat, but she sipped at the tea until sleep finally called her.

When Alice awoke, it was well past lunchtime and her stomach was growling. She gave in and ate the bread, then settled back into bed once more. As the evening came, she heard heavy footfalls approach her bedroom door, but they stopped and returned down the hallway. Alice wondered if her father had hoped to console her but had decided against it.

Alice slept fitfully that night, but after being shut up in her room the entire day before, she was ready to rise when morning came. Though she did not look forward to going downstairs, she did, at least, want some variety from being a recluse. Alice allowed Julia to choose her clothes, not caring what she looked like. Her reflection in the mirror showed a haggard face that Alice had never seen before, and she doubted that the color or style of her gown would make any improvement.

Breakfast was a solemn affair. Mr. and Mrs. Meriwether talked about household business, giving Alice only a precursory "good morning" when she walked into the dining room. Emma, who knew her sister's engagement was off but didn't know the full details, sat silent, too timid to speak when tensions were obviously so high.

The day continued with little enthusiasm for

Alice or the rest of the household. Alice busied herself with a book or a piece of embroidery most of the day, but there was no conversation, and she had a difficult time keeping her mind on anything. Neither of her parents brought up her behavior of two nights ago, nor did they mention the broken engagement.

The routine continued for the remainder of the week. Alice spent her days either eating in the dining room or sitting in the parlor. She left the house only once, and that was to take a walk. Instead of heading down the road, though, she walked around the edges of the pasture behind the Meriwether estate. Alice was too afraid to walk along the road, where she might accidentally run into Ian.

Seeing Ian again, though, was inevitable. On Sunday, as the family prepared to go to church, Alice hoped she might be excused but knew her wish was in vain. She actually suspected that her mother wanted Alice to face Ian as some sort of punishment.

Before stepping out the front door, Alice pinched her cheeks to bring some color to them, but her wan appearance was little improved. She didn't feel penitent, but she certainly looked the part.

Church was not as bad as Alice had feared. The Forbes family always sat in the pew directly opposite the Meriwethers, but Alice kept her gaze straight ahead so she wouldn't risk making eye contact with Ian. She had glanced at him briefly when her family arrived, and that was enough to make her anger flare up again.

When services were over, Alice stayed behind her father, but he paused to speak to Colonel Forbes. Alice kept her head bowed, but she was forced to look up when Colonel Forbes greeted her with stiff civility. Alice mumbled a reply, inclined her head politely, and excused herself. When she turned to leave, though, she ran right into Ian, who had been trying to escape down the aisle, too.

"Oh, pardon me," Alice said, flustered. She

continued past Ian, her shoulder brushing his in her
haste. Ian made no reply and no attempt to stop her,
but as Alice walked out into the sunshine, she knew
there were fresh tears sliding down her cheeks. She
had looked at Ian only briefly, and in that time she had
seen deep concern and sadness in his eyes. Ian had
betrayed her, surely, but Alice had retaliated by
shouting at him, calling his character into question,
and breaking off their engagement. She could have
spoken to him rationally, tried to make him understand
her own feelings in a proper, genteel way. Instead, she
had turned on him just as he had on her.

No matter how angry she was with Ian, seeing
that look in his eyes and knowing it was her own fault
made Alice even more depressed. She had always tried
to please others, often at the expense of her own
wishes, and hurting someone's feelings was
inexcusable. She considered writing Ian a letter to
offer an apology before remembering that Ian and her
father had removed all of her writing instruments.

Instead, Alice continued in her sad routine of
eating, silently working in the parlor, and taking
solitary walks around the pasture. After another week
of such behavior, Alice's mother broached a new topic
one day as the three Meriwether women were working
on embroidery.

"I think a change of scenery might be good for
you, Alice," Mrs. Meriwether began.

"What do you mean?"

"I mean that you have been like a ghost in this
house since...well, for two weeks, and it can't
continue. It is time you started acting like a young lady
of good breeding again. And your father and I believe
it is time you really learn how to be a responsible adult
with household duties."

Alice froze, her needle poised above her white
linen. Several scenarios flashed through her mind at
once: father has arranged a marriage for me, they're
sending me off to be a servant somewhere, or they're

packing me off to a nunnery. Forcing her voice to sound calm and disinterested, Alice asked, "What did you have in mind, Mama?"

"My sister wrote to me recently. Her husband's brother is in need of a governess to watch after his two children. I wrote to her several days ago to enquire whether the position was still open. If it is, you shall be their new governess."

Alice was stunned. Though not as bad as any of the visions she'd had, she wasn't sure how she felt about her mother's willingness to ship her off to another family. Though she knew her aunt's husband, she had never met any of his family and did not know anything about them. "How far away do they live?"

"The Highcroft family lives in Atlanta."

Atlanta! Where there was an airship port and the International and Cotton States Exposition to look forward to! Alice put her head down, biting her lip to keep from smiling. Mrs. Meriwether would be suspicious if she saw Alice's joy at the proposal. Thankfully, Mrs. Meriwether mistook Alice's posture as one of fear and doubt.

"Now, Alice, do not be upset. It is not that far away, and they are a respectable family. You will be well taken care of there."

Alice looked up. "Yes, Mama," she said. "I think it is a good idea. A new place might be just what I need. I would very much like to be a governess."

"Can I come visit you in Atlanta?" Emma interjected.

"Only if your father escorts you," Mrs. Meriwether answered. She turned to Alice again. "You must behave like a proper lady if you go to Atlanta. You will have the charge of two children, and you will be responsible not just for their physical comfort and activity, but for their education, as well. You must be a perfect example to them, and you must be a perfect tenant in Mr. Highcroft's household."

"I will, I promise." Alice realized that planning

her engagement party was supposed to have been her chance to prove herself to Mama. This measure was far more drastic, but much more palatable to her.

That night, Alice lay awake for hours. Finally, though, after two weeks of tears and depression, Alice's wakefulness was due to excitement. Even if she never uttered a word about the New Science, she would still see it in use in Atlanta. She would be able to revel in the inventions around her, even while Mr. and Mrs. Highcroft proclaimed her to be a sweet, well-mannered governess for their children.

That was, Alice reminded herself, only if the position were still open.

The thought brought on some anxiety, and every day for the next three days, Alice rushed to the door if any letters arrived. Finally, on the fourth day, she arrived home from a walk and entered the parlor just in time to see her mother tearing open a letter.

Chapter 6

"Sit down, Alice, as this will concern you," Mrs. Meriwether said. "It is from Mrs. Highcroft in Atlanta."

Alice removed her hat and sat down anxiously, her fingers knotting and unknotting the hat's long green ribbon. She tried to determine the letter's contents from her mother's expression, but found nothing encouraging there. When she had finished perusing the letter, Mrs. Meriwether uttered a short, "Well!"

Unable to wait any longer, Alice said, "What does it say, Mama? Am I to be a governess?"

"You are. They will expect you in Atlanta on Monday. We must have Julia begin packing your things."

"Thank you, Mama! I will make you proud, I promise." Alice could barely contain her excitement. Not only was she going to Atlanta, but she would be leaving on Monday, just four days away!

Unmoved by her daughter's vow, Mrs. Meriwether still spoke sternly. "Keep in mind that this is not a privilege you are being afforded; we are not sending you there for your own amusement. This is a great responsibility."

"Yes, Mama."

"Now go tell your father. He is in his study."

The rest of the house took the news of Alice's departure much differently than her mother had. Mr. Meriwether had always been partial to Alice, and while he was happy for her, he was sad to have his daughter going "so very far away."

Emma was the only person in the family who came close to sharing Alice's enthusiasm. The night after the letter had arrived, Emma came into Alice's bedroom and sprawled on the bed, listing all the things they would do together when she came to Atlanta to visit.

"Don't forget, Mama said that Father has to escort you if you come to visit," said Alice, who was already sorting through her jewelry and hair combs, making three piles: what she couldn't live without, what could stay, and what she would pack if there was extra room.

"I don't care. Once we get to Atlanta, I'm sure he and Mr.—What is it?—Highcroft will smoke cigars and drink brandy together, leaving us to come and go as we please."

"Atlanta won't be like Fairburn, Emma. It's a much bigger city, with a lot more people. I doubt either of us will be going out without a gentleman escorting us."

Emma shook her head. "I am sure that women who live in Atlanta go out very often by themselves. They do not need gentleman escorts, and neither will we."

With the various emotions of everyone in the house, the flurry of packing, and trying to absorb the endless stream of child-rearing advice from her mother, the time leading up to Alice's departure went swiftly.

On Sunday morning, the day before she was to leave, Alice walked into church with her head held high, feeling that she could face Ian without shame.

During the sermon, she looked over at him and was surprised to find his face turned in her direction, staring boldly at her.

As she followed her parents out of their pew and down the aisle following the service, Ian purposely came out and joined her. "May I speak with you?" he asked.

"Of course," Alice said, her face showing confusion at Ian's sudden approach.

As if they were still courting, Ian took Alice's arm in his and led her outside and into the graveyard. Once they were out of view of most of the parishioners, Ian stopped walking and turned to Alice.

"You are going to Atlanta," he said.

"Yes."

"I assume you made this decision since…because other arrangements did not work out as planned." Ian's earlier boldness was turning into awkwardness.

"Mama made the decision for me," said Alice, "but I think it will be good for me."

"Perhaps. Alice…" Ian paused and looked away, as if the right words were hiding under a tombstone. "Take good care of yourself," he finally said. "I feel as if your going away is partially my fault. I wouldn't be able to forgive myself if something happened to you in Atlanta."

Now it was Alice's turn to feel awkward. "That's very kind of you, but I will be under the care of a very good family. Besides, you have no reason to feel at fault." Actually, Alice thought, you do, but I'll forgive you since it means I get to be in Atlanta.

Ian nodded and took Alice's arm again. It felt so comfortable to walk with him that way, so easy being side by side. Ian went so far as to escort Alice all the way to her family's carriage. Once he handed her in, he leaned casually against the door. "Goodbye, Alice. I hope to hear good things from the letters you will send your Mama."

"She will be very happy to share any news with

you," Alice answered, surprised that Ian would care what news she sent of herself. "Goodbye."

Saying farewell to Ian was the first of many partings for Alice, though none of the others held such a mixture of regret and relief. Emma, on the other hand, spent half of Sunday night in Alice's room, torn between lamenting her sister's departure and celebrating her own eventual visit to Atlanta.

When Monday morning arrived, breakfast passed as usual. Instead of retiring to the parlor afterward, though, Alice returned to her room to don a simple brown traveling dress, a matching hat, and a new pair of kid gloves. As Julia helped Alice dress, she remarked, "I don't know what you'll do without me, Miss. You'll have a time of it getting yourself dressed and ready. Who will do your hair?"

Alice smiled. "I may have to do my own hair. I will only be a governess, and I doubt I will get much attention from any of the domestics. I'll miss you, Julia."

Julia blushed and quickly returned to buttoning Alice's dress, but she was smiling, too. "Sure you will, Miss. You'll be missing your Julia every morning when your corset is loose and your hair a tangled mess. There, you're buttoned. Now let's get you downstairs. Your train leaves in just two hours."

Downstairs, Alice found a stern mother and a somber father. Mrs. Meriwether was still firing off advice, sounding very much like a grave preacher. Mr. Meriwether, on the other hand, was quiet.

The endless lecturing continued until Julia came in and announced that Alice's trunks were loaded. Envisioning her clothes, hats, and all of her indispensable personal items piled up on the back of the coach gave Alice a sudden thought: I am not just going to Atlanta. I am leaving my home.

With a sigh, Alice looked around her at the parlor, striving in those last few moments to remember every painting, the pale green of the walls, and the

way the chairs and settee were arranged to
accommodate close conversation.

Mrs. Meriwether ceased her lecturing once they
were in the carriage, but she replaced her homilies
with details. "Don't forget, you'll be picked up at the
station by Mr. Frederick, the coachman. He'll meet
you at the front of platform one. He will see to it that
your trunks are loaded into the carriage. Once you get
to the Highcrofts' house, make sure you change into
your lavender gown for supper. I want you to look
your best when you meet the entire family."

By the time they reached the station, Mrs.
Meriwether had practically outlined every outfit and
every proper phrase that Alice should use in her first
week. Her head spinning, Alice tried to concentrate on
the most important thing: meet Mr. Frederick at the
front of platform one.

The eleven-thirty train to Atlanta was late, so
Alice found herself standing around impatiently along
with the rest of her family. As they waited, Mr.
Meriwether moved next to his eldest daughter.

"You'll want to keep a diary of your stay in
Atlanta, no doubt," he said quietly. As he spoke, Alice
felt him pushing something into her hand. She glanced
down and saw her little blue pocket book. It had only
contained a few drawings, and Alice wondered if they
were still there, or if her father had torn them out and
burned them with the rest.

"Now put it away; you don't want to lose it,"
advised Mr. Meriwether, his eyes glancing quickly
toward his wife, who fortunately was looking away.

Taking the hint, Alice slid the small book into her
handbag. "Thank you," she said quietly, then grinned
suddenly. Mr. Meriwether returned her conspiratorial
smile.

The train finally pulled into the station at noon,
half an hour behind schedule. Only a few people
alighted, and soon it was Alice's turn to board. She
turned first to Emma and gave her a hug and a

farewell. Mr. Meriwether was next, and as they embraced, Alice whispered another sincere "thank you" for the book. Never had Alice thought she would be so grateful for a bundle of blank pages, but to her, it was a sign that her father was on her side. Or, at least, he was not as disapproving as her mother. It was a small victory, but it felt good nonetheless.

Finally, Alice turned to her mother, unsure what to say. She opened her mouth to speak, but Mrs. Meriwether began speaking first. "Write us when you arrive, and let us know about your journey and what you think of the Highcroft family," she began. "And tell me what sort of house Mrs. Highcroft keeps and how many servants they have. Since we have never visited them, I am quite curious."

"Yes, Mama," replied Alice.

"Well, goodbye, dear." Mrs. Meriwether gave Alice a quick embrace. "Be a good girl, remember your manners, and don't do anything unfit for a proper lady."

With those last words of advice and warning, Mrs. Meriwether dismissed her daughter. Alice presented the porter with her ticket and was on board in just a few minutes. She had traveled by train before, but always with her family. It felt odd to settle into a seat next to a stranger, a much older woman who was dozing.

Alice leaned over the woman to peer out the window at her family. Mama stood placidly, while her father and Emma waved and blew kisses. Alice waved in return, and did not look away from their faces until the train moved forward, carrying them out of sight.

The train ride was hot but not terribly arduous. Atlanta was only an hour away, and Alice was content to watch the scenery as the train rolled along. They stopped several times, each town a little bigger than the last as they neared Atlanta. The woman next to Alice continued to sleep, though Alice had the fleeting thought that the old woman might be dead, she was so silent and still. A quiet snore finally dispelled those ideas.

The number of houses lining the railroad track began to increase, until there was a nearly steady procession of them. The track split into two, then became four. Boxcars sat idly on side tracks in a giant shipping yard, and on other spurs engineers backed their engines up to connect to their cargo.

Just as the city began to come into view, the train went underneath a bridge. When the train re-emerged, brick warehouses lining the tracks prevented Alice from getting a glimpse of Atlanta.

The porter entered the car, shouting, "Atlanta! All passengers must exit. End of the line. Atlanta!"

There was a general flurry of movement as the other passengers began to gather their small bags. Mothers collected children who had been running in the aisle, and gentlemen donned their coats.

Alice glanced around her to make sure she had everything. She tied her hat securely under her chin and slid the drawstring of her handbag over one wrist. Finally remembering the pocket book from her father, Alice drew it out with anticipation. She cracked open the book and there, in the first few pages, were her drawings. They were just copies of the Bergfors Device, and although they brought back bitter memories of Ian's part in her disgrace, Alice was pleased that her father had let them remain. These pages, Alice told herself, would never, ever be seen by anyone else, nor would she even tell anyone about them, no matter how trustworthy they seemed. She would not be so foolish twice.

The train gave a final lurch and came to a halt. The woman sleeping next to Alice awoke with a start, glancing first at Alice, then out the window. The activity that followed was some of the busiest Alice had ever seen, as everyone scrambled up into the aisle and headed for the door at the front of the car. Alice waited as the first passengers alighted and she could

walk down the aisle without being jostled by the
crowd. The platform was just as busy and congested.
Porters were shouting directions about the luggage,
which was being unloaded with hasty thumps and
bangs. Everywhere friends and families were greeting
each other or calling out names in an effort to find one
another in the mass of people.

Alice pushed through the crowd, feeling very
small and alone. If Atlanta is going to be like this, she
thought, then I will become quite claustrophobic!

A shadow fell over the scene. Alice glanced up
and saw the most magnificent sight of her eighteen
years: an airship! The vessel was flying at low altitude,
coming to or from the airship port, no doubt, and it
chugged slowly past the train station.

The ship looked like an older model—a Fairlie
S100, Alice remembered—with a wooden structure
slung below the cylindrical balloon by a series of
cables. People sitting on the open-air deck peered
down at the city below them. The engine, Alice knew,
was housed below the deck, and the steam was
channeled through an exhaust port in the rear of the
ship. The balloon itself was a light brown, but the ship
was painted lavender with red trim. Wide red letters
written along the side said, "Airship Tours."
Underneath were smaller letters proclaiming, "See
Atlanta from the Sky!"

A tour by airship! Alice was so mesmerized that
she began to walk in the direction of the ship, as if she
could follow it across town. She paid no attention to
the people moving around her, occasionally pushing
past in their hurry. How could all these people be so
oblivious to the fantastic machine above them? Alice
wondered. As the ship turned and moved away from
the station, Alice glanced at the rest of the sky and got
her answer. Three more airships hung in the air. One
of them was much larger and had the sleek lines of a
newer model, though it was so high in the air that
Alice couldn't tell which model it might be. The other

two were of medium size, but featured completely enclosed passenger areas. The Fairlie was perfect for a tour of the city, but these other ships were obviously for transporting passengers between cities. There was a port in Chattanooga, Alice knew, and one had just opened in Savannah.

Alice probably would have continued to stare at the sky if it weren't for the distinct sound of her name being called. The man's voice came from somewhere in front of her. Alice shook her head, as if to clear it of the airships. Of course, she thought, all I had to do was meet Mr. Frederick, and I've already messed that up!

Alice raised her hand in a wave. "Mr. Frederick!" she called.

Mr. Frederick's bulky frame moved through the crowd with surprising grace, and soon he was standing in front of Alice. He removed his hat and gave her a polite nod. "Miss Alice, I'm John Frederick. Pleased to meet you."

Alice returned his greeting and apologized for not meeting him sooner, but Mr. Frederick laughed. "No worries, Miss," he said. "I'm sure this is a lot to take in for a girl from a small town. But if you're ready, they're loading your trunks onto the carriage now."

Alice answered in the affirmative and followed Mr. Frederick up a long flight of stairs and into the terminal itself. The crowd was beginning to thin, but Alice had little time to look around her as they continued out the wide front doors and over to the curb, where an open carriage sat waiting for them.

"Is all your luggage here, Miss Alice?" Mr. Frederick asked.

"Yes, I just had the two trunks," Alice answered. She climbed into the carriage using a granite carriage step positioned at the curb and immediately pulled out her fan. The busy road was dusty, and a haze hung over everything.

As Mr. Frederick guided the horse through the streets, he kept up a narration of the sights. "We're on

Peachtree Street right now. This is downtown, where
most of the big businesses are. This area was all rebuilt
after the war. The old wooden buildings were burned
when Sherman came through. You know that, right?"

"Yes, sir." Alice was leaning over the side of the
carriage in her eagerness to take it all in. People were
everywhere: hurrying down the wooden sidewalks,
crossing the street, and bustling in and out of shops
and businesses. Most of the people were men, still
wearing their waistcoats and jackets despite the
lingering heat, though here and there Alice caught
sight of a woman conducting business of her own.

They left the congested downtown behind and
wandered through several small neighborhoods and an
industrial area full of huge brick warehouses. After
they passed underneath more railroad tracks, the
houses grew in grandeur. Two-story houses painted in
bright pastels lined the streets, each one boasting
delicate gingerbread trim. The style was the latest
fashion for homes, the very definition of modern
elegance.

"This here is Grant Park," continued Mr.
Frederick. "The family just moved out here about two
years ago. The house is very modern, and the
neighborhood is quite nice. You can go for a stroll
here without having to worry about pickpockets and
the like. I think you'll feel like you're back in a small
town."

Oak and magnolia trees overhung the streets, and
they passed few other carriages. The lawns were all
trimmed and neat, and a smattering of late-summer
flowers bloomed in gardens and in huge planters on
the wide front porches. Unlike downtown, the air was
thick and humid, but not dusty. An occasional breeze
stirred up the leaves in the trees, and Alice was finally
able to let her fan lay idle in her lap.

Mr. Frederick made a couple of turns and shortly
pulled up in front of a pale blue house. A white picket
fence lined the yard, and dogwood trees flanked the

short walk up to the front porch. Mr. Frederick helped
Alice out of the carriage, and she paused to absorb the
lush lawn and ornate house in front of her. The
gingerbread trim was white, and it framed a second-
floor balcony. The house was smaller than the
Meriwether estate, but its opulence was far greater. A
stained-glass window was placed above the oversized
oak front door, which was thrown open as Alice
watched.

    Two children came running out of the house and
up to Alice as if they had known her all their lives.
Among their excited babble Alice could make out
"She's here!" and "Come on!" Laughing, Alice let the
girl and the younger boy lead her by the hand up the
stairs and into their home.

Chapter 7

"I see you met Margaret and Jasper already," said the woman standing in the foyer. As Alice's eyes adjusted to the comparably dim interior of the house, Mrs. Highcroft's form came into focus. She was tall and dignified, her starched collar looking perfectly comfortable on her long neck. Her day dress was simple but made in an ocher linen that complemented her brown hair and green eyes. Alice noted Mrs. Highcroft's sizable emerald ring and matching brooch. Neither was large enough to be gaudy, but they certainly bespoke the family's wealth.

"You must be Mrs. Highcroft," said Alice, dipping her head.

"And you're Alice," Mrs. Highcroft responded warmly. Instead of returning the formal greeting, she extended her arm and shook hands with Alice. "Your mother speaks very highly of you, as does my husband's brother and sister-in-law. I'm sure you'll be a splendid governess. You are very welcome here."

"Thank you. I certainly appreciate your faith in me." There was sincerity in Alice's words: after enduring her own mother's stern affection, Alice wondered how different life in the Highcroft household would be for her.

"Miss Alice, can we show you our nursery?" The youngest one, Jasper, was quickly at Alice's side, tugging on her hand.

"In a moment," responded Alice. "Perhaps you can show me where my room is first."

"Your room will be at the back of the house, next to their nursery. It's upstairs to the right," said Mrs. Highcroft. "I'm sure you are anxious to refresh yourself after your trip. Take your time. Katie, our housemaid, will put the children down for their naps, and when you're ready we'll discuss everything over a bite to eat on the front porch."

"This way, Miss Alice, come on!" Now it was Margaret who was pulling Alice forward. She followed gladly, ready to wash her face and remove her gloves. Mr. Frederick came lumbering up the stairs behind them with the first of Alice's trunks.

Just as Alice and the children reached the second-floor landing, a loud boom sounded from the first floor. Alice let out a shriek of fear, but the others seemed only mildly startled.

"Is everything all right down there?" Alice called to Mrs. Highcroft.

Mrs. Highcroft waved her hand indifferently, but Alice could see the strain in her smile. "It's nothing, I am sure," she replied. "Perhaps just a little incident in the kitchen."

If the noise had come from the kitchen, then Alice presumed that either something had exploded in the oven, or the cook had shot someone. The report had been so loud she had felt the wooden floorboards vibrate.

Shaking off the odd incident, Alice continued to her room at the rear of the house. While Mr. Frederick finished bringing in her luggage, Margaret showed Alice the view from the side and rear windows. The backyard was laid out like an English garden, with perfectly square box hedges surrounding a gravel walk and a fountain. Ivy trailed up trellises that screened the backyard from the view of passersby.

When she was finally left to herself, Alice sat down and really looked at her new bedroom for the first time. It was not overly large, but the high ceiling and light blue paint made it feel open and spacious. The four-poster bed was covered in a quilt that exactly matched the walls, and a fireplace stood opposite the bed. A wardrobe, vanity, and small couch completed the room.

It was, Alice decided, quite nice. She doubted she would spend much time there—perhaps only when she was sleeping or writing a letter to Mama—but it would make a nice retreat when she finished her duties as governess each day.

Alice found the lady of the house on the front porch, a tray of tea and small sandwiches sitting on a table in front of her. Alice sat down in a wicker chair adjacent to Mrs. Highcroft.

"It's quite cool on this porch," Alice began, determined to use her best social manners.

"Yes, we spend a great deal of time out here during the warmer months," said Mrs. Highcroft. "The children are taking their naps, so it should be a quiet hour. My husband is at work—he owns a furniture company just a few miles from here—and Katie is so quiet that you'll hardly notice her coming and going. Our cook keeps to the kitchen, for the most part. She was with my family when I was just a girl, and she doesn't move as easily as she once did."

Alice nodded as she bit into a cucumber sandwich. "How old are the children?"

"Margaret is eight, and Jasper is five. They can be a little rambunctious, but they're good children. Breakfast is at eight each morning, and after that you'll give them their lessons for the day. After dinner, they can play for a while before naptime. Or, sometimes, you may want to go on outings to the park. They go to bed shortly after supper, so you'll have most of your evenings to yourself."

As Alice ate and listened, Mrs. Highcroft continued to chat about the daily routines at the house: when the wash was done, what time Katie would come in to get Alice dressed each morning, and when the family left for church on Sundays. Alice's head was full of new information, but one point stood out above the rest: Katie would help her get ready each morning.

Julia will be glad I don't have to dress myself, thought Alice.

As they talked, Mr. Highcroft appeared at the front gate. He had kind eyes, but the rest of his face was hidden behind a bushy beard that hung down below his chin. "Good afternoon, my dear," he said, greeting his wife. "And who is this? Our new governess, I assume."

Mrs. Highcroft made the appropriate introductions, and Alice was surprised when Mr. Highcroft shook her hand just as his wife had done. Alice wondered if everyone in Atlanta was so informal.

"If you're done with your refreshments, I'll give you a tour," offered Mr. Highcroft. "I left the warehouse early in hopes of finding you here already."

Mr. Highcroft led the three of them inside to the long front hall, where he started opening doors along the left-hand wall. "This is the parlor here, and the dining room, and that door adjoins it to the kitchen." The parlor and dining room were both lavishly decorated, and the furniture looked practically new.

There were three more doors lining the right side of the hallway. The front room was Mr. Highcroft's office, and the middle room housed a small library, though a billiard table took up most of the floor space. Mr. Highcroft skipped the third and rearmost door, which lay directly below Alice's own bedroom.

"What's in that room, sir?" she asked.

"That one? Oh, nothing of consequence," Mr. Highcroft paused. "My younger brother lives with us, and that's his study. He hates to be bothered."

As if on cue, another bang, though slightly less violent than the earlier one, sounded throughout the house. The noise emanated from the mysterious study. Alice managed to hold back a shriek this time, but the alarm on her face was apparent.

"Not to worry," Mrs. Highcroft said. "He's probably just moving things about, changing the furniture arrangement."

A quick look passed between the couple, and Alice knew better than to press the issue. If he can't be bothered to come greet me, Alice thought, let him keep to his study. I don't care if I never meet him.

The children's naptime passed quickly, and Mrs. Highcroft ushered Alice into her new role without hesitation, giving directions to wake them and take them into the backyard for some fresh air.

Alice sat on the back porch while Margaret and Jasper played a lively game of hide and seek. It was hotter in the back, since the house blocked the breeze that blew down the street. It felt strange to look beyond the ivy trellises and into the backyard of another house. Alice could just barely see over the tall vines from her perch. After growing up on an estate with a full acre between her house and the next, it was odd to think of neighbors being so near.

Just as she was thinking about the lack of privacy in her new life, Alice heard a click and a squeak. She turned to her right in time to see a window being raised by two masculine hands. The rest of the man was blocked by the white curtains and afternoon shadows. Still, Alice knew it must be Mr. Highcroft's brother since the window had to open on his study. A faint burning smell floated on the air, and Alice jumped up, afraid that something inside the study was on fire. Since the window was just being used for ventilation and not as an escape route, Alice forced herself to settle back into her chair. She wouldn't worry about it unless the fire brigade came knocking at the front door.

The remainder of the afternoon passed swiftly, and Alice was surprised when a middle-aged woman wearing a simple but crisp checked dress came bustling out to the back porch. "It's getting near supper time, ma'am," she began, not even bothering to introduce herself first.

"You must be Katie," Alice guessed.

"That's right, ma'am. I've got to get you dressed for supper, and the children."

"I'm pleased to meet you," Alice said, surprised at the housekeeper's strictly-business manner. Julia had always been informal and talkative, passing along Fairburn gossip to whichever family member she happened to be near. Except, of course, to Mrs. Meriwether, who was against such frivolity.

Alice called the children to her and they all trooped inside. Katie took the children into their nursery, while Alice retreated to her own room to begin pulling her gowns and other belongings out of her trunks, arranging them neatly in the wardrobe and on the vanity.

Just as her Mama had instructed, Alice chose her lavender gown for supper, though she knew it was too late for making a first impression. Still, she had gotten a welcome reception from the Highcroft family, and Alice didn't want their apparent faith in her to diminish. Katie, as promised, soon arrived to help Alice dress. She then took a brush to Alice's hair, pulling at the blonde locks with little sympathy as she worked out the day's tangles.

Alice emerged from her room with a tightly-wound bun and an aching scalp, but at least she looked better than she had all day. She collected Margaret and Jasper and escorted them into the dining room, where Mr. and Mrs. Highcroft were already seated.

"Alice, you look lovely," said Mrs. Highcroft.

"Thank you," Alice said, surprised and pleased at the compliment. "Where would you like me to sit?" Mr. Highcroft sat at the head of the table with his wife on the opposite end, and the children sat together on one side in what was obviously their usual arrangement.

Mrs. Highcroft indicated the chair adjacent to her, and Alice had no sooner settled in than she heard the chair beside hers being pulled back. She looked over to see a man, no older than twenty-five, with his shirtsleeves rolled up to the elbows and his expensive waistcoat splattered with a dusty white powder. He wore no jacket, and his unkempt brown hair was swept carelessly off his brow.

"Alice, this is my brother Roland," said Mr. Highcroft. "Roland, Alice is our new governess."

Roland gave Alice a quick glance. "Hello." He was clearly uninterested in the new tenant in the house.

Mr. Highcroft said grace, and as they began to eat, Mr. and Mrs. Highcroft kept up the conversation, talking about their day and asking Alice for more details about her journey. Roland remained silent, his brow furrowed as if he were concerned about something.

He wasn't unhandsome, Alice thought, but Roland would never garner a second glance from a woman with his disheveled appearance. He was tall and thin, and his pale, clean-shaven face had angular features that, on the shoulders of a man who cared about his appearance, would have been rather striking.

As soon as he finished his last bite of the bread pudding, Roland gave his brother and sister-in-law a quick nod and left as quickly as he had arrived. During the whole of supper, the only word he'd uttered had been his acknowledgement of Alice.

"Roland is very…scholarly," Mr. Highcroft began. "He gets wrapped up in his work and can be a little…" he paused again, "distracted."

"He really is a very nice young man," said Mrs. Highcroft, "but he does tend to keep to himself."

"I'll be sure not to bother him," Alice promised.

Alice and Katie both got the children ready for bed, then Alice stayed to tuck them into bed and read to them. Once they were asleep, she retreated to her own room. Her mother had asked for a letter, but Alice realized with dismay that she still had no stationery.

Her clothes arranged and her duties as governess finished for the day, Alice wrote about her arrival in the little book her father had returned to her, then blew out her oil lamp and went to sleep early. She was exhausted after such a long day and slept soundly until Katie came in the next morning to wake her.

Alice's first week in Atlanta went by quickly. She easily fell into the routine of giving Margaret and Jasper their lessons, overseeing their playing and afternoon naps, and even walking with them to nearby Grant Park twice. Mrs. Highcroft furnished stationery so Alice could write a satisfactory report to her mother. She didn't mention in the letter that, every now and then, a distant, deep buzzing noise would indicate the passage of an airship. If Alice was lucky, she was outdoors or near a window and could see it glide overhead, destined for the Port of Atlanta.

The only thing out of place in Alice's first week was Roland Highcroft. At every meal, Roland appeared, ate, and left without saying more than a sentence or two. He now included Alice in his nods of acknowledgement, but had no words to spare for her. Strange sounds continued to emanate from his study, and Alice could hear bangs, hammering, and the occasional muffled swearing coming from the room below hers. She lay in bed on Thursday night, listening to the noise that continued until two in the morning.

The next night, Alice prepared for bed in hopes that Roland would go to bed at a decent hour, too, allowing her to sleep in peace. Instead, she heard utter silence until midnight, when the front door squeaked open and closed. Curious, Alice crept to her door and opened it a crack. In the near darkness, she saw Roland come up the stairs, obviously trying to move quietly. He turned and went into his own room on the other side of the staircase, never noticing Alice. Where had he been at such a late hour? Had he been out drinking, or doing something with friends? He hadn't moved like he was drunk, and he didn't seem like the type of person who socialized a great deal. Perplexed, Alice closed her door and returned to bed, her thoughts on the mysterious Highcroft brother.

Alice got a surprise at breakfast on Sunday morning. "Well, Alice, what will you do during your afternoon off?" asked Mr. Highcroft over his coffee.

"Pardon?"

"This afternoon. What will you do with your time?"

"I didn't realize I had the afternoon off," Alice said.

"Did I forget to mention that?" Mrs. Highcroft interjected. "You'll have your Sunday afternoons and evenings off, so you'll have plenty of time to yourself."

"Oh, thank you!" Alice was pleased at the unexpected free time. "I don't know what I will do, though I would love to walk around this neighborhood more. I want to learn where everything is."

Mr. and Mrs. Highcroft gave their hearty approval of Alice's plan, while Roland continued to stare at the far wall in concentration, oblivious to the conversation.

On Sunday, Alice and the Highcrofts had the challenge of squeezing into the family carriage for the ride to church. Jasper sat next to his parents on one side, so Alice found herself squeezed in between Roland and Margaret. Alice felt some surprise that Roland was actually going to church with the family. Even though it was expected, he seemed too distracted to deal with anything that took place outside his study.

Still, Alice noted with approval, he was finally
wearing a complete suit, and his hair was neatly parted
down the middle. He looked much more attractive,
though the bandages wrapped around three of his
fingers stuck out in contrast to the starched clothes of a
gentleman.

After church, Margaret and Jasper spent the
remainder of the day with their parents, who,
following a large Sunday dinner, took them off to visit
some friends who had children of the same age. The
house was eerily quiet: Katie had the afternoon off and
had left the house already, and the cook stayed hidden
in the kitchen. Alice found a book in the library and
tried to read it on the front porch, but the occasional
clanks and bangs from Roland's office were too
distracting.

When it was well past the heat of the day, Alice
finally gave up on her book and left the house for a
walk. She wandered aimlessly through the
neighborhood, enjoying the quiet residential streets.
The sun was already sinking into the tree line when
she turned onto her street to come home.

Two blocks away, Alice saw Roland walking
quickly in the other direction. Once again, he was
leaving the house at an odd hour. Surely he would
miss supper, unless he was going just a short distance.

Alice followed Roland. He had already piqued
her curiosity, and this time she was determined to
know where he went so secretively. She stayed two
blocks behind, and Roland never looked back.

Chapter 8

Alice continued to trail Roland for some distance, coming to the edge of Grant Park and moving beyond the grand houses. Industrial buildings began to appear on either side of the road, and eventually the railroad tracks could be seen far ahead.

A few blocks from the tracks, Roland took a right-hand turn down a much more narrow road. Alice lost sight of him for a moment until she turned the corner, too, and saw Roland disappearing through the front door of a large granite building.

The first floor of the building looked perfectly normal, with wide windows and curtains blowing in the evening breeze. The two floors above, though, had only small slits for windows, and those seemed to be positioned high, near the ceiling. It looked like a fortified castle.

Alice hugged the other side of the street, hoping to be lost in the shadows as she walked past the building. In discreet letters next to the door were the words, "North Georgia Lunatic Asylum."

A lunatic asylum! What could Roland be doing there? Alice's eyes widened as ideas flashed through her mind. Perhaps he worked there at night, or maybe there was a third Highcroft sibling who was a resident there. Or, thought Alice, maybe Roland is half-mad himself.

The asylum was small, and Alice knew that the worst cases wound up at the huge state-run asylum in Milledgeville. Still, she realized suddenly that it was nearly dark outside, and she was a lady standing alone outside a lunatic asylum. A scream issued from one of the high windows, as if some mad person inside had heard her thought.

Alice turned and sped back to the main road. She hurried the whole way home, thoughts of lunatics trailing after her speeding her steps.

The house was dark when Alice arrived: only the candles in the dining room had been lit. The family was taking supper with their friends and were not yet home. Instead, Alice saw two silver trays laid on the table with a cover over each. One was in front of her chair, and the other was in front of Roland's.

What ever would we say to each other if we had to dine alone? Alice wondered.

She sat and uncovered her tray, and began eating the cold meats, cheese, and bread with gusto. Her adventure had made her hungry.

As Alice brushed breadcrumbs off her hands, she turned to an imaginary Roland. "So, dear, did you have a nice time at the lunatic asylum?" She laughed at her joke, but the outburst was cut short. If Roland were to walk through the door, Alice had no idea what she would say to him.

Alice covered the remains of her dinner and left the dining room, but she got no further than two steps up the wide staircase when she noticed that Roland's study door was ajar. Why was Roland sequestered in that room all day, and what could he be doing that made those loud noises? Alice knew she had no right to go inside, but she told herself that just one peek would surely be okay. As quiet as the house was, she would hear Roland's footsteps on the porch if he came back early.

Alice returned to the dining room and picked up a candle. Even though the cook was the only other soul in the house, Alice still crept as quietly as she could to the door of Roland's study. She took a deep breath and held it as she gave the door a gentle push. It creaked quietly, and Alice crossed the threshold with her candle held high.

A desk piled high with assorted papers, blueprints, and gadgets sat near one wall, but it was the hidden contraption in the center of the room that drew all of Alice's attention. It was about six feet tall and three feet wide, and whatever it was had been covered with a thick white sheet. Alice carefully lifted an edge of the sheet to peer underneath, but it was too dark to discern any details, and she was afraid of holding her candle too close to the sheet.

Alice crossed the room to Roland's desk, where an array of gears, wire, and metal scraps lay scattered across the blotting pad. A copy of the American Science Journal was half-hidden under an untidy pile of papers. Alice gingerly slid the magazine out and saw that it was the latest issue.

The magazine clutched in her hands, Alice turned a complete circle as she surveyed Roland's study in the pale glow of the candle. The copper bits, the gears, the magazine: Roland was a New Scientist! He had to be!

Giddy at the idea of living under the same roof as a real scientist and inventor, Alice determined to talk to Roland about his work. It would be hard, she knew, when he was so odd and uncommunicative, but she had to know what kind of work he did.

If he's a scientist, Alice wondered, then why was he at the lunatic asylum tonight?

Shivering at the possible explanations, Alice decided she would speak to Roland in the broad daylight when everyone else was home. The children's afternoon nap would be the perfect time to approach him.

Her mind made up, Alice remembered the Journal that she was still clutching. She sat gingerly on the edge of the desk chair and opened the new issue. The flickering light made the text difficult to discern, but Alice squinted and tilted the magazine toward the candle so she could see every detail.

Half an hour later, Alice was engrossed in an article written by an airship engineer when she had the odd feeling of being watched. Startled, Alice looked up and saw Roland standing in the doorway. She hadn't even heard him come in the front door.

Roland was silent, as always, but Alice jumped up with an apology on her lips. As she stood, though, her arm bumped against the candle and knocked it over onto the desk. The entire room plunged into darkness.

"I'm so sorry," Alice said, her words tumbling out in an anxious jumble. "I was just reading. I didn't mean to invade your privacy. I was curious, and I wanted to read. I'm sorry." As she spoke, the candles still burning inside the dining room cast just enough light to outline Roland's immobile silhouette in the doorway.

Alice picked up the extinguished candle and crossed to the door, but still Roland's form didn't move. "I'll leave you to yourself now," she said. "Please excuse me."

"Why were you in here?" Roland maintained his stance in the doorway.

Alice dropped her gaze, feeling Roland's own eyes on her even though she couldn't see them. "I was curious, and the door was open."

In the silence that followed, Alice offered up another apology. "I'm very sorry, sir. It won't happen again, I assure you."

"You said you were reading. What did you find so interesting?"

"The new issue of American Science Journal." Alice's words came out as a mumble. She felt so humiliated, and here Roland was dragging it out with all of his questions! She wanted nothing more than to flee to the solace of her room.

"Curious reading material for a girl," Roland said.

His words reminded Alice of those spoken time and again by her mother, and most recently by Ian. Her temper flared, overcoming all her other feelings. "I don't see why you should think that," she retorted, holding her head high once again. "There are many very accomplished female scientists, and there is no reason that a girl like me can't take pleasure in reading about the New Science. I have apologized to you for entering your office uninvited, but I will not apologize for my interest in science. Good night, Mr. Highcroft."

Without waiting for a response, Alice squeezed past Roland, brushing against him as he tried to find a reply. "I...You..." He finally gave up as Alice groped up the stairs in the darkness.

Alice's bedroom was in darkness as well. She dismissed the idea of going back downstairs to relight her candle. Instead, she undressed clumsily, slipped on her nightdress, and fell into bed. She was angry, embarrassed, and, now, afraid. What would Roland say to his brother about her behavior? Surely Mrs. Highcroft would write to Mrs. Meriwether about it, and if there was any mention whatsoever that New Science was involved, Alice would probably be on the first train back to Fairburn.

And, Alice thought, I don't want to lose the respect that Mr. and Mrs. Highcroft have for me. What will they say?

Alice lay awake for a long while that night, and she heard the noises of the family returning and eventually all going to bed themselves. When she finally drifted off to sleep, she had fitful dreams about the shadow of a man standing in her doorway.

Facing Roland, let alone the rest of the family, was a horrifying idea. "Please let them be understanding," Alice whispered on her way downstairs the next morning, "and please don't let Mrs. Highcroft tell Mama."

Everyone else was already at the breakfast table, except for Roland, and they all greeted her with their usual cheer. Alice relaxed a little. Roland obviously hadn't had the chance to tell them about last night's transgression. Alice might be able to get through one meal without shame.

Alice's back stiffened self-consciously when she heard Roland enter the dining room behind her. He took his seat as usual, with a brisk good morning to his brother and sister-in-law. Alice gazed down at her plate, as if the ham was wholly engrossing, but she was forced to look up when Roland spoke again. "Good morning, Miss Alice," he said.

There was a faint smile on Roland's lips, and his eyes peered at her as if she were a new invention herself. Alice felt her cheeks flush, and she returned the greeting quietly. The rest of the family didn't notice Roland's subtle expression, but to Alice it was as if he was enjoying a private joke. And without a doubt, Alice thought, I'm the joke.

Much to Alice's relief, Roland reverted to his usual silence during the meal, but every now and then she felt his glance.

"Alice, you have hardly eaten," said Mrs. Highcroft as the plates were cleared from the table. "Are you not feeling well this morning?"

"I feel fine, thank you," Alice answered. "I didn't sleep well last night, that is all."

"Poor dear. It's probably our fault for staying out so late and leaving you here all alone in this house."

Before Alice could answer, Roland spoke up, a hint of indignance in his tone. "She wasn't alone."

Mrs. Highcroft was surprised at the comment and paused for a moment before responding. "You are always busy with your work, Roland. I just meant that Alice had no company to help her pass the time." Turning her attention back to Alice, she asked, "What did you do with your time last night?"

For the second time during breakfast, Alice felt her cheeks flush. "Oh, I just…" Just what? Alice thought wildly. Just snuck into your brother-in-law's forbidden office? "I just read, then went to bed early," she finished. It was mostly the truth.

"Well, nothing wrong with a nice, quiet evening," said Mr. Highcroft, but even as he spoke, Alice knew that his wife noticed the smirk that crossed Roland's face.

Alice was glad when the meal was finished and she could hide in the nursery for the morning's lessons. Roland, thankfully, was back to his usual self at dinner, and still neither Mr. nor Mrs. Highcroft seemed to know anything was amiss.

The weather was cooler than it had been for several days. Though the fall temperatures had not yet arrived, it was clear that the summer was nearly gone. It was the perfect excuse for Alice to propose a walk to Grant Park. The children could enjoy the fine weather, and Alice could enjoy being away from Roland.

The walk to the park was warm, but once they were under the shade of the oak trees, Alice settled comfortably onto a bench while Margaret and Jasper played with some other neighborhood children.

Alice forgot her own worries for a while. The fresh air and steady breeze were calming, and she was happily daydreaming when someone sat down on the bench next to her.

"Roland!" Alice said when she saw who it was. "I mean, Mr. Highcroft. You startled me."

"Miss Alice," Roland replied. He again wore the small smile he had greeted her with that morning.

"What are you doing here?"

"I decided I needed some fresh air to clear my head."

If that was the case, Alice thought, then it was the first time since she had arrived in Atlanta that Roland had left his office in the middle of the day. He had followed her; that much was clear.

"How do you like Atlanta so far?" Roland asked.

"I like it very much, though I have yet to see much of it. This neighborhood and the church are about all I have seen." And the lunatic asylum, Alice added silently.

"You should have an outing on your next Sunday off. They have airship tours here, you know."

"Yes, I know. I saw one when I got off the train. I've always wanted to ride on an airship." Alice was so eager about the prospect that, for a moment, she forgot her awkwardness.

Roland's smile faltered for a moment as he said, "If you like, I'll take you next Sunday. I don't know that James and Mariah would want you to do something like that alone."

"I would like that very much." The words were out of her mouth before Alice could consider them. How could she have agreed so easily to Roland who, just last night, had terrified her? Airships, Alice told herself. Science. They had prompted her to break off an engagement with one man, so it stood to reason that they would get her to agree to an outing with a man who probably despised her.

A pause followed. Roland seemed to have run out of words to say, and Alice thought desperately for something to fill the silence. Every question she thought of, though, stemmed back to the things she had seen in his study. Finally she said, "I am surprised to see you out. I was convinced that you spent almost all of your time in your study."

"I'm not always such a shut-in," Roland said. "You join us at a very busy time in my line of work. I am hoping to give a public demonstration soon and am trying to finalize everything."

"What sort of a demonstration?"

Roland hesitated before answering. "When I am convinced of my success, then perhaps I'll tell you."

Alice pursed her lips at the coy response. "Well, I'd think that you could give me at least a hint. After all, I tolerate the noise of it: often I think you are trying to blow something up in that study!"

"You will have to wait a while longer, I'm afraid."

They lapsed into an awkward silence again. Alice looked over to ensure that Margaret and Jasper were behaving in their play, then stared out at the gentle hills of the park.

Alice hoped that Roland would find something to continue their conversation. When he didn't, Alice decided it was better to bring up the subject of last night than to endure the silence any longer.

"I am surprised that you offered to escort me on an airship tour," she began. "After all, I know you must be very angry with me."

"Angry with you?" Roland looked stunned, but after a moment he laughed. His laugh was heartfelt, and it made Alice smile to hear it. She noticed how his eyes lit up when he smiled, and realized that they were very blue. How did I not notice that when he looked at me during breakfast? Alice wondered. "I am not angry. In fact, I thought you were angry with me," Roland continued. "That's why I determined to extend an invitation to you. I hoped to make you forgive me."

Now it was Alice's turn to look stunned. "Why would I be angry with you?"

"For my behavior last night."

"I am the one who was in the wrong. You have every right to be angry with me. Your behavior was no different than mine would have been, if the situation were reversed."

"I was surprised, but not angry," Roland said. "I was curious why a woman like you would take any interest in my things."

Alice didn't answer. As much as she wanted to

trust Roland, the sting of Ian's betrayal was still too great. Roland knew she was interested in the New Science; she would not elaborate more.

When Roland realized that Alice was not going to respond, he spoke again. "Well, I am glad to know that you aren't angry with me, at least. I may not be the most outgoing person, but I can't stand the thought of someone thinking ill of me."

"You may be assured that is not the case."

"Then let us shake hands on it." Alice took Roland's offered hand. He stood, saying, "I'll leave you to your peace and quiet now. As always, there is more work to be done." With that, he turned and walked up the path, leaving Alice to ponder this new side of Roland Highcroft.

Chapter 9

Roland's friendliness did not end with their meeting in the park. At supper that night, Roland made light conversation with Alice and the rest of the party, though he was still reserved.

When the day ended on such a positive note, Alice went to bed tired but satisfied. Roland had not exposed her transgression to Mr. and Mrs. Highcroft. Tuesday, Alice thought, will surely be a quiet day.

Tuesday morning dawned gray and overcast. It wasn't raining yet, but it seemed inevitable. By the time they were finished with the morning's lessons and dinner, the wind was whipping through the branches of the trees outside, and a slow, steady rain was falling.

Margaret and Jasper were restless as they faced a long afternoon of sitting indoors. Alice did the best she could, pulling out drawing papers and organizing an indoor scavenger hunt for them. Roland even stepped out of his office at one point to give them piggyback rides through the front hall. Alice had to laugh at the sight of the disheveled scientist parading the children around the house.

As the afternoon wore on, the sky continued to darken. It seemed as if twilight had already fallen when Margaret and Jasper lay down for their afternoon nap. Alice even lit a small oil lamp on a table of the nursery to give them some light.

With an hour of free time ahead of her, Alice decided to get her book so she could read in the front parlor. As she walked from the nursery to her room, lightning illuminated the upstairs hall, and the thunder that followed closely after shook the walls of the house. When Alice opened her bedroom door, another flash of lightning lit up the dim interior. Alice stifled a scream when she saw a man silhouetted in the brief light. When her room was thrown into darkness once again, she could still see the outline of the man, a black shadow against the gray gloom.

It all happened in a split second, but to Alice it seemed that she stood there for an eternity. The figure neither moved nor spoke in that brief instance. The shape was too short to be Roland, too slim to be Mr. Highcroft.

With a cry, Alice turned and fled down the stairs. Her feet took her to Roland's study, and she threw open his door and rushed inside without bothering to knock. "A ghost!" she gasped. She stood here, heaving for breath, barely noticing the scene in front of her. Roland's machine sat uncovered, and he had a key winder in his hand. When he saw how distraught Alice was, he rushed over and took her firmly by the shoulders.

"Miss Alice, are you okay?" he asked.

Alice looked down at herself, as if checking for physical damage, then looked back up at Roland. "I saw a ghost." The words came out as a whisper. She only half-believed them herself, and surely Roland would never believe her. He was a man of science.

Roland's face broke into a grin, his eyes crinkling at the corners. Alice expected him to laugh at her next, but instead he said, "That's wonderful!"

Alice blinked. "What?"

"You saw a ghost where, upstairs?"

"Yes, in my room. I walked in just now and it was standing there."

"Just above where we are standing now, then." Roland pulled Alice forward and ushered her into a chair. He sat down at his desk and pulled out a pen and paper. "Tell me, what did it look like?"

When Alice didn't reply, Roland paused and looked up.

"So you believe me?" Alice asked.

"Of course."

"Why are you so excited about it? I'm shaking from head to toe with fear."

Roland's expression changed to one of concern. "Of course you are. It must have been a great shock to you." He got up and crossed to Alice, where he knelt in front of her chair. "Can I get you anything? A glass of wine, or a cup of tea?" Roland was awkward in his gallantry, but Alice appreciated it nonetheless.

"No." Alice raised her hands, but seeing how much they trembled, she let them fall back into her lap. "No, thank you."

Roland had noticed Alice's unsteady hands, as well. He began to reach forward, as if he would take them in his own, but he thought better of it. Instead he said, "You have nothing to fear, truly."

"Perhaps. But fright has driven away my logic for the moment."

"Then I must seek your forgiveness for the second time in as many days."

"Why? It's not your fault that this house is haunted."

Roland frowned. "True, but it is my fault that you saw the ghost. It was a man, wasn't it?"

"Yes," Alice said. "How did you know?"

Roland sighed and stood up. He began to pace in front of Alice, stopping now and then to gaze out of a window half-hidden by boxes piled high. Finally, he began to relate his story. "While this house was being built, a man working on the second story died. He had seemed healthy enough, but he had a stroke and fell, unconscious, from the beams of the house. There have been some odd occurrences in the house ever since we moved in, but nothing alarming. Books that are moved from their proper places, candlesticks that go missing only to be found sitting in the middle of the table later. Once in a great while, footsteps are heard upstairs when no one is up there."

Instead of feeling comforted, Alice's fear grew. How often, she wondered, would this ghost be showing up in her room? Had he fallen from the beams that supported her own bedroom?

"The Spiritualist Movement has brought about some interesting new theories, though you won't find them tested at a séance," Roland continued.

"I'm sure Madame Beauregard would argue otherwise," Alice said to herself.

"What's that?"

Alice looked up at Roland. "Oh, nothing. I had a, ah, unusual meeting with a medium not long ago."

"Really? I'd love to hear about your experience with her. Did you witness anything authentic?"

"Authentically fake," answered Alice. "She was using a Bergfors Device to lift her table."

"Oh, very clever. How was she delivering the steam to the table without the device being seen?"

Alice smiled at Roland's easy distraction. "You finish telling me about the real ghost in my room, then I'll tell you everything I know about Madame Beauregard and her fake ones."

"Right, of course. As I said, the movement has introduced some new theories. One of those is that ghosts are more likely to appear—manifest is the word—if there is some kind of energy source they can tap into. Thunderstorms tend to produce more sightings of ghosts, and it's believed that the spirits somehow tap into the energy of the lightning, harnessing it to manifest."

"Which is why I saw the ghost today, with the

storm," said Alice.

"Partially," agreed Roland, "but not wholly. I've taken these theories to heart and have been working on this new machine." Roland moved to the tall machine in the center of the room. He patted it affectionately. "This is my Ghost Machine."

"Let me guess," said Alice. "It produces some kind of energy that ghosts can use to…manifest, I believe you said."

"That's right! You're more clever than you look! You see, the cogs turn these two drums, which are coated on the outside with a thick velvet. The drums turn opposite to each other, and as they turn the velvet exteriors rub against each other. This steel arm, here," Roland was pointing to a thin rod that moved on a pivot, "drops down and causes a spark generated by the energy built up when the velvet drums rub together."

"How does velvet create a spark?"

"Static electricity," said Roland, obviously proud of his work. "When you were a child, did you ever rub a cat's fur in the dark to see the sparks that flew from your fingertips?"

Alice's eyes widened. "What?"

Roland laughed. "Not exactly a proper pastime, I know. When James and I were young, we had a pet cat. In the winter, when the air was dry and cold, we would blow out the candles and rub our cat's fur backwards. The friction created static electricity, and our hands grounded the energy, creating a spark. This is the same concept, except I'm using the gear-powered drums to create great volumes of electricity."

"And the electricity gives any ghosts in a haunted house the means to manifest," finished Alice.

"Exactly. The machine hasn't been working, though," admitted Roland. "I can't seem to create enough static electricity. With the storm today, I thought I'd try it again."

"Well, it worked," said Alice, "only your ghost

appeared a floor above you.""Yes, so obviously I need
to focus the energy output somehow, so ghosts will
appear here, next to the machine." Roland was quiet,
Alice forgotten for the moment while he inspected the
machine.

Finally, Alice cleared her throat. "Well,
congratulations on your success," she said. "I think I'll
go back upstairs now that I know there won't be a
ghost there anymore. Perhaps next time you can warn
me before you turn the machine on."

"Yes, of course I will," said Roland distractedly.

Alice left Roland's office quietly, as perplexed by
the man as ever.

The storm was beginning to subside, and Alice
had left her bedroom door wide open. In the thin light
that came through her windows, she could see that
there was no one inside, living or otherwise. Alice had
just enough time to collect her thoughts before waking
the children from their nap.

The shock of seeing a ghost was beginning to
subside, but Alice's nerves were still on edge. She
inhaled deeply, thinking over all that Roland had said.
His machine was fascinating, though it obviously
needed to be fine-tuned. She wondered how many
times it had worked in the past, but without a witness
to confirm the ghost. Roland might have been trying to
"fix" his machine for months, when in reality it had
been working all along. "It needs to generate more
static electricity, and that energy needs to be focused,"
Alice mumbled to herself. Even after she had woken
Margaret and Jasper, she was still mentally drawing
diagrams and making improvements to Roland's
Ghost Machine. Still, Alice didn't even consider
offering to assist him in his work. He knew she was
interested in science, but not the depth of her passion
for it. Better to seem ignorant than to risk his
disapproval, thought Alice.

Far from being disapproving, Roland seemed to
delight in having someone in the house with whom he

could converse about his work. His brother and sister-in-law tolerated his scientific endeavors but had never even feigned interest in it, and his niece and nephew were too young for all but the most basic science lessons.

Roland came to supper with the same copy of American Science Journal that he had caught Alice reading. He sat down and handed it to her. "I thought you might want to finish reading this," he said.

Alice blushed but took the magazine with a quiet, "Thank you," trying to ignore the curious looks from Mr. and Mrs. Highcroft.

"Do you enjoy reading such things?" asked Mrs. Highcroft. Her voice held no judgment, but Alice was cautious.

"I always enjoy learning new things," she answered. "It's interesting to read about inventions that may one day change the daily routine for all of us."

"Then you should go on one of these airship tours," said Mr. Highcroft. "They're all the rage. It's a little nerve-wracking at first, but we had an excellent time."

"Yes," Alice said, looking sideways at Roland.

"I've already offered to take Alice on a tour this Sunday, during her afternoon off," said Roland without hesitation.

"Capital!" said Mr. Highcroft, while his wife spoke far more with her raised eyebrows.

Alice finished reading the magazine once Margaret and Jasper were in bed. It was already ten o'clock, but she knew that Roland would still be awake. She padded softly downstairs and knocked quietly at his door.

Roland answered quickly, almost as if he had been expecting her.

"I just wanted to return this. Thank you," said Alice, holding the magazine out but holding her ground on the threshold of the study.

"I never did hear about Madame Beauregard," Roland said.

"And you never did finish questioning me about the ghost."

"Are you too tired to speak now?" Not waiting for an answer, Roland stepped back and waved a hand toward the chair.

Alice glanced behind her, feeling like she was doing something bad. Going into a young man's study at such an hour! What would Mama say to such a thing? Imagining Mama's indignant reaction wasn't nearly enough to keep Alice from accepting Roland's invitation. The more she learned about Roland, the more curious she became.

But, Alice realized as she sat down in the high-backed leather chair, it was more than curiosity. Roland was the first person Alice had met in Atlanta who was close to her age and to whom she could talk without too much reservation.

Roland pulled a second chair close to hers and propped a sheaf of paper on his crossed legs. "Now, tell me exactly where you saw the ghost."

The interview lasted half an hour, with Roland asking very exacting details. What had the ghost looked like? What color were his eyes? Alice regretted having to tell Roland that the ghost had been a mere shadow, a solid form swathed in darkness.

When Roland finally seemed satisfied, he brought up Alice's encounter with the medium again. Alice gladly described the false floor and the pipes running into the fireplace, but she didn't mention that she was the one who had exposed the fraud. That incident had been such a disaster. Earlier, Alice had looked on the night with fondness, since her boldness had inspired Ian to propose. Since the engagement had ended so bitterly, though, Alice now thought the night nothing but a disappointment: to her, to her family, and even to Ian.

Alice spent the children's nap hour with Roland

each day for the remainder of the week. It was becoming easier to speak to him, though most of the time he did the talking, explaining in detail how the Ghost Machine worked and showing Alice other little inventions of his. The Ghost Machine was by far the most ambitious project he had yet undertaken.

Alice was surprised when Roland came to breakfast on Friday morning dressed in a freshly pressed suit. His hair was neatly parted, a pocket watch shone brightly on his waistcoat, and for once his shoes weren't covered with various powders and dusts from his study.

He was positively handsome.

Alice had become comfortable talking to Roland the scientist, with his quirky inventions, disheveled hair, and hastily rolled-up sleeves, but Roland the gentleman was another matter entirely. For the first time since they had met, Alice felt a wave of shyness when Roland wished her a good morning.

"Oh, it's today, is it?" asked Mr. Highcroft.

"Yes. I want to get there early. President Hayes is slated to give the opening speech. I'd hate to miss it," answered Roland.

"You'll have to tell us about it this evening."

Mr. Highcroft seemed content to let the conversation end there, but Alice was not. As Mr. and Mrs. Highcroft spoke with each other, Alice said quietly to Roland, "What's happening?"

"I'm surprised you don't already know," Roland said, his tone teasing. "The Cotton States and International Exposition opens today. Exhibitors have been arriving for weeks now."

Alice's eyes widened. "Of course, it's already September eighteenth! I've been so busy that I lost track of the date."

"It's too bad you can't come with me today for the opening ceremonies," Roland replied.

Alice was distracted for the rest of the day, constantly wondering what was happening at the

Exposition. She missed Roland more than she was willing to admit to herself. After all, he was quickly becoming her only friend in Atlanta.

Contrary to Mr. Highcroft's thoughts, Roland was not at supper to give his report on the ceremonies. He was still not home when Alice tucked Margaret and Jasper into bed, nor had she heard his quiet footfalls on the staircase before she herself went to sleep.

Roland reappeared at breakfast on Saturday morning, still wearing his suit from the day before. It was now rumpled and had streaks of red Georgia clay clinging to it. He looked altogether like his usual self once again, except for frequent yawning and dark circles under his eyes. Mrs. Highcroft was looking at him with disapproval, an expression Alice had not yet seen on her usually pleasant face.

"I'm in trouble," Roland whispered to Alice. She met his gaze with alarm, but saw that the corners of his mouth were turned up in a conspiratorial smile.

"Then you had better be on your best behavior," Alice answered, failing to keep a straight face as she spoke.

Breakfast passed quietly, but as she ushered Margaret and Jasper into the backyard to play, Roland followed. It was still early, and the chill of fall could be felt in the dewy air of the yard. Alice sat on a bench and wrapped her arms around herself. Roland settled in next to her.

"Aren't you going to ask why I'm in trouble?" he asked.

Alice raised her eyebrows at him. "I assume it has something to do with the fact that you're still wearing yesterday's clothes."

"You're very observant." Roland leaned back and looked out across the back yard. He yawned lazily, content for the moment to keep Alice guessing about his misbehavior.

"I also assume you did not come home until very late last night."

"Very early this morning, in fact. About four o'clock."

"Four o'clock! No wonder you are in trouble. What kept you out so late?"

"After the opening ceremonies, I wandered through the Hall of New Science," Roland began. Alice couldn't hide the look of envy that crossed her face. "I met up with Dr. Christophe Liszt. We have been corresponding with each other for two years. He is a member of the Association of Analytically Distinguished Men. You've heard of them?"

"Yes," Alice said. "They are a secret society of New Scientists."

"That's right," Roland was nodding his head with approval. "They live by a scientific code, a method of applying analytical thinking to their experiments. The AAD Men." He pronounced "AAD" as "odd."

A laugh escaped Alice before she could stop herself. "The odd men! I am sure that is not far from the truth."

"They do seem to have a healthy sense of humor."

"How do you know so much about them if you are not part of their secret society?"

"Because my colleague Dr. Liszt is going to sponsor me. I'll be introduced as a potential member and will go to several meetings with them throughout the course of the Exposition. I have to get approval from at least ten members to be inducted." Roland's face was a mixture of pride and nervousness.

"Congratulations," Alice said, hoping that was the right response to Roland's news. "And is that why you were out until four this morning?"

"You sound very much like my sister-in-law right now."

"You are not in trouble with me, I assure you."

"Then, yes, that is where I was. Some of the AAD Men took me out for supper, then drinks after."

"That was either a long supper or a lot of

drinking." Alice was looking hard at Roland now. He didn't seem to be drunk, and he didn't smell of alcohol.

"Both, for some of the men. I wound up in a debate with two other fellows about the proper way to manipulate copper tubes. Before I knew it, the sunrise was only a few hours away."

Alice gave Roland a skeptical look but remained silent.

"Do you still want to take that airship tour tomorrow?" Roland asked, changing the subject abruptly.

"Yes, very much so."

Roland gave a disapproving "tsk" and shook his head. "That's too bad."

"Why?" Alice felt her heart sink. She had been looking forward to climbing on one of those airships since she had arrived in Atlanta. Was Roland going to be busy with the AAD Men, or had some New Scientist found a way to predict the weather?

"Because I'm going back to the Exposition to spend the entire afternoon in the Hall of New Science. I was going to take you, but if you'd rather be floating about on an airship, then I'll have to go alone."

"Do not tease like that! Of course I would love to go to the Exposition." Roland, Alice realized, had quickly learned her one weakness. She doubted that she would have given up a ride in an airship for anything else.

"Then it's settled. Tomorrow after dinner you and I will go see the sights." Without waiting for Alice to respond, Roland stood and went inside the house.

Alice was elated. She had hoped that she might eventually get to go to the Exposition, but to do so during the opening weekend was far beyond her expectations. She had some worry that Mr. and Mrs. Highcroft might not approve of the venture, and she determined to ask their permission during the course of the day. Alice tried not to get too excited until she had a firm answer from them, but she couldn't help grinning as she daydreamed about the new things she would see. Even Jasper noticed Alice's elation, pausing during a game of jacks to ask, "How come you keep smiling at the backyard, Miss Alice?"

Chapter 10

Mr. and Mrs. Highcroft gladly gave their permission for Alice to attend the Exposition with Roland. They praised him for being kind enough to escort her, and they privately rejoiced in the way Alice was drawing Roland out of his reclusive lifestyle.

Sunday morning's church service dragged on, and Alice was convinced that the preacher, whose subject was patience, was purposely being long-winded to test the patience of his own flock. Alice wanted to fidget, but she was too afraid of wrinkling the dark green dress she was wearing. She knew the rich color showed off her pale skin and blonde hair, and she wanted to look as dashing as possible at the Exposition. After all, this would be her first chance to meet New Science's elite, and she wanted to make a good impression.

The preacher should be speaking on vanity, Alice thought wryly.

Finally, the interminable sermon was over and the family returned home for their midday dinner. Alice and Roland both ate in a hurry, as if they could speed up the meal to leave sooner. Unfortunately, the others moved at a leisurely pace, and Alice had to sit and wait while they finished eating.

Alice was so anxious to leave that she was already in the carriage before the table had even been cleared. When Roland joined her, he took the reins with an inattentive hand, and the carriage jolted forward.

The ride to the Exposition grounds retraced much of the journey Alice had taken from the train station. When they would have turned left to take the road to downtown Atlanta, though, Roland went straight. They passed through more neighborhoods, including one full of the grandest mansions Alice had ever seen, before they passed into older, more modest areas.

The first sign that they were nearing the Exposition was the increased traffic. Their leisurely drive suddenly became hectic, as the carriage was lost in a sea of other carriages, pedestrians walking in each direction, and a streetcar rolling along rails in the middle of the street.

They left the carriage in a huge vacant field and joined the throngs of people overflowing the sidewalk. Soon Alice could see the arch of a stone gateway over the tops of the heads in front of her. It was too crowded to see anything else.

Once they walked inside the gate, though, the land sloped gently downward, giving Alice a wide view of the Exposition. While the other visitors scattered in every direction, Alice stood still and breathed deeply, taking it all in. The grounds were beautifully landscaped, with walkways winding past perfectly manicured gardens and long expanses of thick green grass. Wide stone steps flanked by huge urns eased the trek up and down the soft hills. The buildings housing each pavilion were like mansions, though they weren't constructed to last longer than the four months that the Exposition would run. Each pavilion had its own distinct look, from one that looked like an antebellum plantation to another that had a stone façade and thick Romanesque columns. They were scattered throughout the grounds as far as

Alice could see.

As Alice surveyed the scene, she became aware that Roland's eyes weren't on the landscape, but on her. He seemed to be deriving a great deal of pleasure from watching her reaction. Alice turned her head away, feeling flushed. "And where are we going?" she asked quickly.

"Straight ahead," Roland said. He led the way through the crowd, moving slowly but not taking the time to gawk like everyone else. Three times he had to stop and return for Alice, who had paused to look at some building or a roving band of entertainers.

The Hall of New Science was impossible to miss. Its brick exterior was overlaid with a huge framework of massive iron beams. The beams were supporting a maze of copper tubes, gears, whirling metal pieces and, foremost, some of the best New Science inventions Alice had ever seen.

On the right of the wide entrance, one machine lowered a platform through a system of cogs and pulleys. As Alice watched, intrepid fair-goers filed onto the platform, clinging to the narrow railings along each side. With a jolt, the platform was lifted into the air, rising to the second story, where everyone exited onto a balcony.

"I want to ride that!" Alice said, but no sooner were the words out of her mouth than her attention was caught by a fountain to the left of the entrance. A huge brass elephant had been built out of scrap metal, and a stream of water poured from its snout. It would have been rather ordinary, if not for the fact that the elephant was moving. His snout undulated slowly, and his wide ears flapped happily like a kite caught in a breeze. The entire elephant rotated on some sort of turntable.

As they got closer to the building, Alice realized that there were at least a dozen smaller inventions displayed elsewhere among the iron beams. Some were simple, made just for amusement, but others had practical applications.

Alice was rapt. She felt overwhelmed by it all even before they stepped through the doors of the hall, and Roland mistook her awed silence for boredom.

"If you get tired of this hall, we can go elsewhere later," he ventured.

"All right," Alice said, hardly even hearing Roland. Her head swiveled from the left to the right as she tried to take it all in at once.

The inside of the building was open and airy. The ceiling reached above the second story, which was only an inner balcony running around the entire hall. It afforded a bird's eye view of the displays below, and a staircase wound down at one end for those who weren't brave enough to try the people mover outside.

New Scientists had set up their inventions in display areas against each of the four walls of the hall. The middle of the room was open, with an elevated stage fronted by rows of chairs. A chalkboard listed that day's schedule of lectures and demonstrations.

"Which way?" Roland asked.

Alice looked from one side to the other. "Let's go left first," she decided.

They wandered past the first three display areas, where each scientist was engaged in deep conversation with curious onlookers. As they passed the fourth display, where a sizable crowd had gathered, the scientist suddenly broke off his speech.

"Young miss, you made it!" he said happily.

Alice glanced toward him and was surprised to realize that his comment was being directed at her. "Dr. McGuffey!" she cried, recognizing the gentleman.

"Come here, come here," Dr. McGuffey said as the crowd parted to let Alice through. When she was standing next to him, Dr. McGuffey addressed his audience once again. "New Science, you see, sparks the minds of the young and the old, man and woman. This young miss and I may be as different from each other as we can be, yet we are united in our curiosity and desire for advancement." He turned to Alice again. "Now, tell them your name and where you are from."

"I'm Alice Meriwether, and I'm from Fairburn, Georgia, though I'm a governess in Atlanta now," she said. Alice's voice was quiet, the sudden attention making her self-conscious.

"While Miss Meriwether was talking, I was recording her words with my writing engine," continued Dr. McGuffey. He pointed to a large brass lever on his waist-high machine. "Pull the lever, Miss Meriwether."

Alice did as she was told, and the machine began to tick, clang, and shudder. It went on for half a minute, and several of the audience members took a step back as if it might explode, but eventually a piece of paper churned out of the bottom of the machine, landing in a shallow wicker basket. Dr. McGuffey motioned for Alice to take the paper. As she lifted it, she could see typewritten words across the page. They were the very words she had just spoken. With a gasp of surprise, Alice held the paper up for the audience to see.

As if on cue, everyone broke into applause at once. Alice turned to Dr. McGuffey, "Thank you so much for letting me demonstrate your writing machine," she said.

"And thank you for coming to the train station to meet a mad scientist like me," he answered with a wink.

Alice stepped back as the audience surged toward Dr. McGuffey, shouting questions and compliments at him. Alice worked her way toward the back of the tight knot of onlookers, getting her share of greetings and congratulations as she went. When she re-emerged from the booth, Roland gave her a searching look.

"You know Augustus McGuffey?" He had a note of admiration in his voice.

"We met just once. At the train station in

Fairburn."

"He's an AAD Man."

"I'm not surprised. He's said to be very well-respected among his colleagues."

"Yes, he is," Roland said. Now his voice had a thoughtful tone.

Alice and Roland passed many new machines that drew Alice's attention: an automatic water pump, an arithmetic engine similar to Dr. McGuffey's writing engine, and a dome-shaped metal hat with wires sticking out of it. The inventor claimed that wearing the helmet while it was turned on would make you smarter. Alice and Roland both declined the chance to try the device.

They had only gotten a third of the way through all the displays when a loud voice boomed from the direction of the stage. "In five minutes, see the clockwork housekeeper! Dr. Lemuel Bateman's new invention that will revolutionize domestic service!"

Roland looked at Alice. "Shall we?" he asked.

Alice nodded her approval, making a mental note that when they returned to the exhibits, they would pick up at the display featuring an automatic egg cracker.

Alice and Roland filed into chairs about halfway back from the stage. Already a large crowd had gathered for the demonstration. As she looked around, Alice was surprised to see a large number of women in the audience. Of course, she thought, the women would be most interested in a clockwork housekeeper.

A well-dressed gentleman came onto the stage, a brass cone in his hand. A wire of some sort led from the bottom of the cone to a series of boxes on one side of the stage. Alice recognized it as the new Mobile Voice Amplification Machine. The man's voice boomed from the front of the biggest box when he spoke into the cone.

"Ladies and gentleman, scientists and civilians!" he began in his best fairground barker's voice. "You

will never have to pay a domestic servant again!
Giving wages to housekeepers, maids, kitchen help,
and yes, even governesses, has come to an end. Why
give up money, food, and bedchambers to household
help when you can have your very own clockwork
domestics? Just wind them up and set them to their
task. They never tire, they never complain, they never
stop to eat or sleep. When the day is done, just stand
them in a corner, where they will be ready to serve you
in the morning. Dr. Lemuel Bateman is the man you
have to thank for this amazing breakthrough. Visiting
us from the state of Wisconsin, please welcome Dr.
Bateman and his clockwork housekeeper!"

    The red curtains on the stage slid open, and there
stood the diminutive Dr. Bateman and a hulking
clockwork structure. It stood about six feet tall and had
a thick girth, as if it were well fed despite being a
machine. A molded ceramic face gave it some touch of
humanity: the features painted on the face were eerily
lifelike, and the lips turned up in a smile. Alice
repressed a shudder. She couldn't imagine coming
across that vacant stare in the daytime, let alone at
night when the gears had all run themselves down.

    In addition to the disturbing but undoubtedly
feminine face, the clockwork housekeeper was also
clad in a black dress with a white apron. The gears that
made up the hairless head could be clearly seen,
despite a frilly white cap perched on top.

    Dr. Bateman took the conical speaking machine
from the barker and began to speak in a thin, quiet
voice. He was clearly not used to addressing large
crowds of people. Alice could only catch snippets of
what he said, but she watched as he hiked up the
housekeeper's dress to show off the jointed legs
underneath. A gasp ran through the audience. Even if
she was made of gears and metal, it was still improper
to look at a lady's bare legs! Once the initial surprise
was over, giggling and amused murmuring spread
through the audience.

His precursory demonstration done, Dr. Bateman went to the side of the stage and picked up a broom that was lying there. He fitted it into the hands of the housekeeper, firmly wrapping each finger around the broom handle. He then moved behind the housekeeper, which stood a foot taller than him. All the audience could see of him were his elbows as he fiddled with something on the machine's back.

With a start, the clockwork housekeeper jerked to life, its motionless face staring out at the audience. The arms ticked outward and began to move side to side. After four strokes with the broom, the housekeeper moved forward, taking slow steps on its gear-driven legs. It made four more strokes with the brush, then took another step forward.

When the housekeeper reached the end of the stage and dipped the broom to sweep, the bristles swept only empty air. Through some design, the housekeeper knew it had reached the end of the area to be swept. It pivoted to the right and began the sweeping and stepping routine again.

Dr. Bateman's voice was triumphant when he spoke again, and Alice finally heard him clearly. "Internal sensors tell her when she has reached a wall or a stair. She will continue to move in precise lines, getting smaller with each rotation until the room has been swept from the outside to the very center. You will never have to sweep again!"

The audience erupted in enthusiastic applause, and several overzealous women stood up to show their approval.

Alice and Roland looked at each other. "What do you think, Miss Alice?" Roland said.

"I think it has a lot of potential," Alice answered carefully.

"Come now, you can be candid with me."

Alice's reply was cut off when the audience began to cheer again. This time, Dr. Bateman had rolled a washing machine onto the stage. Water sloshed over the sides of the wooden tub. He placed a shirt in the housekeeper's hands, then once again adjusted something on its back. The housekeeper began to dunk the shirt up and down in the water before placing it in the agitator. After several turns of the agitator, the housekeeper pulled the shirt out and fed it through the wringer. Dr. Bateman took the shirt and held it up, droplets of water flying out to sprinkle people in the front row. Another round of applause went up.

"Well, then?" Roland prompted when the audience quieted once again.

"As I was saying, I think it has a lot of potential. But that sweeping is only going to move the dirt around. It didn't gather the dirt into a pile, or sweep it off the stage. The laundry, I admit, is more impressive. Even if you had to hand it articles of clothing, it would save a lot of labor. Still, someone would have to sit there with the machine, so you'd still need some kind of real housekeeper to make sure each task got done."

"A good point," agreed Roland. "But, as you say, it has potential. Within a few short years, clockwork housekeepers might be more fine-tuned and able to work autonomously."

"Certainly."

Roland smiled. "You marveled at the clockwork fountain as we came in, yet you are unimpressed with the clockwork housekeeper that does your work for you."

"I'm not unimpressed," corrected Alice. "I'm trying to be objective. Some of these women will probably put in an order for their very own clockwork as soon as this demonstration ends. But when their new housekeeper arrives, I think they will be sorely disappointed in the amount of work that still has to be done. I just hope they don't dismiss their current housekeepers in anticipation."

"And let's not forget that this clockwork contraption is soaked up to the elbows from doing that laundry. The housekeeper cleans the house, but who cleans the housekeeper? She'll be too rusted to move within the first week."

"Maybe all those out-of-work housekeepers can find jobs as gear cleaners," Alice suggested wryly.

Roland laughed. "You have a shrewd mind, the mind of a scientist," he said. "Shall we move on? I think we've seen the best part of this show."

Alice agreed and they rose to leave. A few other people filed out of the row with them, but those onlookers made a beeline for the front of the stage, where a knot of people had gathered. Dr. Bateman had abandoned the speaking cone and was talking instead to the enthusiastic group before him. His onstage demeanor had improved with every round of applause, and now he was beaming as he continued to show off his clockwork marvel.

Alice expected that they would continue moving through the displays, but instead Roland took her arm and steered her toward the rear of the building. "There's some New Science back here that will impress you," he said. "It's better than a dozen of those housekeepers."

They passed underneath a broad copper sign. The lettering had been neatly punched out with a diamond-tipped auto-tracer, and it read "New Science Dining Room." Inside, people were gathered in twos and threes at small round tables, eating small sandwiches and sipping coffee and tea.

At one side there were two giant silver urns, each as tall as Alice and ornately designed. They sat on large wooden blocks, so they towered over the heads of the people standing in line before them. Steam was pouring out of a vent in the lid of each.

"What are those?" Alice was already walking forward to join one of the queues, not even sure what she was lining up for.

"Do you prefer coffee or tea?" Roland asked.
"Coffee."

"Then you're heading for the wrong line. You want this one." Alice pivoted and moved to the other line, finally noticing the signs hanging on a chain around each urn. One said "coffee" and the other "tea."

"They are certainly the largest coffee and tea pots I've ever seen," said Alice, "but what makes them New Science?"

"Watch."

Alice had a clear view of a man stepping up to the tea urn. There were a series of knobs at the base of the urn, each with lettering that was too small for Alice to read. After a few moments of hesitation, the man pulled three of the knobs out. As they returned slowly to their starting positions, a whirring noise could be heard inside the urn.

A china teacup on a white saucer moved into place below the urn's spigot. Alice couldn't see, but guessed that the cup was moving on some sort of belt. With a hiss of steam, tea burbled from the spigot and neatly filled the cup. The man took his tea and moved away, and the next person stepped up to the machine.

Alice turned to Roland. "It fills your cup for you," she said.

"That's not all. But just wait; it will be your turn soon enough."

When Alice finally stepped up to the giant coffee urn, she saw that the lettering on the knobs labeled them as coffee, sugar, milk, and extra sugar. She gingerly pulled the knobs for coffee, sugar, and milk. The machine spun to life within its gleaming silver shell.

Alice watched, delighted, as the coffee steamed into her cup. "The milk is in it already!" she said, seeing the color of the liquid.

"And the sugar," added Roland, as he made the selections for his own cup. "All the workers have to do is keep its stores of sugar, milk, and coffee stocked, and the machine does the rest."

They found an empty table in one corner and sat down. "Even still," Alice began, "humans have to make the coffee. And usually, they would serve it to us, and we would put the milk and sugar in. So really, it's saving effort on our part, but not on the part of the people serving us."

"A good point. You'll find that a lot of new conveniences and breakthroughs benefit the upper classes. After all, it is primarily the upper classes that do the inventing. We are a selfish lot." Roland's tone was frank. "We want to make our lives better. If it happens to make the lives of the less fortunate better, as well, then that's an added benefit."

"And how does your Ghost Machine benefit others?"

"Well, it will entertain," Roland said, a mischievous look on his face. "It certainly entertained me when you came running into my office so breathlessly."

Alice shook her head at Roland's pertness, torn between amusement and embarrassment.

"It can also help us learn things about life after death," Roland continued, his tone serious again. "And, often, family members want to reach out to someone who has died. The Ghost Machine might give them that opportunity. It's like a séance, really, except you can see the ghost and talk to it directly. Otherwise, you have to put your faith in a medium who may, as you found out, be a fraud."

Alice nodded. "I see. Now if we can get your ghosts to do the sweeping and the laundry, you'll be well on your way to fame and fortune, and I can be idle the rest of my life."

"Planning on sharing my profits, are you?"

"No," said Alice. "I meant I can use your Ghost Housekeeping Machine to do all the work for me. Though I guess, in reality, it would be all my deceased ancestors doing the work."

"I take it back, Alice. You don't have the mind of

a scientist. You have the mind of a mad scientist!"

Chapter 11

The next week for Alice was nearly unbearable, with an unending stream of routine days and boring evenings. She saw Roland only at breakfast, except for several days when he didn't show up at all. He was constantly engaged with other scientists, usually AAD Men, and he kept wild hours, often coming home after Alice had fallen asleep. When he was at home, Roland was in his office working furiously: the sounds of metal being hammered, bent, and fitted together rang out hour after hour.

Alice had hoped to return to the Hall of New Science the following Sunday, but Roland had left the house early that morning, skipping breakfast and church with his family. He had either forgotten it was Alice's day off, or he didn't care. Alice considered going to the Exposition on her own—Mr. Frederick could always drive her over, if he wasn't taking the Highcrofts somewhere—but a thunderstorm rolled in during church, and the congregation exited to pouring rain and muddy roads. There would be no chance of her going all the way to the Exposition in such weather, and Alice knew that she was stuck at home, despite it being her day off.

The following week showed signs of the same

monotony, so Alice determined to ask Roland if she could go back to the Exposition with him on the coming Sunday. She finally did so after breakfast on Wednesday, chasing him after he rose from the breakfast table. He was already stepping into his office when she caught up to him.

"Mr. Highcroft, do you have a moment?" she asked.

Roland turned, surprised to see someone there. "Miss Alice! Of course, I always have a moment for you." Despite his reassuring words, Roland glanced over his shoulder at his waiting Ghost Machine, sitting quietly under its white sheet.

"I was just wondering if you would be kind enough to take me to the Exposition again," Alice blurted out.

Roland smiled. "Of course, though you'll be at the mercy of my schedule this Sunday. I'm attending a lecture at three o'clock. If you come with me, you can either stroll the hall on your own or join me."

"Thank you!" Alice said. "I'll let you get back to work." She retreated quickly and went upstairs to join Margaret and Jasper in the nursery.

Alice silently chided herself while she got the children started on their morning lessons. Why had she felt so shy about asking Roland to take her to the Exposition? She had been shy—no, scared—of him at first, when he was such a mystery, but now they had become friends. Margaret and Jasper were in the middle of reciting their new spelling words when the answer came to Alice. Her outing with Roland had felt almost like a romantic afternoon. The two of them had moved through the crowd as if they were a couple, rather than a kind scientist entertaining his household governess. His easy familiarity with her, his teasing smile, his face turned toward hers as he whispered to her during the clockwork housekeeper demonstration—it all felt very comfortable, yet exciting in its newness.

Alice shook her head to clear her thoughts. No, she told herself, Roland is simply glad to have found someone with whom he can share his New Science. It just so happens that the someone is me. If he had any other intentions, he would not have left me here alone last Sunday!

Alice felt better with that resolve, and she turned her attention back to the children in time to correct Margaret's spelling of "observe."

Roland and Alice had time only for a few bites of dinner on Sunday before they had to leave for the Exposition. Mr. Highcroft was usually firm about everyone staying until the end of the midday meal, but he made an exception on account of the lecture Roland was attending.

As Alice stood in the hallway adjusting her hat, Katie bustled by on her way out for the day. She handed Alice an envelope as she passed. "I forgot to give you this, Miss. It arrived a day or two ago."

"Thank you, Katie." Alice looked down and recognized her mother's handwriting on the envelope. She and her mother kept up a regular correspondence, though both sides were usually full of trifling matters. Alice, not wanting to relay even a hint of New Science, hadn't even mentioned her first trip to the Exposition. Mama, on her side, had such an aversion to gossip that she only wrote about the most mundane happenings: in her previous letter, she had gone into great detail about Emma's new dress.

Alice had just broken the seal on the envelope when Roland came up. "Are you ready? Good, we must be going. Mr. Frederick already brought the carriage around." Without waiting for a word of answer, he opened the front door and began to step out. Remembering his manners at the last possible moment, he stepped back and let Alice go out first.

Roland was full of nervous anxiety as the carriage clambered toward the Exposition. His hands wouldn't sit still in his lap, and his gaze kept shifting to his pocket watch.

"Are we late?" Alice asked.

"No, not at all."

"Then why do you continue to check the time?"

"Professor Crowfoot is giving this lecture," answered Roland, as if that would answer all. Seeing Alice's confused look, he added, "He is the current president of the AAD Men. I have to convince him that I'm every bit as innovative as the current members."

Alice nodded, letting Roland return to his silent fretting. She wasn't sure how attending a lecture would convince this Professor Crowfoot of Roland's intelligence. Maybe there would be an exam given at the end of the lecture, Alice mused. The idea of a room full of wizened old scientists and young thinkers like Roland bending over a piece of paper, sharpened pencils scratching away, made Alice giggle quietly. She put her head down so Roland wouldn't notice, and her eyes landed on the unopened letter still lying in her lap. With a sigh, she pulled it out and began to read. "My Dearest Alice," it began.

> I hope and pray that all continues to go well for you in Atlanta. It gave me great pleasure to read in your letter how much you like Margaret and Jasper and how well they are getting on in their lessons thanks to your tutelage. The Highcroft family is very respectable, and I hope that you are learning by their example and by the example of the society they keep.
>
> Mrs. Highcroft sent me a letter that arrived the same day as yours. She tells me that you attended that big exposition there in Atlanta, and that you were escorted by her brother-in-law. She speaks very highly of him as an educated, well-mannered young man,

and I am glad that you were able to
attend something as exciting as the
exposition. You must write and tell me
all about your visit there.

The letter continued, with Mrs. Meriwether's
usual account of family doings. As she read, though,
Alice's thoughts kept straying to the line informing her
that Mrs. Highcroft had given a report on Alice. A
favorable report, no less! She was relieved that there
was no mention of Roland's being a scientist, and she
was frankly surprised that Mrs. Highcroft spoke of him
so highly. She wondered if Mrs. Highcroft really
regarded Roland as a well-rounded gentleman, or if
she was saying that to allay any worries Mrs.
Meriwether may have. Either way, Mama hadn't
objected to Alice's friendship with Roland. Alice felt a
great sense of relief without even realizing that
Mama's opinion on the matter had been worrying her.

Alice re-read the first two paragraphs of the letter
at least three times before she finally put the letter
away, tucking it neatly into her handbag. By then, they
were nearing the Exposition. The crowds were not so
great as they had been on opening weekend, and they
reached the front entrance more quickly than before.
Since Mr. Frederick had driven them this time, they
were able to get out right in front of the entry gate.
Roland asked Mr. Frederick to pick them up at five,
then led the way inside.

Alice still felt a sense of wonder at the place even
though she had been there before. Roland's anxiety
and hurry meant they were nearly an hour early for the
lecture, so they strolled at a more leisurely pace this
time. One squat building looked like a shack in
comparison to the grand buildings towering over it, but
the smell of barbeque wafted out. Long tables were
lined up outside, where people ate carefully, trying not
to drip any of the barbeque sauce onto their clothes.
Alice felt her stomach growl at the scent; their quick
dinner hadn't been enough for her taste.

As they neared the Hall of New Science, a handsome gentleman walking in the opposite direction stopped and addressed Roland. "On your way to Professor Crowfoot's lecture, then?" he asked.

"Jacob! Yes, we're making our way there now. You're heading in the wrong direction for it, though."

"That's because I've got an even bigger meeting to attend." The man, who was near Roland's age, was clearly proud of himself. "The Atlanta Journal is interested in buying one of my clockwork newspaper boys."

"Congratulations!" Roland said with sincerity. Alice smiled but remained silent, and the man seemed to notice her for the first time. "Jacob Masterson, pleased to meet you. And you are?" he said, extending his hand to Alice.

"Alice Meriwether," she answered.

Jacob shook Alice's hand warmly and kept his grip while he turned and raised his eyebrows at Roland. Roland kept his face serious as he answered, "My assistant."

"Well," Jacob said, turning his eyes back to Alice, "you have the finest assistant in the entire hall, I daresay." Finally, he released Alice's hand.

They parted soon after, and Alice turned to Roland once they were out of earshot. "How do you know him?" she asked.

"We went to school together."

"Hmmm," was all Alice answered. She was tempted to add that Jacob had held her hand for an awfully long time, but if Roland hadn't noticed it, then she wouldn't mention it. Something about Jacob's manner had made Alice uncomfortable, as if his inquiring eyes had appraised her a little too thoroughly.

Alice had expected to sit in front of the stage at the center of the hall again, but Roland walked right past it to the staircase at the rear of the building. He turned to Alice as they began to walk up the curving steps. "I guess we should have ridden the platform outside. I forgot how excited you are to try that," he said.

"Next time," Alice answered.

The second floor of the hall had seemed to be nothing but a long balcony running along all four sides of the building, but when they reached the top Alice realized that there were a number of doors along the back wall. Each was labeled with a number: they headed for Lecture Room 3.

The room was small, with space for only about twenty chairs. There were two open windows on the outside wall, making the room much less stuffy than the hall itself.

Roland selected two chairs in the second row. The front row was already full and people were still coming through the door at a steady pace. Once all the seats were full, men began to stand along the back wall. The cool breeze from the windows was stifled by the mass of bodies in the room, and Alice began to wish for her fan. As she looked around, she realized that she was the only female attending the lecture.

Alice's attention was brought back to the front of the room by the entrance of Professor Crowfoot. He was in his late fifties, and his white hair still had streaks of black in it. His skin was deeply tanned and he had a weathered look, a stark contrast from the usual fair-skinned pallor of scientists. Unlike them, Professor Crowfoot appeared to actually leave his laboratory once in a while. He also didn't have the look of a man who grew up wealthy. There was a hardness to him that the other scientists lacked. In fact, Alice realized, in any other setting Professor Crowfoot might look rather intimidating. His large size and haggard appearance had probably made him a threatening presence in his younger years. Judging by the way the entire room fell silent and every back was a bit straighter when he entered, Alice guessed that Professor Crowfoot was still a threatening presence.

His voice matched his stature, a deep, craggy voice that commanded instant attention. "Harnessing energy is the topic of today's lecture," he began, skipping any kind of greeting. "We've learned how to create energy through steam, the winding of gears, water pressure, creating sparks, even riding stationary bicycles to power a conveyor belt." As he spoke, Professor Crowfoot began to pace back and forth, looking out at the sea of faces like a general surveying his troops. "But," he continued, "we are still learning how to harness that energy, to capture it and utilize it without losing vast quantities of it."

The lecture went on for close to an hour. Alice found the whole thing fascinating, though much of the terminology and concepts were far beyond her understanding. It was like watching an opera: she could follow the basic story but couldn't comprehend the minute details.

Near the end of his lecture, Professor Crowfoot's eyes searched the audience. "Where is Dr. Bateman?" he said.

Alice recognized the man who stood up as the same Dr. Bateman who had demonstrated the clockwork housekeeper. He had a small contraption in his arms, housed inside a wire birdcage. There were a variety of gears and wires running through the bottom of the birdcage, and a yellow-feathered model bird sat on a swing at the top. Dr. Bateman came up front and stood next to Professor Crowfoot, holding his birdcage aloft so everyone could get a good look.

"Dr. Bateman is trying to perfect his clockwork canary," Professor Crowfoot began. "He has a finite space in which to work since he wants it all contained within the birdcage. When the winding gear is primed, it does more than just turn gears. Two of the gears have flint cogs, so they generate sparks as one turns the other. Those sparks are fed through wires which power the amplifier for the bird's voice."

As he spoke, Dr. Bateman wound the machine

with a brass key and set the whole thing into motion. The bird turned its head and flapped its wings, but with even less grace than the clockwork housekeeper. It certainly wouldn't take the place of having a real bird as a pet. Its voice, though, was a true feat of New Science. The notes that warbled out of the metal beak were melodious, ringing cheerfully through the room thanks to the amplifier. After just a few seconds, though, the voice began to falter, lowering to a whisper.

"The energy from the sparks is strong initially, but as the gears wind down, too much of the energy is being lost, and the amplifier fails," Professor Crowfoot continued. "How do we harness more of the sparks' energy?"

Silence hung in the air as everyone waited for Professor Crowfoot to give the answer. It soon became apparent that he wasn't going to speak, though, and that he expected someone in the audience to offer a solution. There was much clearing of throats and scratching of heads as the other scientists thought, but no one ventured a guess.

Professor Crowfoot pointed at the birdcage. "Remember, there is a small space in which to work. Any additions or changes have to be small. How do you make a higher percentage of the sparks feed into the wire?"

"Put a dynamic reflector around the sparking gears, so sparks that fly in the wrong direction will be redirected to the wire."

Every head turned to look at the intrepid scientist who had finally offered up an answer, and Alice was amazed to realize it was her voice that had rung out through the room. The surprise on everyone's faces was no comparison to her own expression. Alice's hand came up to cover her mouth as her eyes met Roland's. His shocked look reminded her of Mama's face when Alice had disrupted the séance. I should learn to keep my mouth shut, Alice thought. Why must

I always blurt things out at the wrong time?

The following silence seemed interminable, and Alice was relieved when Professor Crowfoot began to speak again. "What about our space constraints?" he asked, his dark eyes fixed on Alice.

Alice slowly lowered her hand and took a deep breath. "Well," she began, her voice now quiet and timid, "dynamic reflectors can be shaped according to the space, so long as they are concave enough to properly redirect the energy. And other scientists have proven that energy capture can be improved by as much as twenty-five percent with a reflector only one-eighth of an inch thick."

A couple of the other scientists nodded in agreement. Alice knew some of the men in the room must have read the same article in the American Science Journal, but apparently she was the only one who remembered its contents.

Professor Crowfoot smiled, but it only made him look more menacing. "And how does a girl your age know such things?" he asked.

Alice should have told the truth, but even among fellow New Scientists she was afraid to admit how much she had read and studied on her own. She glanced at Roland. "Mr. Highcroft is working on his new machine and has been looking for a way to harness static electricity," she said. Well, she told herself, that part was true, at least.

Now Professor Crowfoot's eyes turned to Roland. "And has the dynamic reflector aided you?"

Roland answered the professor, but his gaze was fixed on Alice as he spoke. "I haven't had a chance to implement it yet," he said slowly. "I've been busy working on some other bugs in the machine."

"Mr. Highcroft is right," Professor Crowfoot said, addressing the audience once again. Alice frowned. "I was right," she mouthed silently as Professor Crowfoot continued. "A dynamic reflector is a thin piece of copper with an even thinner backing of lead.

Bend it to reflect electric sparks in the proper direction, and you'll see an increase in captured energy. It takes precision tuning to get the most power out of it, but I assure you that the results will be worth the effort."

The lecture broke up shortly after, and as the other men collected in groups or left, Professor Crowfoot made a beeline for Roland. "You must be as brilliant as I've been told, but I didn't realize you were also so humble. Next time speak up; don't make your assistant do the talking for you."

"I was curious to hear what other solutions might be offered up. A dynamic reflector isn't the only choice," said Roland.

"No, but it's the best choice." Professor Crowfoot appraised Alice before turning back to Roland. "You are lucky in your choice of an assistant. I fear, however, she won't be able to attend tonight's AAD Men reception with you since it's for gentlemen only. You'll have to tell us about your accomplishments yourself."

Roland's expression changed from nervous to excited at the mention of the reception. "Thank you, sir. I'll be happy to attend, and I'm sure you'll be tired of hearing my bragging by night's end."

"Yes, well, till tonight, then." Without a second look at Alice, Professor Crowfoot turned away to address several scientists who were waiting impatiently for his attention.

Roland smiled broadly all the way out the door, along the balcony, and down the stairs. He was still smiling when they sat down in the café, fresh cups of machine-made coffee in front of them. "I just got invited to tonight's AAD Men reception by Professor Crowfoot!" Roland said, as if Alice hadn't been standing right there when it happened.

"Yes, I recall," she said. "Congratulations."

"Thank you." Roland leaned toward her to whisper, his face turning serious. "But, Alice, why did

you lie to him? You didn't hear about dynamic
reflectors from me."

Alice shrugged, trying to act casual, but her voice
betrayed her nerves. "I read an article about them."
She hesitated before continuing. "At home, I wasn't
allowed to read the American Science Journal, so I
guess I wasn't ready to confess it to a room full of
strangers."

Alice watched Roland, wondering what he would
say to her confession. He surprised her by simply
answering, "Of course, if you hadn't spoken out like
that, I wouldn't have gotten invited to tonight's event.
So, thank you."

"I'm glad I could help." Alice gazed at Roland as
he happily sipped his coffee, staring into space and
dreaming, no doubt, about becoming an AAD Man
himself. As she watched, he suddenly blinked a few
times and sat straighter, suddenly alert.

"Not allowed to read the Journal!" he said, more
to himself than to Alice. He finally turned to her, an
expression of utter disbelief on his face.

"That's right."

"But why? How could your parents possibly
object?"

"Because a lady's place is in the home or working
in her community with other women of good society,"
Alice echoed her mother's words. "New Science is an
unhealthy interest for young ladies who should be
more concerned with making a good marriage."

Now Roland looked offended, as if Mama herself
was standing there, lecturing. "Unhealthy! Marriage!"
He shook his head. "You should have told them you
wanted to marry a scientist and were simply looking
for eligible bachelors within the pages of the Journal."

Alice relaxed and laughed at Roland's joke. She
started to make a quip about hoping to find a
marriageable scientist here at the Exposition, but she
realized it might sound too suggestive. Instead, Alice
merely smiled and drank her coffee with much more

enthusiasm.

Chapter 12

Roland was even more reluctant to leave the Hall of New Science than Alice. Even though they were supposed to meet the carriage at five o'clock, and it was twenty minutes till already, Roland proposed that they see the final demonstration of the day before leaving.

It seemed as though everyone at the Exposition was crowding into the hall to see the new steam-powered Horseless Carriage. It looked like a carriage, but it was much larger and sat on wider wheels. The passenger compartment was from a traditional carriage, but a platform on the back of it housed a water tank and the massive steam engine. At the front, where the coachman sat, reins had been replaced with a row of levers. Each lever, it appeared, led to one of the carriage wheels. A trail of steam puffed languidly from the engine as it waited to be driven.

The Horseless Carriage sat on the floor in front of the stage, and all of the seats had been moved to make room for the demonstration. People were standing everywhere: around the demonstration area, on the stage, and along the upper balconies. As Alice and Roland squeezed into a small space at the side of the stage, more people crowded behind them. By the time the Hall's giant clock sounded five, the crowd was seven people deep downstairs and three people deep on the balcony.

Alice could barely see the tall man in a long lab coat who stepped up to the Horseless Carriage. He looked immensely proud of himself, and he spoke loudly into the voice amplifier. Since they were right next to the speakers, the scientist's voice echoed painfully in Alice's head, and she covered her ears.

"Welcome, welcome! Welcome to the demonstration of the world's very first functional Horseless Carriage! I am Dr. Higgenbottom, and this is my crowning achievement!" As he waved his hands in triumph, the crowd began to cheer. Roland leaned over and had to shout into Alice's ear to be heard over the clamor. "He's terribly proud of himself, isn't he?" Alice nodded in agreement before clamping her hand over her ear once more.

Dr. Higgenbottom continued to speak, describing the components of the Horseless Carriage piece by piece, pausing after each point to let the crowd show their enthusiasm. His voice rose in pitch as he explained the levers. "And now, my assistant, Donald, will drive the Horseless Carriage!" A wild roar went up for the young man who now came into view, swinging up onto the buckboard with all the grace and style of a hero in a storybook. Donald waved and made a show of settling onto the high seat and readying his hand on the brake lever.

The showmanship was too much for Alice, who sighed impatiently. All she wanted to see was the machine in action. The crowd surged forward, pushing Alice and Roland ahead of them. Alice glanced back and realized the crowd had grown even more. In front of them, the demonstration area was slowly shrinking.

"Ready, set, go!" Dr. Higgenbottom shouted into the voice amplifier, and the only thing louder than his voice was the pop of the steam engine as Donald released the brake lever. Steam began to churn out of the engine in earnest, but for a moment nothing happened. Finally, the heavy carriage began to inch forward. The audience gasped to see the carriage move without a horse. Even Alice could appreciate the significance of the invention: aside from trains and trolley cars, every other mode of overland transportation relied on horses.

As the Horseless Carriage picked up momentum, Donald adjusted the levers so it turned to the right. He moved in a wide clockwise circle, barely missing some of the intrepid audience members who had stepped forward for a better view. Alice joined in the cheering, excited to see an invention she had read about but had never actually seen.

The carriage continued to move faster, going now at a pace that matched a horse's trot. Donald drove competently, making wide circles around the demonstration area. He slowed to a crawl, stopped completely, then lurched forward again. Shouts of, "Faster, faster!" rang through the audience, and Donald complied. The engine began to roar as the Horseless Carriage went faster, steam billowing into a cloud that hung inside the hall like an approaching storm.

Alice looked at Dr. Higgenbottom just in time to see his face go pale. He stood transfixed, his eyes on his invention. She followed his gaze and saw the front left wheel shuddering under the weight and the speed. Already Donald was fighting to make the machine steer straight, but he showed no signs of decreasing the speed.

A high, shrill shriek began to sound, like a giant tea kettle. It was nearly drowned out by all the other noise, but its piercing wail was instantly recognizable to the scientist and his assistant. Their eyes met, panic and dismay on their faces.

Whatever Dr. Higgenbottom shouted at Donald couldn't be heard, but surely he hadn't suggested what Donald did next. The front wheel began to wobble even more violently, nearly pitching Donald from the buckboard. Not willing to ride it out, he jumped from the Horseless Carriage, landing in a heap and knocking down five or six bystanders.

The driverless carriage continued to speed forward, now moving in great rolling hitches toward the stage. The whine of the steam engine increased, the pressure inside the reservoir nearing its breaking point.

With no one to steer, the carriage veered to the left, and Alice saw it coming directly toward her. The audience finally realized the carriage was out of control, and their initial shock transformed into panic. Screams erupted from the women, and men were shouting directions to clear the area. Alice looked all around her, but there was nowhere to go. The Horseless Carriage was in front of her, and on every side the crowd of people still pressed on her as everyone tried to flee in a different direction.

Suddenly, a strong arm clamped around Alice's waist and yanked her hard to the left. Her feet came off the floor as her slender body was lifted into the air. She realized that it was Roland who was holding onto her, and when her feet touched the floor again, he pushed her away from the carriage. They were in the open space of the demonstration area, and there was enough room for Alice to take several running steps before a crowd of people once again barred their way.

"Get down!" Roland shouted behind her. Alice complied, sinking to her knees. Roland followed her movement, kneeling down behind her and wrapping his arms around her shoulders.

No sooner had Roland positioned himself between the carriage and Alice than the great steam engine exploded. The damaged front wheel buckled under the force, and though Alice couldn't see the wreck, she could hear the creak of breaking wood and the clatter of falling structures as the machine bit into the corner of the stage, just a few feet from where she and Roland had been standing a moment before.

Looking in front of her, Alice could see that
everyone else had cowered to the ground, too. Behind
her, though, a man screamed in pain as hot water
showered him. Alice could hear his heavy footfalls
nearing them, and a second later she was facedown on
the floor, her body pinned there by Roland's. The
injured man had run right into Roland in his blind
haste.

The entire hall was utterly silent for a moment,
save for the quiet clink of metal shards falling to the
ground. Alice felt a warm rivulet of water running
along her left arm. It wasn't scalding, so it must have
come from the reserve water tank on the Horseless
Carriage. She twisted her head to look at the water and
saw that it was red.

Chapter 13

At that instant, the silence broke and chaos once again erupted. People stood and fled the hall, their screams and cries muffling Alice's small voice. "Mr. Highcroft!" she shouted, trying to turn her head far enough to see his face. "Roland!"

Feet were running past, inches from Alice's face. She felt Roland's body rock as people stumbled over his prone form. The crowd was too thick and too fast to even attempt getting up; she knew they would just be knocked down again. Alice shut her eyes and prayed, the tears on her cheeks matching the heat of the blood trickling down her arm.

Suddenly Roland's mouth was pressed against her ear. His voice was quiet, but firm. "It's all right. Just stay still. It will be over soon."

Alice tried to nod as Roland's grip tightened around her body. His weight pressed against her back, making it hard to breathe, and she was lying awkwardly on his forearms and hands, but still she was grateful for his protection.

The onslaught of panicked people was soon over, as Roland had promised, but it seemed to Alice that they had cowered on the floor for an hour. Soon people were hurrying in the other direction, not to escape but to tend to those too injured to move. Roland rolled off of Alice and sat up. He took her shoulders and pulled her up next to him, putting one arm around her. They huddled together, Alice's head resting against Roland's cheek.

If only Mama could see me now, Alice thought wildly. She would never approve of us being so familiar with each other! Alice fought the urge to laugh. Well, she told herself, this isn't a normal social setting, so it must be all right.

To her surprise, Alice burst into tears. Roland patted her back awkwardly, unsure how to react as she turned her face into his shoulder. She clung to his torn coat, and he sat quietly as Alice's tears slowly stopped. "I'm sorry," Alice mumbled into his collarbone.

Roland's voice was weary. "I thought I was going to cry myself," he said.

"I forgot!" Alice sat up suddenly. "You're bleeding!"

"I think a shard of metal from that blasted machine did it." Roland slid his arm from Alice's shoulder and held it out. His coat sleeve was soaked with blood.

"Let's get this off you and see how bad it is," Alice said. The sight of the blood made her stomach lurch, but she clenched her jaw and helped Roland slide his coat off. His white shirt looked even worse, and Alice gingerly rolled his sleeve up to reveal the deep gash on his upper arm.

Roland looked at Alice. "You're bleeding, too," he said, nodding at her own arm.

"No, that's your blood. I about fainted when I saw how much you were bleeding. I couldn't tell if you were even conscious until you spoke."

Roland gave Alice a wan smile. "Were you terribly worried about me?"

"Yes." Alice pulled out her handkerchief and folded it into a neat square, which she pressed against Roland's arm. "This isn't going to do much good. We need to get you a proper bandage."

Alice stood up slowly, her limbs stiff and tired. Roland refused any help in getting up, and as he rose she took a moment to survey the scene around them.

It looked as though a battle had raged through the hall. People were scattered everywhere, some lying on the floor, a few sitting and nursing wounds, and others stood together in tight knots. One half of the stage had collapsed, and the failed machine itself rose up like some great carcass. Steam still issued slowly from the ruptured engine, and every now and then a clank or a click sounded from it.

Several of the people closest to the wreckage appeared to be unconscious, and one man's torso stuck out from a pile of wooden beams. He cried for help even though five men were already busy clearing the beams to free his legs.

The sound of quick footsteps behind her made Alice whirl around, and she found herself face to face with a nurse. Several other nurses and a doctor accompanied the woman, and each had a large bag of medical supplies. The group had fanned out across the area.

The nurse addressed Alice. "We came from the Medical Station as soon as we could," she said briskly, already pulling supplies from her bag. She gave Roland's arm a quick exam and, satisfied that none of the metal shards were still in the wound, she bound his arm quickly and efficiently with a white bandage. Roland barely had time to thank her before she picked up her bag and hurried over to someone nursing a sprained ankle.

"I'm sorry I suggested we stay for the demonstration," said Roland. Alice just nodded and followed Roland as he picked a clear path through people and Horseless Carriage parts. "And I ruined your dress," he added.

"I wouldn't worry about that," Alice said. She stopped on the front steps of the Hall of New Science, almost surprised to see that it was still daylight out. The sun hovered above the distant line of trees at the edge of the Exposition grounds. Alice breathed in the fresh air and felt the breeze refresh her senses. After a moment she turned to Roland. "If you hadn't acted so quickly, I would have been in the middle of that wreck. Thank you."

Roland looked away briefly, then turned back to Alice. He opened his mouth to speak, paused, then tried again. Alice felt certain that his simple "you're welcome" wasn't what he was going to say initially.

Before she could wonder what Roland had really wanted to say, two men with "PRESS" badges on their coats swept up. One spoke to Alice, the other to Roland. "I'm with the Atlanta Journal," said one. The other introduced himself as a reporter with the Atlanta Constitution.

"What happened in there?" they asked in unison.

Roland and Alice looked at each other, seeing the weariness in each other's faces. Roland turned to the reporter addressing him. "We were too far away to really see what happened," Roland lied. "Some gentlemen inside will give you a better story."

The reporters dashed inside, each looking for the most sensational details.

Alice and Roland moved slowly through the crowd of people working their way to the Exposition's exit. Everyone gave them a wide berth, and many of the women gasped with shock and disapproval at their disheveled, bloody clothes.

There was a throng of carriages on the street outside, all waiting patiently for their passengers. After some searching they found Mr. Frederick, who gaped in silence when he saw them. Roland explained briefly as he and Alice climbed into the carriage. They rode home in silence, each too tired to speak.

Alice was relieved when they arrived at an empty house. She didn't know who the Highcrofts were visiting, but she was thankful that she and Roland were spared another explanation of their appearance. They parted at the top of the stairs, each repairing to their bedrooms to clean up and change clothes.

The family returned home while Alice was folding her stained dress into a tight ball. She wasn't sure whether she should throw it away, toss it into the fireplace, or try to clean it. She had just stuffed it into the back corner of her wardrobe when there was a quiet knock on her door. It was Margaret, who told her that supper would be in fifteen minutes.

Weary as she was, Alice was glad to know there would be a full supper tonight. Her stomach growled at the thought, and it seemed like days since she had eaten a hurried dinner to make it to Professor Crowfoot's lecture on time.

Alice was anxious to check on Roland. She knew the bleeding wasn't as severe as it had seemed at first, but he had been run into and tripped over so much while he was protecting her that she was worried about the severity of his other injuries. He might not have felt the pain at the time, but by now his muscles would be sore and his body bruised.

When dinner was served, Roland was still missing from his seat next to Alice. "Is Mr. Highcroft not feeling well?" Alice tentatively asked his brother, not knowing how much Roland's family knew yet of the day's adventure.

"Oh, I believe he's feeling just fine," answered Mr. Highcroft. "He had a function to attend tonight. Something having to do with the Exposition."

"Oh," was all Alice could answer. After all they had been through, she couldn't believe that Roland had left the house to attend the AAD Men reception. Of course, she reminded herself, getting accepted into that society was one of his greatest desires, so he would have limped there with a broken leg if need be.

Alice's own bruises were beginning to make themselves known. Her knees and elbows were particularly tender after being thrown so roughly to the floor at the Hall. She wished very much that Roland was there next to her to offer some measure of silent comfort.

After supper, Alice sat on the couch in her room with a book. She was determined to stay awake until Roland returned so she could make sure he was all right. As the hours ticked by, though, Alice's weariness overcame her, and she fell asleep on the couch. She woke up some time in the night and slipped into bed, but her dreams were full of people running, trampling both her and Roland under them.

Roland was, at least, at breakfast the next morning, and Alice knew that the circles under his eyes were only slightly darker than her own. When he passed a plate of toast across the table to Jasper, Alice saw him wince with pain.

"How was your reception last night?" she asked, forcing herself to sound cheerful.

At least Roland's eyes lit up at the mention. "It went very well. Professor Crowfoot was most attentive to me."

"I'm glad to hear it."

"Thank you." Roland hesitated. "He asked about you. So did Jacob Masterson."

Alice wasn't sure what to make of that information, particularly the latter part. "That was kind of them," she said, feeling it was the safest answer.

"Professor Crowfoot was quite impressed with you. He says you retain knowledge exceedingly well."

"And Mr. Masterson, was he also impressed with your new assistant?" Alice put the emphasis on the last word, her sarcasm obvious.

"You could say that. He asked me if you were engaged or if you had any beaus."

Alice blinked, torn between laughter at the inquiry and a feeling of unease, considering who had been asking. Something about Jacob Masterson just hadn't sat well with her, whether it was the way his hand lingered on hers or the way he had looked at her so boldly, as if she were a conquest.

"I told him I thought you were unattached," continued Roland, his voice dropping.

Alice merely nodded and returned hastily to her breakfast. She was all too aware of the eyes of Mr. and Mrs. Highcroft on both her and Roland.

During naptime that afternoon, Alice knocked on the door of Roland's study. The door did not open for many long seconds, and Alice was beginning to think that Roland was out or simply ignoring anyone who wanted to see him. When he finally did open the door, he moved stiffly.

Once she was inside the study with the door safely shut behind her, Alice leaned toward Roland. "Are you all right?" she asked.

"I feel like I've been run over by hundreds of people," he answered.

At Alice's concerned look, Roland continued. "I'll be fine in a few days, but I had some terrible dreams during what little sleep I got."

"I had the same nightmares. Was I in your dreams, as well?"

Roland raised his eyebrows. "That's a rather forward question, isn't it?"

"I meant, it's just that, well, I dreamed about yesterday, too, and you were in the dream, just like you were there when it really happened. So I just wondered…"

Roland smiled. "You were there. But then, I've dreamed about you before."

"About me?"

"Yes." Roland would say no more on the subject. Instead, he just gave Alice that small smile that looked so teasing and changed the subject. "Come and see the changes I've made to the Ghost Machine."

Alice complied, and she was very conscious of

how close the two of them stood as Roland pointed out the new dynamic reflector nestled behind the velvet drums. "It's taken me hours to get it positioned just right, but I think it will generate enough electricity now."

"I haven't seen any more ghosts in my room, though," said Alice. "Is it still not working properly?"

"Until I get the machine tuned better, I don't want to turn it on. I didn't want to frighten you with any more unexpected guests."

"If you forewarn me first, I don't think I'd mind too much. Or just let me sit down here while you test it."

"I don't want it popping up in the nursery, or any other room of the house, for that matter. James and Mariah know I'm building a big machine, but they don't know what it does. Nor, I think, do they want to know."

Alice was surprised. "Do they not approve of your pursuits? Mrs. Highcroft spoke very highly of you to," Alice stopped, the words, "my Mama" on her lips.

"To...?" Roland prompted.

"To me," Alice supplied in a hurry.

"She's a kind woman. And to answer your question, James and Mariah don't disapprove of what I do, but they're not at all interested in it. I gave up trying to entertain them with my work years ago."

"I'm sorry to hear it," Alice said. "I know what it's like to have ideas you can't share with your own family."

"I have you now, though, don't I? And you, I'm afraid, will have to listen to me ramble on behalf of the entire family."

Alice was more than happy to hear Roland's latest plans for perfecting the Ghost Machine. She watched as he pointed out possible fixes for getting ghosts to appear in front of the machine, rather than above.

The only interruption came from Katie, who came in to give Alice a letter that had just arrived. To her surprise, Alice saw that the handwriting on the elegant envelope was not from her mother. She tore it open eagerly and pulled out a thin sheet of stationery that held only a few neatly-written lines.

"It is an invitation!" said Alice, scanning the sentences quickly. "The League of Women Scientists is giving a lecture in the Hall of Women on Friday, and they would like me to attend. I wonder how they got my name and information?"

"You turned more than a few heads during Professor Crowfoot's lecture," said Roland. "Not to mention, you are acquainted with Dr. McGuffey. Perhaps he recommended you."

Alice sat down on the couch, her eyes still on the letter, and Roland settled in beside her. "It's too bad I can't go," she said.

"Then again," Roland continued, as if he hadn't heard Alice, "it's possible that I told Mrs. Crowfoot about you, since she's the head of the League of Women Scientists. It's also possible that I already told Mariah that I will help watch the children on Friday so you can attend."

Alice looked quickly at Roland, almost expecting him to be joking. He was amused, certainly, but she could tell he was in earnest. She threw her arms around his neck. "Oh, thank you!" she said.

Roland stiffened at Alice's unexpected hug, and only then did she realize what she had done. She hastily withdrew her arms and slid away from him on the couch. "I beg your pardon," she mumbled.

"You need not apologize to me." Roland shifted so that the gap between his body and Alice's disappeared. "You are a passionate woman, Alice. I have never seen a woman so enthralled by science. How could I not help foster that passion?"

Alice's heart beat faster at Roland's closeness, but she realized there was no romantic gesture behind

Roland's actions.

And why should there be? And why should I care? Alice wondered. I am not in love with him.

Yet, as she sat there in silence, alone with Roland in his study, her thoughts strayed to the warmth of his arm around her in the middle of the Horseless Carriage wreckage. She thought of his teasing smile, his penetrating blue eyes, and the way he leaned toward her when he was excited about their subject of conversation.

I am falling in love with this man, this scientist, Alice thought.

That realization was quickly followed by another: and I must not let him know, because he doesn't feel the same about me.

"Mr. Highcroft," Alice began, feeling the need to say something before the silence stretched on any longer.

"Please, just Roland. After our adventure together yesterday, I don't think there is any need for us to be formal."

"Roland, then. Thank you. You've been so kind to me."

Roland was about to respond when the grandfather clock in the hall chimed the hour. Alice leapt from her seat. "I must wake the children," she said. "I will see you at supper." With that, she left the room as quickly as she could, too confused about her own feelings to stay any longer.

Chapter 14

The Horseless Carriage disaster made front-page news in both the morning and evening papers. At supper, Mr. Highcroft asked Roland and Alice if they had witnessed it. They both confessed that they had, but after a silent look passed between the two, neither mentioned just how close they had been to the danger. Roland's wound was safely concealed under his shirt, his sleeves rolled up less high than usual so the bandage wouldn't show.

Roland changed the subject deftly by mentioning the invitation Alice had received for Friday's lecture at the Hall of Women. Both Mr. and Mrs. Highcroft were delighted and expressed their enthusiasm for Alice's warm reception among the scholars at the Exposition. If Mrs. Highcroft was still writing to her mother, Alice hoped she would forget to mention the unexpected honor. Of course, the invitation was not wholly a surprise to Mrs. Highcroft, to whom Roland had already spoken about watching the children.

"He never has time to watch them," she said. "It must mean a lot to him that you attend, Alice."

"It means a lot to me, as well," Alice answered.

Friday could not come fast enough for Alice. The week crept by, and Roland's continued absence only made things worse. Alice knew he was doing even more with the AAD Men in his quest to get approval to join their society, but she couldn't help feeling a little resentful. She had to remind herself that it was only through his generosity that she was going to attend the lecture on Friday.

Friday finally arrived, and Alice left just after dinner for the three o'clock lecture. Roland saw her off, standing on the front porch with Margaret and Jasper. Once Mr. Frederick dropped Alice off at the front gate, she felt slightly nervous at being alone in a sea of so many people, but the freedom of wandering on her own soon overshadowed any other feeling.

The Hall of Women was a large building with columns across the front and a great domed roof. Alice was early enough that she could wander around the first floor, taking in the exhibits featuring accomplished women.

The lecture was being held in a meeting room upstairs, and Alice chose a seat near the front of the crowded, stuffy space. Most of the women were older, probably in their thirties or later, and Alice was fascinated by their appearances. Several were very genteel, with feminine dresses that signified wealth. Others were clearly uninterested in appearance, with simple garments and buns pinned haphazardly on their heads.

The woman who stood up to greet the audience looked like she was well past middle age. Her graying hair was wound in a coil at the nape of her neck. A pair of spectacles sat on the end of her long nose, and her green eyes flashed behind them.

"Welcome," she said crisply. "I am Melvina Crowfoot, president of the League of Women Scientists. You are all here today because you care about science. You realize, as do we, that a woman's place can be in the home and in the laboratory."

As Mrs. Crowfoot took the stage, Alice breathed deeply and settled back into her chair, feeling blissfully at home among like-minded women.

Melvina Crowfoot's lecture was more of a current events lesson as she profiled women in science. Several of the women were there, rising from their seats for heartfelt applause. At the conclusion, Mrs. Crowfoot encouraged the women who were not yet members of the League to introduce themselves.

Alice lined up behind several other women, and when it was her turn, she offered her hand to Mrs. Crowfoot. The lady gave her a firm handshake and peered at her keenly. "So, you're that young man's assistant, are you?"

"Well," Alice began, but Mrs. Crowfoot continued.

"My husband was most impressed with your ability to regurgitate information, but can you think for yourself?"

Alice felt her pride swell. "Of course. I have plenty of drawings of my own design." Or I used to, anyway, she added silently.

"But they're still just drawings, aren't they? Haven't actually built them yet, have you?" Mrs. Crowfoot looked like a snake ready to strike.

"No, not yet," Alice admitted.

"Of course not! And do you know why? Because you are just an assistant to this man! You must break free, be your own scientist! Tell him you will not tolerate being his lackey any longer! You are an intelligent woman with ideas of your own! You must be free of his tyranny!"

Alice took a step back as Mrs. Crowfoot's voice rose, her tone righteous and demanding. Alice thought about replying that she was, in fact, not really Roland's assistant, but she feared that might bring on another tirade. Instead, she smiled brightly.

"Thank you for your encouragement," she said.

"The next time you see him, you tell that man that you are not going to be trapped, like electricity inside a Taylor's Cone. You will not be held down because you wear petticoats and a corset!"

Alice gasped. "A Taylor's Cone! Yes!" Her voice was nearly as loud as Mrs. Crowfoot's, and the League president mistook Alice's excitement for shared indignance.

"That's right! You tell him!" shouted Mrs. Crowfoot.

"I will. I'm going to go home right now and tell him. Oh, thank you, Mrs. Crowfoot, thank you!" Alice took the woman's hand and shook it heartily. As she turned to exit, she realized the entire room had fallen silent as they listened to the loud exchange. Now they erupted in cheers and applause for Alice, who, they were certain, was striding out the door so she could go confront the male scientist who was holding her back.

Alice giggled as she hurried her way back to the Exposition entrance. She knew Mrs. Crowfoot had mistaken her outburst and found it exceedingly funny. She was still laughing when she found Mr. Frederick and climbed into the carriage.

"What's so funny, Miss?" he asked.

"She never even asked me what my drawings were of," Alice answered. "She didn't even care to know what kind of science I like. For all she knows, they're worthless designs."

Mr. Frederick began to ask for clarification but thought better of it. He just shook his head and turned his attention to the reins.

When the carriage glided to a stop outside the house, Alice jumped out before Mr. Frederick could offer his assistance. She flew up the steps and through the front door, shouting Roland's name. When there was no response, she went out the back door and found him seated on the porch, the children playing in the yard.

"Roland!" Alice's shout died on her lips when she saw him seated just a few feet away.

"What's wrong?" Roland jumped up, alarmed.

"A Taylor's Cone! She said it, and it just clicked

into place. A Taylor's Cone inverted at the top of the machine to channel the energy into one spot. The ghosts will appear beneath it."

Roland stood for a moment, stunned, then he and Alice both spoke. "I can't believe I didn't think of that!" they said in unison.

"But you did think of it," said Roland, looking at Alice with clear admiration.

"Not until Mrs. Crowfoot mentioned one, and it just seemed so obvious."

"You told her about the Ghost Machine?"

"No. She told me to tell you that you can't keep me trapped in your Taylor's Cone of servitude just because I'm a woman. Or something like that. She was very adamant that I quit being your assistant." Alice laughed at the memory. "Of course, I'm not really your assistant, but I couldn't get a word in edgewise with her."

Roland laughed, too, and reached out to squeeze Alice's arm. "Everyone seems to think you are, though, and why not? You've just given me the solution that could make the Ghost Machine successful. I think you've earned the title."

Alice's smile widened. "Thank you. Just don't tell Mrs. Crowfoot. She'd be terribly displeased."

Roland gave Alice a curious look. "You really must tell me about this lecture. Perhaps over supper. For now, you must excuse me, but I've got a lot of work ahead of me, thanks to you."

"Thank you for watching the children," Alice called as Roland left for his study. When he was gone, she sat down in his vacated chair, feeling very out of breath, but excited.

Alice could hardly believe her luck! Mrs. Crowfoot's shocking attitude had led Alice to a solution that would most likely work to make ghosts manifest right next to the machine. As excited as she was about that, Alice was just as giddy at the thought of being Roland's assistant. A real assistant to a New

Scientist! Alice sighed. The only disappointment was that she had no one to whom she could speak or write of her afternoon. Mama was, of course, out of the question, and a letter to Emma could too easily fall into Mama's hands.

Fortunately, Alice was able to share her excitement with someone: at supper, Roland announced to the family that Alice was officially his assistant. He praised her knowledge and hinted that his machine would soon be functioning because of Alice's input.

"Well done, Alice," Mr. Highcroft said approvingly.

"She needs a lab coat if she's going to be working with you during her time off," said Mrs. Highcroft. "Otherwise, every dress she owns will be ruined." Alice smiled at Mrs. Highcroft's practical approach.

As supper continued, Roland asked for details of Alice's visit with the League of Women Scientists. She related Mrs. Crowfoot's message, imitating the woman's harsh voice. Margaret and Jasper laughed at the mockery, but Mrs. Highcroft was shocked that a woman could feel that way, especially about her own brother-in-law.

"It was such an honor for them to invite you, but perhaps they are not as good of society as we thought," she cautioned.

"I think you are right, ma'am," Alice answered. "I appreciate all they have accomplished, but they act as if they are more capable than men. To talk to Mrs. Crowfoot, one would think there was some sort of conspiracy afoot."

"For my part, I'm glad you have put me in my place," Roland said, straining to keep a straight face. "You must lead this venture from here on out. You are always right, while I am always just a man. Just speak, and I will do as you command."

On the whole, it was the most enjoyable supper Alice had ever eaten in her life. The laughter and teasing that night would have never been tolerated in the Meriwether household, but it came easily and comfortably with the Highcroft family. Roland especially was the source of Alice's happiness. Never had Alice felt so companionable with another person. Their shared interest, his unassuming manner, and her respect for him as a scientist combined to increase her feelings for him. Alice went to bed that night wondering if an assistant had ever fallen in love with her New Scientist before, and if so, what the outcome was. It was one experiment Alice was afraid to try.

Roland was again so busy with the AAD Men that he had no time for Alice that weekend. Instead, she spent Sunday afternoon in her bedroom, making plans. A letter had arrived from her Mother on Friday. Amid the excitement of Alice's afternoon, she didn't even open it until Saturday.

There was still no mention of Alice's involvement with Roland and all the time she had spent at the Hall of New Science. Still, Alice knew that Mrs. Highcroft continued their correspondence: the two mothers had agreed that Emma would come to spend a week with Alice.

Alice was delighted at the news—and surprised that Emma was being allowed to come without her father—but Emma's visit would also mean that Alice had to act more reserved since anything she said or did might be reported back home. She would have to spend less time in Roland's study and be less open in conversation with him at mealtimes.

In spite of that, Alice was still looking forward to the visit, which had been set for the second week in October. It was just one week away, and Alice sent a reply to her mother to acknowledge the plan.

On the Friday night before Emma's arrival, Roland knocked on Alice's bedroom door. It was already past ten o'clock, and the rest of the household had retired. Alice herself was in her dressing gown, sitting in bed with a book.

Alice opened the door a crack. "Yes?"

"You must come at once!" Roland said.

"Let me get dressed."

Roland waved his hand dismissively. "Don't bother. I want to show you now; I am too excited to wait." Without waiting for Alice's answer, he pushed the door open and took Alice by the wrist, towing her behind him down the stairs and into his study. With her free hand, Alice pulled her dressing gown tight around her throat, trying to cover her thin nightgown underneath. She tried to move silently, afraid that they would wake Mr. and Mrs. Highcroft, exposing their impropriety. Walking around the house in her dressing gown, and with a man, no less! Alice was shocked at her own behavior, but Roland hadn't really given her a choice. In fact, he seemed oblivious to the fact that she was hardly dressed and her small feet were bare.

Inside his study, Roland stopped and gestured grandly at the Ghost Machine. "What do you think?" he asked.

Suddenly Alice understood his enthusiasm. Roland had already gotten a Taylor's Cone and fitted it to the machine. Though scientists usually pointed the brass contraption upwards or at an angle, this one was suspended from the top of the machine and pointed straight down. It was tall enough for a grown man to stand underneath. Below, a circular piece of steel lay on the ground.

Alice observed the machine for a moment. "The electro-static energy is harnessed by the dynamic reflector and fed through these copper wires to the Taylor's Cone, which allows the energy to be concentrated beneath it for minimal loss," she said.

"The smartest assistant any New Scientist ever had," Roland answered, clearly proud of her. "Of course, you're responsible for both the dynamic reflector and the Taylor's Cone. I don't know what I would have done without you."

Alice's reply sounded nonchalant, but she was inwardly beaming. "You would have found the answers yourself."

"If the Ghost Machine works, Alice, I would be happy to name you as my co-inventor."

Co-inventor! Alice could hardly believe Roland's words. Still, she shook her head. "I only made the suggestions. You're the one who built the machine."

"Now we just have to find out how well it works. I'm going to arrange a demonstration soon at one of the haunted places here in Atlanta. I've got a whole list of them from my interviews with the lunatics. Can you imagine? Ordinary people who saw ghosts, but their families thought they were mad and put them in an institution. Such a shame."

"So that's why you went to the lunatic asylum!" The words burst from Alice's mouth. The mystery solved at last!

Roland raised his eyebrows. "Yes," he said slowly.

Alice felt her cheeks redden, and she pulled her dressing gown even tighter around her body in her embarrassment. "I followed you one night," she confessed, her voice barely above a whisper. "I was out for a walk early one evening, and I saw you further down the street. You left the house at such odd times, and I was so curious about you."

Roland's face was inscrutable. "What did you think when you saw me go into the asylum?"

"I didn't know what to think. That place frightened me." Alice was speaking to Roland, but her eyes were fixed firmly on the carpet beneath her feet.

Roland moved toward Alice. He put one hand under her chin, gently lifting her face so she had to look into his eyes. "That was the night I found you in my study, wasn't it?" he asked.

Alice nodded, not trusting herself to speak. The

shame and guilt of getting caught in Roland's study came flooding back to her.

"You are a woman of many secrets, Alice Meriwether," Roland said quietly. "I wonder, what other secrets do you have?"

Roland searched Alice's eyes so deeply that she felt certain every secret she'd ever had must be laid bare to him.

"That night was the only...I have never...I shouldn't have..." Alice's words came tumbling out, her mind in a rush to conceal her true thoughts about the man before her.

"I am glad you did," Roland said, surprising Alice into silence.

He explained further, his teasing smile turning his lips up as he spoke. "If I hadn't found you reading my American Science Journal, I may have never learned of your interest in New Science. To this day, I might sit by you at every meal with only a cursory greeting because I would have no idea how much our passions are aligned. If you hadn't been in my study, I may have never taken you to the Exposition with me, I would still be baffled with the Ghost Machine, and I would have never gotten the AAD Men dinner invitation from Professor Crowfoot."

Alice knew she was still blushing, but for a very different reason than before. She had not expected Roland to offer such praise, and the compliments made her self-conscious. She tried to look away, but his hand on her chin kept her face firmly fixed on his.

"You say you came here to be a governess, but sometimes I think you really came to help me." Abruptly, Roland reached into his pocket and held out his hand. A small gold locket in the shape of a heart lay in his palm. "I want you to have this," he said.

"For me?" Alice took the locket and opened it, and a tinkling sound issued from its clockwork innards. "It is a music box! But so very small."

"One of the scientists at the Hall makes these.

You never have to wind it. I thought you might like the idea of wearing it on a chain. That way you can always keep what matters most to you close to your heart."

"You," Alice breathed. She closed the locket as she spoke, and her word hung in the sudden silence.

"I what?" Roland prompted.

Alice paused. "You…are very thoughtful. Thank you."

Roland smiled. "You're welcome. It is the least I can do for my brilliant assistant. Now you will always have science close to you, wherever you go. Even when you go home, your Mama won't know, but you will."

"Yes, I can keep science close to my heart," said Alice. Of course Roland had meant science, she chided herself. How could I have assumed otherwise? He always means science! Maybe he has no interest in anything else. But then, Alice thought, have I ever given any indication that I care about anything else?

"Roland, why not test the Ghost Machine here before your demonstration?" Alice asked, changing the subject.

"Who says I haven't? I take it you haven't had any late-night visitors in your room recently?"

"Only you, this evening." Alice sighed. "I should get back to bed." She reached a tentative hand out and placed it on his arm. His skin was warm beneath his shirtsleeve, but Alice could also trace the outline of his bandage with her fingers. She was going to thank him for his gift, but instead she blurted, "You're still hurt!"

"It's on the mend," Roland assured her.

Alice frowned, but nodded. "Off to bed then. Thank you for my locket."

Alice walked slowly up the stairs to her bedroom, hoping that, for any reason, Roland would call her back. Instead, she fell asleep with the locket open on her pillow, its quiet notes lulling her to sleep.

Chapter 15

Alice yawned discreetly into her gloved hand as she stood on the train platform with Mr. Frederick. Katie would be watching the children all day, and though the station clock read 12:30 p.m., Alice felt like she was still struggling to wake up.

When the train finally puffed into the station and came to a stop, Emma was one of the first passengers to alight. She bounded from the steps of the train car, looking around her with a wide-eyed joy which, Alice knew, must have been on her own face when she first arrived in Atlanta.

Alice waved to get her sister's attention, and Emma hurried over, holding out her arms to hug Alice. "What a big city!" Emma exclaimed.

"Yes, it's nice to see you, too," Alice answered, smiling.

Mr. Frederick moved away to see to Emma's luggage while Alice guided Emma inside the terminal. Emma talked the whole time, relating news from home and her plans for seeing every street in Atlanta by the time a week had passed.

The two girls waited inside until Mr. Frederick returned to tell them that the carriage was loaded and ready to depart. As soon as they walked into the daylight, arm in arm, Emma's stream of chatter abruptly ceased. "Oh, my," she said.

"It is very different from any city we've visited in the past, is it not?"

"Yes. It's so busy. I've never seen so many carriages at once." Suddenly Emma's eyes were drawn upward, high above the street. "Oh, Alice, is that one of those airships?"

"It is."

"It's fantastic, isn't it? And look, you can see the people on it. How lucky they are, floating up in the air like that. No wonder you love them so much."

Alice couldn't conceal her smile of satisfaction. "They give tours around the city in them. If you like, we can do that tomorrow, after church. Sundays are my day off, so I won't have to watch the children."

"I would like that very much."

Emma's answer reminded Alice of her previous conversation with Roland about the airship tours. She hesitated before saying, "If you don't mind, Mr. Highcroft's brother had expressed interest in going on a tour, as well. I'll ask him if he'd like to join us."

"Alice, do we have to have some stuffy gentleman escort?"

"He is not an escort, he is my friend. We made plans to take an airship tour some time ago, but haven't been able to do so yet."

"All right, then," said Emma. "Would this be the Mr. Highcroft who took you to the Exposition?"

"Yes."

"Hmmm." Emma gave her sister a wicked smile. "You are not content to be engaged to just one man, I see."

"I am not engaged to anyone, nor do I foresee myself becoming engaged to Mr. Highcroft," Alice answered stiffly. She climbed into the carriage then and changed the subject by asking Mr. Frederick to narrate the journey, as he had when Alice had arrived.

Once Emma had settled into the Highcroft house

and changed out of her traveling clothes, she and Alice spent the afternoon walking around Grant Park. Now that it was October, the weather was significantly cooler during the day, and they had a pleasant time catching up with one another. Alice still had to conceal many details of her adventures, but she enjoyed describing the Exposition grounds to Emma.

Roland was not at supper that night, which greatly disappointed Alice. She also realized that she was nervous at the prospect of introducing him to Emma, though not sure why she should feel that way. Perhaps Emma would dislike him and carry a negative report home to Mama, or, most likely, Roland would assume he could discuss New Science with Emma as easily as he did with Alice. That scenario would certainly be revealed to Mrs. Meriwether.

In the meantime, Emma got along well with the rest of the family, and she was welcomed heartily by all of them. She was sharing Alice's bed for the duration of her visit, and as they lay there that night, Emma was still talking excitedly. "Such lovely manners, but so different from how we were raised. Mr. Highcroft shook my hand, like we were old friends," she was saying, when Alice suddenly shushed her into silence.

"Roland is home; I heard the front door just now," Alice said, sitting up.

"Who is Roland? Oh, that Mr. Highcroft, you mean. Do you call him by his Christian name to his face?"

Instead of answering, Alice swung her legs over the edge of the bed and stood up, smoothing her nightgown. "I will go ask him about the airship tour tomorrow."

"Alice! You are in your nightgown!" Emma's tone was shocked, and Alice was surprised how much she resembled their mother on the rare occasions that she scolded.

"That's why I'm putting on my dressing gown."

"But you can't go speak to him like that. It's improper."

Alice glanced at her sister in the dark room. "It's the big city, Emma. Things are different here." She hoped Emma would accept that excuse.

As she expected, Roland had gone straight to his study. She tapped on the door quietly, and when he answered, Roland didn't seem at all surprised that it was Alice who had come to see him. He silently waved her into the room and didn't speak until he had shut the door behind her.

"You must have exciting news to relate, coming here like this," he said. "I thought wandering about in your dressing gown was against all your moral principles?" Roland was clearly amused.

"Well, you have already seen me like this once, so I don't see that it makes much difference anymore," Alice answered stiffly.

"Of course it makes a difference. I'll become so used to it that I'll expect you to attend breakfast dressed like this."

"Don't tease. I merely came down here to ask you something."

"Let's have it, then."

"My sister Emma arrived from Fairburn today. We want to go on an airship tour tomorrow during my afternoon off. Since you had promised to take me, I thought I'd ask if you want to come, as well."

"I can't," Roland answered. "I have to meet with several other scientists tomorrow."

Alice was disappointed but tried not to let it show in her expression. "I feel guilty, taking the tour with Emma rather than you. We planned it so long ago."

"Yes, but I've been dragging you all over the Hall of New Science instead of taking you on an airship, one of the things you most want to do. Just promise to wave down at me when the ship flies over the Exposition."

"I will." Alice turned to go, then stopped. After a

moment's hesitation, she turned back to Roland. "I do have a favor to ask," she began. "Emma doesn't care for the New Science as I do. She's not against it like Mama is, but she's likely to relate everything that happens during her visit."

Before she could continue, Roland interrupted. "I won't let her know how much time we've spent at the Hall or even discussing science. But Alice, she's going to know what I do."

Alice couldn't help smiling. "I lived here for a week before I figured it out."

"But this Monday night is my demonstration of the Ghost Machine. That's why I'm meeting other scientists tomorrow: I am inviting AAD Men and other accomplished gentlemen to the demonstration."

"Then you found a place that's haunted?" Alice asked, her concern about Emma forgotten for the moment.

"Yes, a wonderful house in the Kirkwood neighborhood. The family there had committed their son for claiming to see a soldier wandering the halls, but then they began to see the soldier, as well. They removed him from the lunatic asylum, but not before I'd had a chance to interview him."

"That's excellent news! I'm sure the demonstration will be a huge success for you."

"You must attend, of course," Roland said, as if it were obvious. "Your sister may not know your role in perfecting the machine, but I know, and you must attend. Of course, if you go, then she must come, as well."

"Of course, I want to attend," Alice said, but the hesitation was still clear in her voice.

Roland took a step closer to Alice. "You will attend. If you try to back out of it, then I will march directly up to your room and tell your sister everything right now!"

Alice laughed and held her hands up in surrender. "All right; I will be there."

Emma was already asleep when Alice returned to the bedroom. She was glad as it saved any awkward questions about her relationship with Roland, at least for one night.

Roland made no mention of Alice's late-night visit during breakfast the next morning, but he was very courteous to Emma. After welcoming her to Atlanta and asking about her journey the day before, he made small talk with her about the city, the Exposition, and what to expect the first time on an airship. Alice was surprised to hear him converse so easily about subjects other than science. Clearly, he knew how to act every bit the gentleman. When Mrs. Highcroft had written to Alice's mother about Roland's good manners, she had been honest.

Roland's kindness to Emma continued throughout their crowded ride to church, and Alice felt a stab of jealousy. He rarely took such considerations with her, and she wondered why he hadn't shown these gentleman-like manners when she had been the new girl in the house.

After dinner, the two girls and Roland piled into the carriage. Mr. Frederick was going to drop Roland off at the Exposition before taking Alice and Emma to the airship port. Roland sat across from them, pointing out interesting places to Emma along the way. As they neared the Exposition entrance, another carriage sailed past. The man inside the open chaise was holding a birdcage, and the clockwork bird inside was singing triumphantly. Doctor Bateman's bird was working properly at last, presumably thanks to the addition of a dynamic reflector. Alice and Roland turned to each other, both opening their mouths to exclaim, when Emma's question of, "What is that thing?" made them check their comments.

"A clockwork bird," Alice said.

Emma pondered this for a moment, then said, "How nice. You wouldn't have to feed it, and it would only sing when you wanted it to."

Alice and Roland both laughed heartily at Emma's easy acceptance of the New Science invention, but neither one explained their amusement. When Roland finally climbed out of the carriage, wishing them an enjoyable tour, Alice motioned him over. She leaned down and whispered, "I will tell her about the Ghost Machine on the way to the tour."

Roland answered as quietly, his lips brushing Alice's ear. "Good luck." He pulled back and looked at her significantly, then offered Emma a bright smile. "Have fun, Miss Emma. Wave at me when you fly over the Exposition!"

Alice felt another pang of jealousy as Emma was given the same admonition that Alice had received the night before, but she kept her face inscrutable.

As soon as the carriage began to move again, Emma spoke up. "Whispering good-byes to each other, are you? I think you must be engaged to Mr. Highcroft."

"I am not. If you had paid any attention, you would have noticed that Roland paid a great deal more courtesy to you today than he did to me. I assure you that he never makes such small talk with me."

"No, and why should he? The two of you are already on such good terms that you go visit him in your dressing gown! I'm sure you've both moved far past the stage of making pleasant conversation."

Alice elbowed Emma at this pronouncement, glancing sharply at Mr. Frederick and hoping he hadn't overheard. Even if he had, Alice hoped he was discreet enough not to repeat it.

"Would you like to know what Roland and I were talking about last night?"

"Oh, do tell me, dear sister. Did he profess his love for you?" Emma was giggling now.

"Don't be silly. He told me that he is having a demonstration tomorrow evening, and he wants both of us to attend."

"A demonstration of what?"

"A machine he has built."

Now Emma was frowning. "What sort of machine?"

"It's a surprise. Only myself and a few others know what it does. If it works, it will open a lot of doors for Roland."

"He built it, you say?"

"Yes."

"Invented it, you mean."

"Well, he did design it, yes."

"Mr. Highcroft is an inventor, then." Emma paused. "He is one of these scientists, isn't he? You are living under the same roof as a scientist! Does Mama know?"

"No, Emma, and you can't tell her! Roland keeps to himself; he's always shut up in his study, and I am with the children all day. I only found out because he had left his study door open, and the machine was sitting right there in the middle of the room."

Emma eyed her sister suspiciously, knowing Alice too well to believe her claims of mere friendship with Roland. She still believed there was some romantic involvement between the two, which she made clear with the look on her face.

"Admit what your relationship really is with Mr. Highcroft, and I promise I won't utter a word about him or his machine to Mama," Emma said.

Alice sighed. It went against her inclination to divulge the truth, but Alice had to hope that Emma would keep her promise. "I am his assistant," Alice said.

"What does that entail?"

Alice shrugged. "Mostly, he talks and I listen, and sometimes I make suggestions. I think Roland just likes having someone to talk to about the machine; it helps him to think out loud."

Emma nodded, satisfied at last with Alice's answer. "Mama would hate it, you know, but I am happy for you. I know how much you love that stuff."

Now it was Emma's voice that dropped to a whisper. "And he's a handsome man, Alice! Are all of these science men so good looking?"

Alice relaxed and gave Emma a playful tap with her fan. "Certainly not! Most of them are much older than us and hardly handsome. One scientist we saw at the Exposition was quite frightening in appearance. I daresay you'll meet a lot of them at tomorrow's demonstration, and then you can decide for yourself."

"Perhaps at least one of them will be handsome and single, then," said Emma. She spent the rest of the carriage ride gazing out at the streets and buildings going past, no doubt dreaming about a roomful of young, attractive scientists hoping to find an "assistant" of their own.

The airship port was an impressive sight. The ticket windows and waiting room were housed in an elegant and modern central station on the ground. It was smaller than the railway station but more lavishly decorated. The ceiling had crown molding and a great crystal chandelier hanging from the center. All of the benches were padded with red velvet, and the brass fixtures along the walls were all gleaming. There were four airship platforms, one above each of the four corners of the station. A wide wrought iron staircase wound up to each one.

Alice bought their tickets for the three o'clcok tour, then she and Emma took a seat in the waiting area. An interesting mix of people ambled past. Most passengers were wealthy since airship journeys were much more expensive than traveling by train. The women were wearing the latest styles in rich brocades and silks, while the men wore their top hats at rakish angles and had ornate watches hanging from their waistcoats.

The airship crews, on the other hand, reminded Alice of the drawings of pirates she had seen in storybooks. The men who stoked the fires to keep the steam engines running were covered in black soot, and their clothes were covered in patches and badly-darned rips. One captain came down the platform stairs with the air of royalty. His long wool coat was dark blue with gold buttons that matched the coat's epaulettes. Unlike the crews, the captain had an air of importance. His gray beard was neatly trimmed, and Alice saw ladies curtsey gracefully as he passed. A swarthy man followed the captain like a guard, his long hair tied back in a ponytail and a pistol tucked into his leather belt.

"Have you ever seen such a man?" Emma asked, leaning close to Alice to avoid being overheard.

"No. He is certainly more elegant than a train captain, isn't he?"

"Not the captain, silly. I mean that vile man following him! I wouldn't want to meet him after the sun goes down."

As if he had heard them despite being on the other side of the station, the swarthy man suddenly looked over. Emma froze as his eyes first met hers, then Alice's. Emma dropped her head, but Alice continued to gaze at him. Surely this man had once been a pirate! Alice had read references to airship pirates in the magazines, but she had always assumed they were just legendary characters. Men had spent so little time in the air and, for the most part, stayed within the newly-established shipping lanes, so outlandish stories were bound to crop up about the unknown stretches of sky.

The boarding call for the three o'clock tour finally broke the spell, and Alice rose quickly. She was so anxious for her first airship ride that she fairly sprinted up the stairs and had to wait at the top as Emma followed at a more leisurely pace. Once Emma joined her, Alice turned to the airship hovering at the edge of the platform. A wide ramp led up onto the open-air deck, and already people were filing in, handing their tickets to the porter who stood there with one foot on the ship and the other on the ramp. He swayed easily with the ship's gentle rocking.

Waiting in line for their turn to board seemed to take an eternity, but finally Alice handed over her ticket. She accepted the porter's proffered hand to steady her as she took her first step onto the wooden deck. The ship bobbed slowly, and walking was much easier than on a moving train.

Alice led the way to two seats near the rear of the deck and against the edge of the right-hand railing. It wasn't until she settled into her seat that she noticed Emma's face.

"Are you all right? You are so pale!" Alice said.

Emma just nodded and tightened her grip on the chair back in front of her.

Alice pulled out her fan and waved fresh air toward Emma, hoping it would do her some good. She couldn't understand how Emma could feel so nervous. Certainly, they were hanging in the air and held up only by a giant balloon, but for Alice that fact generated excitement.

After most of the seats had been filled, the crew of the ship went to work: the ramp was raised, unseen men stoked the fire underneath the deck, and black smoke billowed from the smokestack at the rear of the ship. At the front, the captain turned the wheel, and the ship slowly pulled away from the platform. Alice saw first a few inches, then a foot, then a yard of the ground beneath them. As she watched, the carriages and people moving along the streets below became smaller, shrinking as the ship rose higher. A tour guide standing at the front began pointing out landmarks, but Alice peered toward where she assumed the Exposition must be. All she could see from their current place in the sky were the tops of trees, with leaves beginning to turn yellow, gold, and red. As she strained her eyes to see the hidden Exposition, Alice's only regret was that Roland wasn't there to share the experience with her. Granted, he had been on the airship tour in the past, but somehow Alice felt that it would have given him great pleasure to see her reaction to finally being on one of the great ships.

Thinking of not being with Roland reminded Alice that she was with her sister, and she turned with concern to Emma. Thankfully, she had relaxed somewhat, but her hands were now in a tight knot in her lap, and she stared forward rather than out at the scenery. Alice put one of her hands over Emma's. "I hope you won't be too nervous to wave at Roland," she said.

Emma gave Alice a thin smile. "I don't think flying is for me. I hope his new machine is not a flying contraption."

"I assure you that it won't require you to step foot onto anything that flies. In fact, we'll be inside a house for the demonstration."

"Don't waste your time comforting me; I'll be all right," Emma said. "You will miss the whole tour if you don't look the other direction."

Alice gladly turned her attention to the city below her, though she kept her hand on her sister's folded ones. Eventually, they came to the Exposition. Alice convinced Emma to lean over so they could both look straight down while Alice pointed out each building.

"And that one there, with the metal bits reflecting the sunlight, that is the Hall of New Science," Alice told her. "That's where Roland is right now."

The girls raised their arms simultaneously and waved down at the building, and several people around them chuckled to see the girls waving at someone so far below.

Other than the thrill of being on an airship, floating over the Exposition was the highlight of the tour for Alice. The touring ships only sailed over the busy downtown areas, so they never got close to Grant Park and the Highcroft residence. Alice did get a thrill while watching a train pull into the station, recollecting her own amazement at stepping off the train to see a tour ship overhead.

Emma was one of the first passengers off the ship, despite sitting so near the rear of the deck. Alice followed at a leisurely pace, hoping to extend her time on board by as many seconds as possible. The end was inevitable, though, and she soon joined her sister for the walk down the spiral staircase and back into the station.

Mr. Frederick wasn't supposed to pick them up in the carriage until four-thirty, and they only had ten minutes to wait according to the steel clock hanging on one wall. The sisters got cups of tea from a small café opposite the ticket windows and sat down. Their cups had long been empty and the clock read five-fifteen before Mr. Frederick finally appeared, looking harried and apologetic.

"So sorry, Misses, but Mr. Roland asked me to fetch him first and, well, you know how that can be," he said, panting from his rush inside the station.

"Then where is Mr. Highcroft now?" asked Alice, peering behind Mr. Frederick's broad frame.

"He finally turned up, only to tell me to go on without him as he was staying late at the Exposition. Lord only knows how he'll get home tonight."

"I daresay he'll find a way," said Alice.

Roland arrived home sooner than expected, having gotten a ride from some scientist friend of his, and he was at supper. He looked exhausted but happy, and as the main course was served, he leaned toward Alice and said quietly, "It is all in place; tomorrow will be the start of a new life for me." He took a hearty bite of cucumber salad, and after swallowing he added soberly, "That is, if it works like it's supposed to."

"I am sure it will," said Alice. She noted that Roland paid much less attention to Emma at this meal, and her spirits lifted considerably.

Roland's words echoed through Alice's head as she fell asleep. The Ghost Machine demonstration could completely change his life if it went well. He would be assured entrance into the AAD Men, and in the course of a couple hours Roland could become the next New Science sensation. That night Alice dreamed of seeing Roland's portrait on the front of the American Science Journal.

Chapter 16

Roland was anxious at breakfast on Monday, and he hardly spoke, even to Alice. As soon as he had finished eating, he made his excuses and disappeared into his study. Less than an hour later, two burly men showed up at the front door, ready to load the Ghost Machine onto their flatbed carriage. Roland insisted on keeping the white sheet over the machine, making the loading more difficult and drawing the attention of the entire household. They all congregated on the porch to watch the men grunt and huff their way through the process.

Once the machine was securely strapped down, Roland walked up the porch steps. Alice assumed he was heading for his study, but at the last moment he stopped and turned to her. "You will be there?" he said.

"Of course," answered Alice.

"Seven o'clock."

"We'll be there by six-thirty so we can get the best seats in the house."

Roland nodded, satisfied with Alice's assurances, and turned to leave.

Calls of "good luck" and "we'll see you tonight" rang out as Roland climbed onto the flatbed next to his precious machine.

"He is leaving very early for this demonstration," remarked Emma as they returned to the house.

"I'm sure he is nervous and wants to go over the entire machine once it's been delivered," said Alice.

The rest of the day passed slowly, but finally, after a walk to the park that seemed to take many miles and many hours, it was time to prepare for that night's outing. Alice put on her lavender gown, the same one she had worn for her first supper with the Highcroft family. She had only worn it once since that first night, and she wanted to make sure she looked like a lady, despite being a scientist's assistant.

Roland had left his study door wide open, and throughout the day no one had bothered to close it. Now Alice peeked in, marveling at how much larger the room looked without the bulk of the Ghost Machine dominating everything. It was then she noticed the dark brown jacket draped over the back of Roland's desk chair. Alice shook her head, recalling Roland's usual rolled-up sleeves that morning. He would, no doubt, want to look like a gentleman that night even more than she wanted to look like a lady. Alice took the jacket, folding it carefully to ensure it didn't get wrinkled on the carriage ride.

True to her word, Alice, Emma, and the Highcroft family arrived at the house hosting the demonstration with nearly thirty minutes to spare. A small crowd of scientists had already gathered, and Alice made a beeline for Roland, handing his coat to him as she said hello.

"You are a lifesaver," Roland said, sliding his arms into the coat. "I would have looked half-naked standing in front of everyone in just my shirtsleeves."

"So do you mean that you are half-naked at home, when you come to supper dressed that way?" Now Alice had the teasing smile that she usually saw on Roland's lips.

Roland's face flushed, but then his expression

changed to match Alice's. "This coming from a woman who arrives at my study door in naught but her dressing gown?"

"You didn't give me a choice the first time!" Abruptly Alice turned serious and she nudged Roland. She spoke now to someone who had just approached behind him. "Good evening, sir."

"Good evening. You must be Mr. Highcroft's assistant. I remember you from Professor Crowfoot's lecture." The man extended his hand to shake Alice's. "Gordon Smith, from New York University."

"Pleased to meet you, sir," Alice said, then excused herself so the two gentlemen could talk.

Alice joined Emma and the rest of the family in the large parlor. They were already seated in the third row of chairs, which had been laid out neatly for the occasion. The Ghost Machine sat at one end of the room, the white sheet still in place.

"We decided to save the best seats for the scientists," Mr. Highcroft explained as Alice took her seat. "I have a feeling their opinion is going to matter more than ours."

Alice nodded and took a deep breath. She had felt Roland's nervousness when she spoke to him, despite his lighthearted teasing. Now she could feel her own tension growing, as well, and there was a knot in the pit of her stomach. To distract herself, Alice sat back and gazed about the room. The house was an older one and was much larger than modern homes in the city. It even made the Meriwether estate in Fairburn seem modest in size.

The parlor was outdated but still lavish, and the yellow and green striped wallpaper set off the gilt frames and family portraits hanging on the walls. The old but ornate furniture that normally occupied the room had been pushed against the back wall to make room for the portable chairs.

Alice was pondering the portrait of a particularly grim-looking subject when a smooth male voice interrupted her thoughts. "Miss Alice, I had hoped to see you here."

Alice glanced up to see Roland's friend Jacob Masterson, but at the moment all she could remember was the way he had sized her up on their first meeting. He had that look in his eyes again. "Oh, Mister…" Alice faltered.

"Masterson, Jacob Masterson. I must not have made a strong enough first impression."

"On the contrary, Mr. Masterson. You invented the clockwork newsboys. It's just that I've met a great deal of people the last couple of months, mostly scientists, and I'm afraid I need to write down a list to keep everyone straight."

Jacob's attention turned to Emma, who was gazing at him with open admiration. However much his manners made Alice uncomfortable, even she could agree that he was handsome, a perfectly-tailored suit showing off his muscular frame. "And who is your beautiful friend?" he asked Alice.

"My younger sister, Emma Meriwether. Emma, this is Mr. Masterson. He and Roland went to school together."

Jacob gallantly took Emma's hand and kissed it. As Roland had done just a day before, Jacob's attentions were suddenly fixed on Emma, and Alice was momentarily forgotten. It wasn't jealousy Alice felt this time, though. She was relieved not to have him leering at her, but she worried about how her sister would hold up under his flagrant flirtation.

Emma was melting. She batted her eyelashes and answered all of Jacob's questions with a giggle.

Thankfully, a flurry of activity from the front of the parlor interrupted Jacob and Emma's tête-à-tête. Roland was standing up there, looking composed. He appeared perfectly calm and, Alice noted, perfectly handsome.

"Here we go," Jacob said, moving to sit behind Emma and Alice.

Alice thought she must be feeling all of Roland's anxiety for him. Her breath came in short gasps, and she fanned herself constantly despite the comfortable temperature of the room. The only thing that could make her feel better now was to see the Ghost Machine work properly.

The room quieted, the most recent arrivals sat down, and Roland began to address everyone. "Ladies and gentlemen, distinguished scientists, thank you for coming to tonight's demonstration of my new machine. The Spiritualist Movement has become a sensation throughout America, indeed throughout the world. Until now, we have had to rely on the intercession of mediums to relay messages from the other side. We hear the supposed words of the departed spoken by a stranger's lips, and we have to believe that flickering candles and clattering tables are the result of a spirit who has come to communicate.

"But what are table rapping and trances when compared to the fully-formed manifestation of a spirit? To a ghost who appears right before your eyes? You don't have to worry about being hoodwinked by a medium because you can see the spirit before you; you can recognize the echo of its human form with your own eyes!"

Alice was struck by Roland's speech, and she suspected that much of his preparations that day had gone into practicing the exact words he would say. The speech was obviously working: the audience was silent, and more than a few people were leaning forward with anticipation.

"Unfortunately, ghosts don't manifest on demand. We can't predict where or when they will appear, or even if they will manifest as anything more than footsteps, a cold breeze, or an object moved from its usual place," Roland continued.

"Until now. Thanks to the advancements achieved through New Science, we can now generate the energy a spirit needs to manifest, and we can focus that energy to one specific place to ensure that the ghost appears directly before us. Ladies and gentlemen, allow me to introduce the invention that will change our perception of the afterlife, that will transform the Spiritualist Movement and give new life to those who are dead: the Ghost Machine!"

With a flourish, Roland whipped the sheet off the machine, and it rose before all of them, every metal surface gleaming. Murmurs broke out among the crowd, but they were only given a few moments to admire the metal contraption. As Roland released the already-wound cogs, several other scientists stood to lower the gas lamps and blow out the candles in the room. The parlor was plunged into near dark as several ladies gasped in fear.

"The home you are now in was built in 1852," continued Roland, talking over the hum of the churning cogs. "It was used as a make-shift hospital during the War, and many good Confederates died within these walls. The bodies were eventually moved to a cemetery, but at least one spirit remained behind."

Now the cogs were moving faster, and small sparks were beginning to form where the velvet surfaces of the two drums rubbed against each other.

"That soldier has been spotted numerous times over the years since the War, but only briefly or out of the corner of the eye. In this parlor, though, visitors sometimes hear phantom moans of a wounded, dying man. Once, a young family member went to the cook to ask for water, explaining that the sick man in the parlor had asked for it. Concerned, the cook came into this room and found no one."

Now the sparks were really flying from the velvet drums. Roland continued speaking, and his voice took on a resonant tone as he addressed the empty air of the room. "Tonight we want to speak with the Confederate soldier who lingers in this house. We want to see your face, to ask you questions, and to give you our help. If you are here, use the energy of this machine to your advantage. Please, show yourself to us!"

There was a pause. In the dark room the sparks looked like tiny lightning bolts flashing out of the blackness. The only sound was the whir of the cogs and the hum of the velvet drums rubbing against each other.

Alice thought she saw a flicker beneath the Taylor's Cone. She blinked and peered at the spot where, despite the dark, she knew the Cone was positioned. Yes, there! Another brief flicker of light, then another and another. A cold draft of air washed over Alice, and as the temperature dropped, the flickering increased. Like pieces of a puzzle, the flashes formed the head and torso of a man, though the image was too blurry to see details.

Transparent legs began to form, and then the upper half of the ghost seemed to solidify. Already Roland was cranking the gears to keep the Ghost Machine wound. The ghost was clearly a Confederate, though his gray uniform was torn and stained. The face was haunting. Sad eyes surveyed the room from sunken sockets, and his emaciated face was hidden beneath a scraggly beard. He looked at the audience with mild curiosity, as if they were on display, rather than him.

The ghost appeared to be a solid man from the waist up, though he emitted a pale glow that made him visible in the darkness of the room. His legs were still transparent. Alice could hear the intake of breaths all around her, but no one spoke.

It was Roland who broke the silence. He finished winding the cogs and stepped forward, his silhouette visible in front of the sparks. "Can you tell us your name?" he asked quietly.

The soldier's eyes now turned to Roland, and his mouth began to move silently.

"He's saying 'Robert,' I think," someone in the front row offered.

"Yes, and the last name looks like 'Hampton,'"

offered another.

"Is your name Robert Hampton?" Roland asked.

The ghost nodded.

Before Roland could ask another question, there was a startled scream from the back of the room. Every head turned away from Robert Hampton and toward the sound. A woman's face was illuminated in the ghost's glow as she stood and waved her hands. "Robert Hampton!" she shouted. "My dear uncle Robert!"

Even the ghost himself was staring at the woman with incredulity. Roland's mouth was hanging open, but finally he asked her, "You recognize this man?"

"Yes! I knew he looked familiar to me," she said, her voice now choked with tears. "My daddy's brother Robert used to bring us girls such lovely sweets when we were children. But he went off to the War and was killed."

Alice watched the ghost as the woman spoke and saw him nod and smile softly when she mentioned the sweets. His mouth pronounced one word that was clear to all those watching him: "Isabella."

"He says your name is Isabella?" The hesitance was clear in Roland's voice.

The woman screamed again. "My name! He remembers me!" With that, she took a great heaving breath and pitched forward in a faint. Several people around her caught her and eased her back into her chair.

Immediately, the room broke into chaos. Several other women stood and screamed, while others proclaimed their belief in the Ghost Machine. A few men shouted, as well, including one scientist who boldly offered to buy the machine for two hundred dollars. Everyone else was murmuring to each other, the ghost temporarily forgotten.

Even Roland was too stunned to think of Robert Hampton's spirit, standing there beneath his Taylor's Cone. As the Ghost Machine began to wind down,

Robert's image flickered and began to fade. Roland turned to him just in time to say, "Thank you, Robert Hampton." The ghost gave a polite nod and vanished, and the room was once again in complete darkness.

Someone called for lights, and the flames on the gas lamps on the walls were raised. As the audience calmed down—and Robert Hampton's niece finally revived enough to sit up without the support of more than two men—Roland spoke. "As you see, the Ghost Machine allows us to make a personal connection with the spirit of the deceased, something that just can't be accomplished by a medium. I assure you that I was unaware we had a relative of this ghost in our audience tonight, but I think this lady's testimony proves how much the Ghost Machine will change the Spiritualist Movement."

Immediately scientists began waving their hands, anxious to ask questions. The man who had offered to buy the Ghost Machine repeated his offer.

"I thank you, but it is not for sale. Perhaps, in time, I will build more for the purpose of selling them."

Alice recognized the rough voice that spoke next, though she hadn't seen Professor Crowfoot come in. "That Taylor's Cone was most effective. Did it make much of a difference in your ability to make the ghost manifest?"

"It made all the difference," answered Roland. "Prior to that, we had no way to specify where the ghost should manifest. A ghost popped up a full flight of stairs above the machine once, giving my assistant quite a scare. Her bedroom happens to be above my study."

The anecdote drew a round of laughter, but Roland soon continued, looking right at Alice as he spoke. "It was her idea to use the Taylor's Cone," he said, a note of pride in his voice.

Many eyes turned toward Alice then, including Emma's, who looked at her sister with surprise.

Jacob Masterson leaned forward, his chin nearly resting on Alice's shoulder as he spoke quietly into her ear. "You're even more valuable than Roland let on. I must try to steal you away from him."

Jacob's hand came up to rest on Alice's other shoulder, and she fought the urge to shake him off. Instead, she smiled tersely. "Thank you, but Mr. Highcroft doesn't have to worry about me decamping," she said.

"Perhaps I could learn to be a scientist's assistant," Emma said wistfully, looking meaningfully at Jacob.

Jacob just laughed, and suddenly he rose from his chair and raised his voice to address Roland. "You won't sell your machine, but how much for your assistant? I see she is as intelligent as she is beautiful."

Alice wanted to slide down onto the floor to hide. Even Mrs. Highcroft sent a disapproving glance toward Jacob. Roland had a ready answer, though. "It is not in my ability to dole her out," he said. "Alice can be assistant to anyone she pleases. For that matter, I believe she'd be a capable scientist herself." The look Roland gave her as he spoke overcame Alice's embarrassment, though she was determined not to forgive Jacob just yet.

"That's too bad, because she has already turned down my proposal," Jacob said. Roland started at the words, and Jacob clarified. "Don't look so alarmed; I only mean my proposal to be my assistant, not a proposal of marriage. Not yet, anyway."

Alice was glad she had decided not to forgive Jacob just yet. If he had made her uncomfortable before, then she truly disliked him now.

Thankfully no one else spoke up, and Roland concluded by thanking everyone for attending. He received a round of enthusiastic applause and was soon surrounded by his fellow scientists, wanting to know the minute details of the Ghost Machine.

Mr. and Mrs. Highcroft worked their way through

the knot of people to congratulate Roland, but Emma
and Alice stayed a distance away, each holding one of
the children by the hand. Roland looked up and
mouthed, "See you at home."

The carriage ride home was a jovial affair. Mr.
and Mrs. Highcroft were both vastly impressed with
their relation. They had never seen a machine of his
that worked so well, and it was the first large-scale
project he'd ever undertaken.

Even Emma, impressed by both the machine and
Jacob Masterson's charisma, offered her own praise of
the Ghost Machine and New Scientists in general.

Alice put Margaret and Jasper to bed, but the rest
of the household was too excited to retire for the night.
A light supper was brought out, and afterward
everyone gathered in the parlor, hoping Roland would
return before too long. At eleven o'clock the sound of
creaking wheels could be heard, and soon after, the
same deliverymen who had taken the Ghost Machine
that morning came in, laboring just as much to return
the machine to the study.

Roland followed them, his jacket off and his
shirtsleeves rolled up, as usual. He had a wide grin on
his face and looked slightly overwhelmed by the
night's events and the praise of his peers. Everyone
greeted him enthusiastically, none more so than Alice.
In her excitement, she forgot herself again and caught
him in a tight hug. "I am so proud of you!" she said.
"Congratulations. I knew it would work!"

Roland returned the hug. "Thank you, Alice. I
could not have done it without you," he said into her
ear.

Suddenly, the two of them realized that Mr. and
Mrs. Highcroft and Emma were all staring at their
affectionate display. Roland cleared his throat
uncomfortably and Alice stepped away quickly, her
face flushed. Instead of looking angry, though, the
others looked as if they were on the verge of laughing.

"Come, let us toast to Roland's success," said Mr.

Highcroft, breaking the awkward silence. A tray holding a bottle of wine and five glasses was already sitting on a sideboard, and Mr. Highcroft made a show of uncorking the wine and measuring it out into each glass. When everyone had a glass in their hand, Mr. Highcroft held his aloft. "To my brother Roland and the successful demonstration of his invention. I'm very proud of you."

Everyone gave their heartfelt agreement and sipped the wine before settling into seats around the room. Alice sat on the settee and was pleased when Roland took a seat next to her.

The conversation revolved around the night's events, especially the appearance of the ghost and the coincidence of his niece being in the audience.

"I never expected such a dramatic turn of events," Roland said. "It certainly made the machine's debut sensational, didn't it? A few of the men actually suggested I had planted her there."

"I hope you convinced them otherwise," said Mr. Highcroft.

"I believe so. The woman came over to speak to me, and they realized she really was a stranger to me."

"Roland, who is this Mr. Masterson fellow?" Mrs. Highcroft asked suddenly.

"Jacob and I went to school together. He's far more accomplished than me," Roland answered.

"More accomplished in New Science, maybe, but not in manners." Mrs. Highcroft was frowning.

"Has he offended you? He can be rather brash at times."

"His comments about Alice were quite out of line."

"Oh, that," said Roland. "I'm sure he was only trying to joke."

"He was not," Alice said quietly, but it was enough to reach Roland's ears. He turned to her, and now he was the one frowning.

"You think he meant it?" he asked.

"I really did turn down an offer to be his assistant," Alice answered.

"You would learn a lot from him. He's skilled, and he's from a very wealthy family, so he always has enough money to build extravagant contraptions. Working as his assistant would be a great opportunity for you." Roland sounded almost sad as he spoke, as if Alice were going to leave for Jacob's laboratory right that moment.

"I agree with Mrs. Highcroft. His manners are not what they should be," Alice said firmly. "You don't have to worry about me going to work for him, or anyone else."

"I thought he had fine manners," interjected Emma.

"Flirtation does not imply good manners," Alice said.

Roland chuckled then, raising his glass in a mock toast to Jacob. "He always charms the prettiest girls," he said. He turned to Alice and added quietly, "And the smartest."

Once everyone's glass was empty, the party broke up for bed. Mr. and Mrs. Highcroft went ahead, but Roland lingered, discreetly taking Alice's arm to delay her.

"Will you come to my study with me?" Roland asked.

"Of course. Emma, I'll meet you upstairs."

Emma simply raised her eyebrows and smiled knowingly before she turned and went up the staircase.

Roland ushered Alice into his study, his hand still on her arm, and shut the door behind them. They were barely seated before Roland began. "I am going on tour," he announced.

"Pardon?"

"At least, I hope I am. Dr. Smith from New York University was there tonight, and he is interested in bringing the Ghost Machine there for public demonstrations."

Alice clapped her hands. "Roland, that's great news! Congratulations!"

"He's an AAD Man," Roland continued, "and he's talking about getting some of the Men in Washington, D.C., to coordinate demonstrations, as well."

"Washington and New York. How wonderful!" Alice was delighted for Roland, but with a sinking heart she realized it would take him away from her. Life in the Highcroft household would be very quiet and dull without him there.

"It will probably be a few weeks before I hear anything definite about the plan," Roland said. "We may wind up not going anywhere at all. In the meantime, at least, the AAD Men will be helping me stage public demonstrations here in Atlanta. People will pay good money to see the Ghost Machine."

"You just have to find a haunted place," said Alice.

"I don't think that will be a problem. Four people at tonight's demonstration offered me their homes. I won't need to return to the lunatic asylum for ghost stories anymore."

Chapter 17

As expected, Roland was absent during much of the following week. The Ghost Machine had made him something of a celebrity at the Hall of New Science, and suddenly he was engaged for supper every night. During the day, he was busy trying to line up public demonstrations, and he was asked to present a lecture at the Hall on Friday.

Despite Roland's absence, Alice was far from bored. Having Emma there to help her with Margaret and Jasper provided some much-needed company, and Emma's sudden acceptance of the New Science— thanks largely to Jacob Masterson's charms, such as they were—meant that conversation between the sisters flowed easier than ever.

"I never disapproved of the New Science," Emma was saying on Friday afternoon as they sat in the parlor, "I just didn't care about it. But now I see why you are so interested."

"Just don't tell Mama or she'll march right into this house, take you home, and shut you up for the next five years," warned Alice.

There was a sudden loud knock on the door, and both girls jumped. They each had a vision of Mama standing on the porch, her fist pounding demandingly on the door and a look of cold disappointment on her face.

When Katie ushered the visitor into the parlor where Emma and Alice sat, they saw that it was not Mama after all, but Alice's dismay was hardly lessened. It was Jacob Masterson.

Emma and Alice rose to greet him, Emma doing so with much more enthusiasm than her sister.

Jacob bowed grandly and settled into a chair. "Good day, ladies. I had hoped to find Roland, but the two of you are quite the consolation prize."

"Roland has been spending most of his time at the Hall of New Science," Alice said, adding, "as I'm sure you are aware."

"Me? No, it's not my job to keep track of his schedule. It's hard enough to keep all of my own appointments." Jacob turned to Emma. "And how are you this morning, Miss Emma?"

"Very well, thank you," Emma said, blushing. "It's fortunate that you stopped by. I've been hoping to learn about some of this New Science."

"Then I shall have to take you to the Expositon to see all the new inventions for yourself," Jacob said easily. "Although your sister will have to accompany us."

"Oh, Alice, can we?" Emma asked.

Alice sighed, wavering between a polite answer and an honest one. "I don't know that we'll have time to go before you leave," she said. Then she turned to Jacob, her face teasing but her voice serious. "I am used to being escorted to the Exposition by a gentleman."

Jacob's head flew back as he laughed heartily. "You accuse me of not being a gentleman!" he said. "Tell me, is Roland your ideal of a gentleman? Too engrossed in his scientific pursuits to take notice of the beautiful girl who follows him everywhere. His eyes so fixed on gears and levers that he doesn't see the fine figure before him. If that is your definition of a gentleman, then I hope you never accuse me of being one."

Alice stood up and stared at Jacob with incredulity. To come into the house and speak of Roland in such a way was unacceptable! She tolerated his flirting but would not allow him to degrade Roland. Alice was on the verge of asking Jacob to leave when a voice spoke from the doorway. "I didn't expect to find you here, Jacob."

Jacob turned in his chair, his manner as smooth and confident as ever. "Roland, welcome home. We were just talking about you."

Roland glanced from Jacob to Alice, who was still standing. How much had he overheard? Alice hadn't even heard the front door open. Roland's eyes narrowed but he came in and took one of the empty chairs. "Why are you here?" he asked frankly.

"To tell you the good news," Jacob said, winking at Alice as he spoke.

The gesture had its intended effect on Roland. He started and stared at Alice with wide eyes. "What news?" he said slowly, his eyes still fixed on Alice.

"I'm providing the remainder of the funding for your northern tour," Jacob announced, grinning broadly.

"What?" Roland asked at the same time Alice gasped.

"You said yourself last night that all you were missing was the rest of the funding," Jacob continued. "So I'm providing it. I'll get the standard cut of the profits from the Ghost Machine demonstrations, and you'll get to be the rich and famous scientist you always wanted to be."

"I…" Roland began. "I don't know what to say. Thank you." Roland stood and strode across the room so he could shake Jacob's hand. "Thank you!"

"You are so thoughtful, Mr. Masterson," said Emma, smiling sweetly.

Only Alice remained silent. She was torn between

dislike and gratitude. That such a disconcerting man should be the one to make Roland's tour possible! And, she thought, how appropriate that he should be the one taking Roland away from me.

Alice was still standing, and now she spoke quietly. "Please excuse me," she said and hurried from the room. She walked as calmly as she could up the stairs and into her bedroom, but once there she sank down onto the bed, her hands pressed to her eyes as if she could keep out the thoughts of Roland leaving. It wasn't just that which had prompted her to leave the room, though. Alice's feelings about Jacob made her distrustful of him, and she suspected that he had an ulterior motive in putting up the money for the tour. As Roland had been searching for the right words to say, Jacob had given Alice another wink. He would certainly turn a profit on the venture, but there was some other motivation, too.

Alice knew she couldn't mope for too long. Her pocket watch told her it was time to wake Margaret and Jasper from their nap, so she smoothed her skirt and patted down her hair. She forced a smile onto her face as she entered the nursery.

By the time she ushered the children downstairs, Jacob and Roland were both gone. Alice proposed a walk to Grant Park to take advantage of the fall weather. Emma joined them, and as they walked toward the park she spoke quietly to Alice. "That was very odd of you," she said, "to leave like that just when Mr. Highcroft had been given such good news."

"I couldn't stay in there another minute. I don't trust Mr. Masterson, Emma, and you should be careful not to get drawn in by his charms."

Emma exhaled impatiently. "I know what I'm doing, thank you." After a pause, she added, "And that still doesn't explain why you left the room so abruptly. Mr. Highcroft tried to follow you; thank goodness I was there to tell him that a man can't go traipsing into a lady's bedroom."

At least that bit of news made Alice feel a little better.

"I'm still waiting for your explanation," Emma prompted.

Alice sighed. "I feared I might say something rude to Mr. Masterson. I'd hate it if he changed his mind about funding Roland because of something I said. Also…" Alice stopped the words, "It means Roland is going to leave," from passing her lips.

"Also, what?" Emma said. When Alice remained silent, Emma shook her head. "Don't bother, I already know. It's written all over your face, sister. You never looked this way with Mr. Forbes, even when you were engaged to him."

Alice thought about protesting, but realized anything she said would only serve to confirm Emma's suspicions. Instead, she changed the subject. "Look, the leaves are finally starting to fall. Margaret, Jasper, we can look for pretty-colored leaves to take home."

Roland was not at supper that evening, and although Alice saw him at breakfast on Saturday morning, he was much too busy discussing the plans for the tour with his brother. He had no time to notice Alice's subdued manners.

Emma was scheduled to return to Fairburn on Tuesday, and, unknown to Alice, she and Jacob had made arrangements to attend the Exposition on Sunday. Alice was expected to go with them. She would have made her excuses to stay home if not for her concern about Jacob's impropriety. Not that he had really done anything improper yet, Alice told herself, but he seemed like the kind of man who might. She wasn't going to let him take Emma anywhere unescorted.

As expected, Jacob flirted endlessly, from the time his carriage picked the girls up until the time they returned home. To Alice's discomfort, though, he spent as much time teasing her as he did Emma. Alice couldn't figure out if he really liked either one of them, or if he just flirted with any girl that was nearby. She decided it must be the latter.

Emma was in raptures over everything they saw, especially in the Hall of New Science. One of Jacob's mechanical newsboys was on display, and he delighted in showing Emma how it worked. She didn't understand much of the technology behind it, but her enthusiastic exclamations more than made up for her lack of knowledge.

Meanwhile, Alice was looking everywhere, hoping to find Roland. She had only seen him at breakfast during the past two days. He had already hosted another successful demonstration of the Ghost Machine and had more demonstrations scheduled for the next month. Between that and his impending tour, he seemed to have forgotten all about his assistant. Less than a week ago, Roland had been so grateful to Alice and so quick to praise her for her part in the machine's completion. Now, he was once again the stranger living downstairs.

Emma's departure on Tuesday was harder than Alice had expected. She loved her sister and was sorry to see her go after such a short visit, but she was especially sorry to lose a companion, knowing Roland wouldn't be there to keep her company when she got home.

The two sisters embraced on the platform. "You won't tell Mama about all the New Science?" Alice asked.

"If you won't tell her about Mr. Masterson," Emma answered.

Alice's eyes narrowed. "What do you mean?"

"He's asked me to write to him since I'm going home. I don't think Mama would approve."

"No, she wouldn't. Take care, Emma. Don't give your heart away to a man like him."

"Alice, you worry too much about me. I doubt I can get into much trouble with stationery and a pen."

After their final good-byes, Emma climbed into
the nearest train car. Alice waved until the train had
rolled out of sight before returning to the carriage.

It was over a week before Alice even saw Roland
again. He came to breakfast on a Thursday morning, a
shadow of whiskers on his cheeks and his hair even
messier than usual. He was wearing his jacket for a
change, but one sleeve was ripped.

"Good morning, Roland. Do you still live here?"
Mr. Highcroft asked with gleaming eyes.

"Gracious, what happened to you?" Mrs.
Highcroft blurted.

Roland slumped down in his chair, and Alice saw
that his right hand was wrapped in a strip of cloth.

"I had a demonstration last night at a house on
Peachtree," was all Roland said. When it became clear
that his family expected more detail, he continued.
"The ghost showed up, but the family living at the
house had neglected to mention it's not a nice spirit. I
was standing closest to the machine, and that ghost
sent me flying across the room. I don't think I've ever
even met a living man with that kind of strength."

"What happened to your hand?" Alice asked.

"In my effort to stop my fall, I put my hand out
and wound up finding the pot-bellied stove."

Alice wanted to comfort Roland, and her hand
came up to squeeze his arm. Remembering his recent
absence, though, Alice stopped herself. If Roland
wanted no more to do with her, then she wouldn't
force her friendship on him.

Whether Roland slept all day or changed and left
the house, Alice didn't know. After supper, during
which he was again absent, Alice went out to the back
porch and sat down. The evenings were getting cooler,
but the chill air felt refreshing. The sun was setting
much earlier now, and it was nearly full dark already.

The last few lightning bugs of summer flitted among the plants, and a mockingbird trilled from its perch in the back of the garden.

As Alice sat there in thought, idly fingering the gold locket that Roland had given to her, the back door squeaked open and Roland came out. He took a seat next to Alice, hesitating as he did so. The silence between them stretched, and finally Roland spoke quietly.

"We haven't spent much time together lately," he said.

"No," Alice replied, her voice just as quiet and grave.

"It's just that there's been so much happening all at once."

"And I'm busy with Margaret and Jasper all day," Alice supplied.

"I didn't realize how much I missed you until last night. I had no one to take care of me and had to wrap up my hand by myself."

Alice smiled despite her dejection.

"Do you think your sister would like to come back to Atlanta?" Roland asked suddenly.

Alice frowned at the sudden change of subject. Roland was admitting to missing her presence, and now he was talking about her sister? "Perhaps," she said slowly.

"She was very good with Margaret and Jasper, and I know James and Mariah were quite taken with her."

"But they already have a governess."

"For now. But someone will have to take your place beginning December first."

"I was unaware that my tenure here was coming to an end."

"Of course it is," Roland said, as if Alice was slightly daft. "If your sister is willing, she can take your place then."

Alice shook her head. "I don't understand. Mr.

and Mrs. Highcroft don't want me to be governess anymore because they prefer Emma?"

"They consider you family already," assured Roland, "but they know you'd rather be on the tour than stuck here at home."

Finally, all the pieces fell into place for Alice. "Wait, you want me to go on the tour with you?"

"Of course. That was always the plan." Roland looked at Alice's face for a long moment. "You thought I was going without you," he said. It was a statement, not a question, and Alice only nodded her head.

"I just assumed you knew," Roland said.

"No. I thought you were leaving and I was going to be here alone." Alice couldn't believe that she actually said that out loud to Roland, but he didn't waver.

"I can't do this without my assistant," he said, then held up his injured hand with a grimace, "as evidenced by my disaster last night."

Alice smiled again, though she was still in shock at the proposition. She reached out and took Roland's uninjured hand in her own. "Thank you," she said. There were no words to convey her joy at this sudden turn of events, but the expression on her face told Roland all he needed to know. He squeezed her hand and smiled back at her, and Alice felt her heart begin to race. She could only see Roland's face in the last vestiges of twilight that crept under the roof of the porch, but she thought she saw him inch closer to her.

"Alice," Roland said quietly. Before he could say more, though, the back door banged open. It was Jasper, and he was crying. "Miss Alice, I had a nightmare!" he wailed.

Alice rose and scooped Jasper into her arms, making soothing noises as she did so. She looked down at Roland and gave him an apology, excusing herself so she could take Jasper back to bed.

When Jasper finally slept quietly again, Alice

crept down to the back porch, but it was empty. Whatever Roland had been about to say, she would have to wait to hear.

Chapter 18

Roland's tour was scheduled to begin on December first, just three and a half weeks away. It would be a very short time, Alice knew, to convince her mother to allow her to go.

In the end, though, getting Mama's approval was easier than expected. Mr. Highcroft wrote to Mr. Meriwether, asking permission for Alice to accompany Roland on the journey and requesting Emma's presence in the Highcroft household. Mrs. Highcroft sent a letter to Mrs. Meriwether, too, and with both husband and wife offering such praise of both Alice and Roland, as well as such enthusiasm for the tour, it was impossible to say no. Mrs. Meriweither didn't like the New Science, but she liked appearing ungracious and stubborn even less. Of course, that didn't save Alice from a flood of letters, admonishing her to be on her best behavior and to act like a lady at all times. Mrs. Meriwether continued to warn her daughter of the dangers of New Science, but her tone now held the attitude of, "Well, if you must do it, then do it with class."

As November progressed and the leaves on the trees began to change colors in earnest, Alice was happier than she had ever imagined she could be. She spent each Sunday afternoon in the Hall of New Science, and even those who didn't know her name knew that she was Roland's assistant, while others called her the Ghost Machine girl. She attended lectures, where she was now welcomed with the male scientists instead of being stared at as an oddity. When Alice wasn't in a lecture, she was making the rounds, looking at the inventions on display by the scientists with whom she was becoming acquainted.

Occasionally, Alice was given a weeknight off to go to one of Roland's Ghost Machine demonstrations, though often the entire family would attend. The Ghost Machine had become a part of Atlanta's social scene in its own right, and now admission was being charged for the privilege of seeing it in action. Jacob Masterson may have sold his mechanical newsboys to the Atlanta Journal, but the papers they waved with clockwork arms contained enthusiastic articles about Roland's most recent demonstrations.

Even Roland was much happier now that he had a successful invention and an adoring crowd. He was still the disheveled, rumpled scientist at home, but in public his demeanor was becoming more polished and stylish. Alice spied more than a few ladies eagerly asking him questions at the conclusion of demonstrations, and she guessed they weren't talking to him to learn more about the science of the machine. Alice had to laugh at their feigned interest.

Roland was busier than ever between demonstrations nearly every night and preparations for the tour, but since the night he and Alice had talked on the back porch, he had made a point of reserving time for her. Often it was only a few minutes of conversation during a meal, and there were several nights when she only saw him at some late hour after everyone had gone to bed. Roland would creep up to her bedroom and tap quietly at the door, and when Alice answered, he would whisper a joking, "Good morning!" The two of them would quickly exchange news with each other, Roland teetering on the threshold as if he might fall inside at any moment.

However short their time was together, Alice rejoiced in it. She had been happy for Roland's success since that first demonstration, but now her joy was untainted by the jealousy and sadness of being left out of the tour. Even Mr. and Mrs. Highcroft added to Alice's happiness. They had been instrumental in securing permission for Alice to join the tour, and she understood why Roland had said they practically thought of her as family. Even her duties as governess had a freshness to them, and Alice knew she would miss Margaret and Jasper when she resigned at the end of November. Leaving the children was the only sad prospect in an otherwise happy month.

Two weeks before the start of the tour, Roland held a private demonstration at the house, open only to his own family, Alice, Emma, and several carefully selected scientists. Jacob Masterson was there, as was Dr. Gordon Smith, who was arranging the demonstrations in New York City. Professor Crowfoot, as head of the AAD Men, was invited, too, and he brought along his outspoken wife. She greeted Alice with a cold eye, silently accusing her of still being only a scientist's assistant.

Like his other demonstrations, this one did not disappoint. The ghost Alice had glimpsed in her bedroom so many weeks before stood in front of her once more, though now he looked like a real man, not just a shadow.

As Alice gazed at the ghost, she realized she was becoming jaded to the spectacle. How quickly she had gotten over the shock of seeing ghosts and of witnessing Roland communicating with them!

The only shock of the evening was a pleasant one: after the demonstration, Professor Crowfoot put down his cup of coffee to announce that Roland was being inducted into the AAD Men the following week.

The news was as much a surprise to Roland as it

was to the rest of the party, and everyone offered him their hearty congratulations. "If there were AAD Women," Roland said to Alice, "I'd nominate you."

"But Mrs. Crowfoot would shoot down your nomination, on account of me being just an assistant," Alice whispered back, glancing sidelong at the woman as she did so.

With the tour just two weeks away, Alice soon found herself nearly as busy as Roland. In addition to watching Margaret and Jasper, she had to find time for packing and for getting several new dresses and cloaks. It would be cold in Washington, D.C., and even more frigid in New York, and Alice's Georgia wardrobe had nothing appropriate for winter up north.

Emma returned to Atlanta five days before Alice's departure. The overlap allowed Alice time to catch Emma up on what the children were studying in their lessons, and to let her get back into the rhythm of the Highcroft household. As Roland had promised, Mr. and Mrs. Highcroft welcomed Emma warmly, simultaneously lamenting the impending loss of the other sister.

The two sisters had been reunited for scarcely three hours before Jacob dropped in for a visit. This time, he didn't hide under the pretense of coming to see Roland. He acknowledged that he was coming to make sure Emma had arrived safely.

The two of them fell into their flirtatious ways instantly although, Alice thought, there was a level of intimacy between them that had not existed before. During Emma's prior visit, she had simply received Jacob's attention with little more than fluttering eyelashes and smiles, but this time she spoke as coyly as Jacob.

As soon as they were alone in Alice's bedroom that evening, Alice asked her sister about her relationship with Jacob. Emma denied anything improper, admitting only that they had exchanged a few "friendly letters" during her absence.

Knowing she would get no more out of Emma—
and that her misgivings about Jacob would only fall on
deaf ears—Alice tried to ask Roland about the
situation. She wasn't comfortable giving away her
suspicions about Emma's attachment, so she simply
asked whether Jacob had any romantic interest in her
sister. Roland looked at her blankly, replying that he
didn't think Jacob was attached to any woman, let
alone Emma.

Alice knew she had been overly optimistic to ask
Roland about it. He didn't even recognize her own
affection for him, so how would he ever notice
something between his friend and her sister? If he was
blind to the one, it stood to reason that he was blind to
the other.

Alice's mind was eased over the next few days:
she was far too busy to let her thoughts linger on her
sister, Jacob, or even on her own feelings for Roland.
She had never completed packing with so much
enthusiasm.

Chapter 19

December first finally arrived with a brisk breeze that made the red and yellow leaves scurry down the road as if they were late for their own adventure. Alice put on her new dark blue traveling skirt and bodice; a lined black cloak was draped over the bed for her departure. Even Alice's gloves and leather boots were new.

"You look very elegant," Emma commented as soon as Katie had finished dressing them both. She appraised her sister as if noticing for the first time that Alice had indeed grown into a woman.

"Thank you. You're looking well today, too," Alice answered. Emma had chosen a pretty dress of deep orange, a perfect match for the fall scenery.

"Well," Emma said, smoothing her dress self-consciously, "I want to look nice at the port. I fear it may be one of my last public appearances, since being a governess takes up so much time."

"Don't worry. You'll have every Sunday afternoon free for making public appearances. And you can show off at church as much as you like."

Both girls giggled at the idea of preening in church, and Alice hugged Emma suddenly. "I'm going to miss you. I've never been so far from all my family before."

"You'll be having too much fun to miss me," Emma assured Alice. "I'm certain you'll come back with plenty of wild tales."

On their way to breakfast, Alice promised to return with stories of violent ghosts, fainting women, and scientific disasters at the most prestigious parties.

The entire family wanted to accompany Alice and Roland to the airship port, despite the fact that it required them to borrow a second carriage so that there would be room enough for all of the people and luggage. Emma and Margaret rode with Roland and Alice, and they were rewarded for it with the full story of the mechanical carriage. It was the first time that Alice had related the story to anyone, and she was amused when she realized in what a heroic light it shed Roland and how embarrassed he was about it.

As soon as their carriage pulled into the port, Alice knew exactly which ship they would be taking to Washington, D.C. The balloon was massive, its great bulk floating over the station silently but ominously, throwing everything below into shadow. The passenger compartment slung below the balloon was huge as well, and even from a distance Alice could see that it was a luxury ship.

Roland hurried off to make sure the Ghost Machine had been delivered and loaded safely, rushing from the carriage before it had quite come to a stop. As for Alice, she felt just as much awe as she had the first time she had spied an airship over Atlanta's sky. Taking the tour with Emma had been one thing, but climbing aboard such a huge structure and going so very far on it was what had filled her daydreams. As she studied its shape and sleek lines, Alice knew the ship was an Aeronaut 200, the only ship to make the journey from New York to San Francisco in just five days.

When she finally tore her eyes away from the ship, Alice saw that Emma, with Margaret's hand in hers, was already walking inside the terminal. Mr. and Mrs. Highcroft followed with Jasper in tow.

Alice hurried to catch up with everyone, but she stopped short as soon as she went through the wide doors of the terminal. It seemed as if the entire Hall of New Science had shown up to see them off: Alice even saw Dr. McGuffey standing in the crowd. After a moment, Alice realized they must all be AAD Men, because Professor Crowfoot stood at the head of the group.

Roland's face appeared among the crowd a moment later, and by his relaxed expression Alice knew he had successfully checked on the Ghost Machine. Glasses full of champagne began to appear and were passed around. When everyone, including Alice, had a drink in hand, Professor Crowfoot stepped forward.

"To our newest member, and the successful inventor of the revolutionary new Ghost Machine, Roland Highcroft!" he shouted. "May your journey bring you knowledge, success, and a few dollars to finance your next project!"

An appreciative cheer went up, but Professor Crowfoot continued to speak. "And to his assistant, Alice Meriwether. You'll have your hands full taking care of Roland, my dear."

This time the cheers were mingled with hearty laughter, and the gathered scientists gladly drank from their glasses. Other passengers and their families looked on the festivities with wonder, speculating on who the celebrated pair was and why they were important enough to warrant such a sendoff.

Alice had barely drained her glass when the boarding call for their ship sounded from the amplifiers. Mr. Highcroft offered his best wishes to Alice, shaking her hand, but Mrs. Highcroft hugged her with real affection. Margaret and Jasper did the same.

"You must write and tell me all about it," Emma

said. "I want to know what ladies our age are wearing
in the other cities."

"I promise," Alice said, embracing her sister.
Emma began to respond, but suddenly her gaze
focused on something over Alice's shoulder, and she
smiled sweetly. Alice turned and saw Jacob there. She
greeted him stiffly and turned back to Emma, but her
sister's attention was entirely fixed on Jacob. Shaking
her head, Alice picked up the small bag she was taking
on the ship with her and walked toward the spiral
staircase. As she went, she received farewells and
handshakes from the scientists who had lined up to see
Roland on his way. Where Roland was, though, Alice
didn't know. Thankfully, she had her ticket and had to
be satisfied with seeing him once they were both on
the ship.

Alice walked up the staircase slowly, careful not
to trip on the hem of her new skirt. She looked out
over the sea of people when she reached the top,
seeing them waving excitedly. Caught up in their
enthusiasm, Alice waved back, and she was smiling as
she walked across the platform to the waiting airship.

The interior of the Aeronaut 200 was much like a
sleeper car on a train. The long ship was divided into
compartments, each of which sat four people. A deck
below the passenger deck contained the engine room
at the rear, the kitchen in the center, and the crew
quarters at the front. The captain sat at the front of the
passenger deck; the small bridge of the ship was
separated by glass walls so curious passengers could
watch the captain as he spun the maple ship's wheel.

Alice had the layout of the Aeronaut 200
memorized since she had copied its design onto her
drawing papers, but actually seeing the interior of the
ship was nearly overwhelming. The wooden walls of
the compartments shone from layers of polish, but they
were no match for the gleaming brass rails that lined
the hallway. The thick carpeting was a rich mauve, and
even the small gas lamps that would light the hall after

dark were specially designed to fit snugly against the walls.

A porter escorted Alice to a compartment on the left side of the ship near the front. Alice was the first to arrive, and she sat next to the window after stowing her bag in the rack above the seats.

Despite her excitement, Alice was conscious of each minute that ticked by. Where was Roland?

Alice turned when the door of the compartment opened, but it wasn't Roland who stepped inside. Instead, it was Dr. Smith from New York University. Since he was making the arrangements for the Ghost Machine demonstrations in New York City, he had decided to accompany Roland and Alice on the tour. And, Alice suspected, since New York University had laid down a large sum of money to help fund the tour, Dr. Smith was there to ensure everything went according to plan.

Dr. Smith greeted Alice congenially and took the seat opposite her. She had only met him in passing, but he seemed to be a pleasant man with good manners. He was in his early forties, Alice guessed, and his round head was mostly bald already. From her conversations with Roland, Alice knew that Dr. Smith did very little inventing of his own. Instead, he was considered to be a theoretical scientist: his ideas were so advanced that the inventions to match them were impossible to make. But, Dr. Smith hoped, his theories might influence the current New Science trends, so that in twenty, thirty, perhaps one hundred years, those impossible inventions might be possible.

Alice and Dr. Smith made light conversation until Roland finally arrived. His eyes were wide and he was out of breath, and when he sat down next to Alice, he let out an audible sigh.

"Problems getting on board?" Dr. Smith asked, holding back laughter.

"I've never received such a sendoff in my life," said Roland. "I think I shook hands with every person in the port, gave a quote to both the Journal and the Constitution, and then a dozen men felt it necessary to raise me up on their shoulders."

"You're quite the celebrity today."

"Quite," agreed Roland. As he spoke, he reached into his breast pocket and withdrew a small stack of calling cards. "What do you think? And every one from a lady."

Alice laughed out loud at the boldness of the women who had handed their calling cards to Roland. Most probably didn't know anything about him other than that he was handsome and very popular. "I'll make sure you have written a letter to every single one of them by the time we reach Raleigh," Alice said.

Roland winked at Alice. "You should be worried. I believe this is their way of applying to be my assistant."

Dr. Smith chuckled. "Yes, they'd be happy to assist you in spending the money you'll be making on this tour. Take care, Roland, or you'll have women throwing themselves at you the moment we hit the ground again."

"Good thing I have Alice here to fend them off."

"Yes, but who will keep Alice at bay?"

The three passengers in the compartment turned to look at the person who spoke from the doorway. Alice gasped in dismay, but Dr. Smith and Roland expressed only surprise.

"Jacob! What are you doing here?" Roland was the first to recover from Jacob's sudden appearance.

"I'm investing a lot of money in you and your machine, Roland. I'm going to make sure I turn a nice profit." Jacob turned his attention to Alice. "And this will give me more opportunity to convince your assistant to become mine." He put emphasis on the last word.

Alice was torn as she watched Jacob sit down. On one hand, she was relieved that he and Emma would be separated for the duration of the tour. After all, their dangerously flirtatious relationship was the only concern Alice had felt as she boarded the ship. On the other hand, being trapped in a small compartment with Jacob for the next two days sounded like a form of torture. And however deep their friendship might be, Alice could see that Jacob's comments about Alice made Roland bristle. Roland tried to hide it, but years of learning each other's nuances made it apparent to Jacob. The more uncomfortable Roland was with Jacob's behavior, the more Jacob was likely to tease Alice.

It's going to be a very long ride to the layover in Raleigh, thought Alice.

The porter walked down the hallway just then, shouting that they were shoving off, and soon after, a slow yet distinct shudder marked the ship's transition from stationary to sailing.

The tip of Alice's nose brushed the glass as she stared out the window. Below, the entire port seemed to have emptied, and everyone was waving up at the departing airship. Alice spied many ladies waving white handkerchiefs, and she wondered which ones had given Roland a calling card.

The ship turned to the north, and Alice saw a section of Atlanta into which she had never ventured. Soon they were gliding over the gold, yellow, and red canopy of trees. Small towns appeared beneath them from time to time. The airship rose still higher, until the lowest clouds passed underneath. The landscape below was changing as the small hills of Atlanta turned into broader, higher ones. Off in the distance, Alice could barely see the Blue Ridge Mountains standing up from the horizon.

Thankfully, Dr. Smith was adept at guiding the causal conversation between the four companions. Every time Jacob made a comment to Alice that held suspicious implications, Dr. Smith would interject smoothly with some new topic of conversation. Alice gave him many grateful looks and saw Roland do the same more than once.

Roland and Jacob were soon locked in a debate about the future of armies, and whether clockwork soldiers would be a viable option by the turn of the century. Dr. Smith's head nodded and he began to doze, and even Alice found her mind wandering. She pulled out a book she had brought along and began to read, stopping only when a late dinner was served. Each passenger got a small silver tray nearly overflowing with roast beef, okra, greens, and bread. Alice balanced her tray gingerly on her lap, hoping she wouldn't spill anything onto her new clothes.

When the attendant returned to collect the empty dinner trays, Alice asked him where they were.

"About halfway through South Carolina, Miss," he answered in a thick Northern accent.

"Such a long way to go," said Alice after the attendant left. "This is the furthest from home I've ever been."

"And we're not even halfway there," said Roland.

"Tell me, Dr. Smith, since you live in New York, what prompted you to accompany us to Washington?" Alice was merely making polite conversation, so she was surprised at Dr. Smith's answer.

"To keep an eye on you, of course."

"I beg your pardon?" Alice raised her eyebrows and peered at Dr. Smith, wondering if he was in jest.

He laughed, but his reply was in earnest. "You and Roland certainly couldn't make this journey alone," he explained. "Both of you so young, and unmarried! It wouldn't have been proper. Roland's brother asked if I'd come on the entire tour to be a chaperone."

Jacob laughed heartily. "I don't think you have to worry about these two." He pointed at Roland, "He only cares about science, and I don't think he's yet realized that Alice is a woman." Jacob's gaze turned next to Alice. "And she doesn't even know what a proper gentleman is."

"But I certainly know an improper gentleman when I see one," said Alice, her tone icy.

"I didn't think I had anything to worry about from you, anyway," said Dr. Smith. At Roland's surprised look, he clarified. "Or from you, either. But appearances can be everything, and we don't want to be improper. I'm surprised you didn't already know my purpose among this party, Alice. After all, your mother and father would never have allowed you to come otherwise."

Alice nodded and made a polite reply. She had been so excited about going on the tour that she hadn't even thought about the logistics of it all. It had only been the night before that she realized there would be no Katie to dress her each morning. Mrs. Highcroft had been very comforting, assuring Alice that the fine hotels at which they would be staying employed women who helped female guests with such necessities.

Alice fell asleep at some point during the long afternoon. She awoke to find that she and Roland were alone. "Where are the others?" she asked, covering a yawn.

"In the smoking lounge at the back of the deck," Roland answered. "I should have told you why Dr. Smith was coming with us. I wasn't keeping it a secret intentionally; I just forgot to mention it."

Alice waved her hand at Roland, dismissing his concern. "I don't mind. He's right about you and me not being able to travel alone. Well, we could, but it just wouldn't be right since we aren't married."

Alice blushed as the last few words left her mouth, and even Roland's pale cheeks reddened slightly. She turned her head away and gazed out the window, but Roland seemed to have been waiting for just such a subject to come up between them.

"Just what sort of offers has Jacob made you, anyway?"

Alice turned back to Roland, her embarrassment

gone. "I don't trust him," she said, lowering her voice to a whisper even though they were alone in the compartment.

Roland frowned. "He's always been a flirt," he began, as if he needed to make excuses for his friend.

"He flirts too much for my taste."

"Too much? So you like a little flirting, then." Roland's tone was teasing, but now it was his turn to flush and turn his gaze away. It was the first time in weeks, Alice realized, that the two of them had conversed about anything other than the upcoming tour. Their recent talks had all been so serious, full of planning and preparations. It felt good to hear the lightness in Roland's voice again.

"It depends on who is doing the flirting," Alice said boldly.

Roland's tone turned serious again. "I could have a talk with him, if you like."

"No!" Alice said, a little too adamantly. "That would just make it worse. He loves making both of us uncomfortable. Has he always been that way?"

"Not to me, no. I guess we have you to thank for his recent behavior."

"Oh, dear," Alice muttered. The conversation came to a halt with the return of Dr. Smith and Jacob.

Alice spoke very little for the rest of that night's flight. Her mind was too engaged in analyzing Roland's words and his awkwardness at the mention of flirting. Supper was merely an assortment of cold meats, cheeses, fruit, and bread, and after she finished eating, Alice realized she was ready for a soft bed. Flying by airship was exciting, but it was conducive to stiff legs and a sore back.

It was ten o'clock by the time the airship lowered gently next to the platform at the Port of Raleigh. Alice was glad to alight after their seven-hour journey. There was only one platform, and the terminal below was much smaller and simpler than the one in Atlanta.

There were two hotels just one block from the

port, and Alice followed her gentlemen escorts without much thought. They went into the lobby of the Raleigh Arms Hotel. Alice paused, wondering what to do next: she had been inside hotels before, but she had never actually spent the night in one.

Roland sensed Alice's hesitation and pointed toward an arrangement of furniture in front of a roaring fire. "Have a seat; I'll get your room for you," he said.

Alice thanked him and gladly sat down. The crackling of the fire and the flickering flames were hypnotic, and Alice could feel her eyelids drooping. She suspected that she could easily fall asleep, were it not for the sparsely-stuffed settee. *I hope the beds are more comfortable,* she thought.

Alice heard Roland call her name, and she turned to see him standing behind her, holding a key aloft. She rose and took it gratefully. Jacob and Roland would be sharing a second-floor room, and Dr. Smith took the room between theirs and Alice's. Apparently, Dr. Smith wasn't going to take any chances when it came to being proper.

As Mrs. Highcroft had promised, a maid came to help Alice undress. Five minutes after the maid left her room, Alice was asleep.

Five hours after that, Alice was wide awake.

Chapter 20

Several pairs of footsteps were moving quickly down the hall, and Alice heard a door shut with a thud. Her first thought was that a fire had broken out and everyone was fleeing the building. Alice was suddenly alert, a feeling of panic rising in her chest.

Alice opened her door a few inches and peered into the hallway. A middle-aged couple was walking past, and they were both fully dressed.

Do you have to get dressed to exit the building even if it's on fire? Alice wondered. Instead of asking the couple that question, she asked, "Is there an emergency?"

"Not at all," said the woman. "But someone up on three awoke when a ghost appeared in their room. The desk clerk said that a young scientist staying here can make ghosts appear, so everyone is going to the room to see the demonstration."

Alice frowned. It was four in the morning, for one thing, and the Ghost Machine had been left in the cargo hold of the airship, for another. Still, Alice was curious to see what was happening on the third floor for herself. She retreated into her room and dressed herself as best she could.

It wasn't hard to find the room, but getting inside

was impossible. It was already full, and a crowd was standing outside in the hallway. Everyone unable to see the demonstration stood silently, listening to the startled noises made by those within the room. Before a full ten minutes had gone by, applause erupted from the room, and people began streaming out. Every witness wanted to talk about the Ghost Machine's successful demonstration, and they found willing ears in the hallway.

Once the room had been cleared, Alice edged her way past all the people and peeked inside. The Ghost Machine stood in the center of the room, and her traveling companions were right next to it, grinning broadly and congratulating each other.

"What's this about?" Alice asked, forgetting her manners in her surprise. "It's four in the morning!"

Roland shrugged and gave Alice a lopsided smile. "Apparently the desk clerk is the cousin of a man who saw a demonstration in Atlanta. He recognized my name in the register."

"Yes, but how did the machine get here?"

"Some men volunteered to go unload it and haul it over here," Jacob said. "We paid them handsomely, but more than made up for it in the donations we've just been given." Alice noticed for the first time that Jacob had a sizable stack of money in his hand.

Alice shook her head, torn between amusement, annoyance, and admiration. Of course, her first thought was why hadn't they bothered to wake her up so she could share the experience, too?

Too tired to argue, Alice simply said, "I'm going back to bed. I'll see you all at breakfast." Without waiting for a reply, she turned and followed several other hotel residents back to the second floor. This time, it took her a lot longer than five minutes to fall asleep.

The Ghost Machine was broken. There was no indication of it until the party arrived at the airship port, bleary-eyed and quiet after the previous night's activity. When Roland presented his ticket to the porter at the gangway leading to the ship, the porter gasped.

"Mr. Highcroft, sir," he said in a whisper loud enough for Roland and his companions to hear. "There was some trouble with your device this morning."

"Trouble?" Roland asked, suddenly alert.

"The men who returned it from the Raleigh Arms had a little difficulty loading it back onto the ship. One of them let his side drop as they carried it, and the whole thing toppled over."

"How serious is the damage?" Roland's alertness had turned to alarm.

"Not sure, sir. I don't know how that stuff works or what it even looks like when it's not broken." The porter paused, leaned toward Roland, and spoke even more quietly. "It seems the men had been drinking, sir."

"Show us to the cargo hold. We'll work on it during the flight."

Alice and the others followed the porter onto the lower deck. The cargo hold was bright enough with its wide doors thrown open, and it was immediately obvious that the Ghost Machine was bent. The top half of it leaned at a slight angle, and several of the copper wires leading to the Taylor's Cone had been ripped free.

Roland ran his hands over the machine, assessing every inch of it. "That has to be straightened, new wire there, hammer out these dents..." Roland spoke to himself, taking note of the repairs he would have to make.

Alice turned to the porter. "We'll need lanterns as soon as the cargo doors are closed," she said. "And bring us a tray of coffee, please. I expect we'll be needing it."

"Yes, ma'am. Of course." The porter turned and scurried out. Already Roland had put his bag on the ground and was pulling out his tools.

Dr. Smith pulled a small notebook from his coat pocket. "First, Roland, let's list every repair that needs to be made. Then we can prioritize and get to work on the worst of the damage. The cosmetic blemishes we'll save for last."

The last item was entered on the list as the cargo doors shut with an echo that bounced throughout the hold. The room was suddenly dark, and even as Alice groped for a nearby steamer trunk to get her bearings, the airship cast off and the floor lurched beneath her feet. There were sharp sounds of metal scraping against wood as Roland's tools began to slide across the floor.

Suddenly a bright light flared and Jacob's face came into view, a match held in front of him. With his other hand, he reached out to steady Alice.

As the ship settled and began steaming along, the movement slowed to the usual gentle shifting of an airship in flight. The match burned down, and Alice was grateful when Jacob had to let go of her in order to strike a new one.

The pile of burned matches reached four before the porter finally returned bearing two lanterns and one long brass object that looked like a telescope. The porter handed it to Dr. Smith gingerly. "Careful. It's a torch, but the flame is at the back, and the light comes out the front."

When it was lit, a bright, concentrated circle of light came from the torch, much brighter than the glow of the lanterns. "Ever seen one of these, Miss Alice?" Dr. Smith asked. When Alice shook her head, he continued. "The flame is refracted through a series of glass lenses to concentrate the light. Simple construction, but exceedingly clever."

"It would be more clever shining on the underside of the dynamic reflector," Roland suggested with impatience.

The work went slowly. Roland soon shed his coat and rolled up his sleeves. He ran his hands through his hair in frustration every time he stopped to sip at his coffee, and soon Alice smiled as his appearance.

"What can you find amusing about all this?" he asked her.

"After weeks of seeing you all dressed up and proper, it's nice to see you looking quite yourself again."

Roland responded with a wan smile. "If we can't get the machine working, we'll be selling those nice suits to buy our passage back home."

"Nonsense. These repairs are minor and you're more than capable."

Roland's smile grew. "Thank you, Alice."

Even in the dim light, they could see Jacob's sarcastic expression. "There isn't enough room in this hold for so much sentiment. Alice, I dream of the day when you offer me such encouragement."

The journey—and the hours—continued on. It was excessively cold in the cargo hold, and Alice kept her cloak wrapped tightly about her. In the early afternoon, the porter brought trays of dinner down for the four of them. Roland barely touched his food, and Alice had to take bites with one hand while holding a lantern aloft with the other.

When the last item on Dr. Smith's repair list was complete, Roland stood back and sighed. The Ghost Machine looked just as it had the night before.

"Now let's just hope it still works," he said.

Roland triple-checked the straps holding the machine in place before he agreed to return to the passenger compartment. Alice was grateful to finally sit down. Her black leather boots were fashionable but not comfortable for standing for such long periods. A flask of brandy appeared—Alice suspected it was Jacob's—and the men each took a long drink from it. Another light supper appeared soon after, and all four of them ate with enthusiasm.

The journey from Raleigh to Washington, D.C., was not quite as long as the first leg from Atlanta, and the sun had just set when the ship began to descend. As they flew over the city, the gas lamp-lit streets of Washington shone in straight spokes radiating out from the Capitol building. The interior of the great building glowed brightly, its windows flooded with light.

"Electric light fed by great steam-powered generators," explained Dr. Smith. "They have the same at the White House, where our president lives."

"We'll have time to do some touring tomorrow since we don't have a demonstration until Thursday," Roland told Alice. "I never took you on an airship tour in Atlanta, so maybe I can make it up to you with a tour of Washington."

"I'll be happy with anything we do tomorrow, as long as it doesn't involve standing on my feet all day in a cold, dark cargo hold."

"Come now," Jacob interjected. "Being trapped in the dark with three gentlemen is a singular experience. I imagine your sister will quite enjoy your next letter to her."

Alice didn't answer, but she smiled inwardly at the disapproving look that Dr. Smith leveled at Jacob.

The Washington, D.C., airship port was even larger than the one in Atlanta. There were at least a dozen platforms, though two of them had wide signs that read "Government Use Only." Several other ships had recently docked, and the terminal was crowded with travelers.

Alice struggled to keep up with her three traveling companions, who moved through the crowd with assurance. Finally, she reached out and discreetly took hold of the back of Roland's coat. When he surged forward, he realized part of his attire was being held back.

"Afraid of being left behind?" Roland asked.

"Yes."

Roland smiled and offered his arm. "I promise not to lose you," he said as Alice gratefully slid her arm through his.

Outside the port, a long line of carriages for hire waited to take passengers to their hotels. Alice joined the queue with Jacob and Dr. Smith, but Roland hesitated. "You three go ahead. I'm going to make sure the machine gets unloaded and transported without any more trouble," he said.

Without waiting for a reply, Roland turned and quickly disappeared inside the port.

Alice was much too tired to take in the scenery as their carriage clattered along the streets of Washington. Thankfully, the journey was short, and they were soon at the Jefferson Inn. The lobby was ornate and brightly lit with gas lamps along each wall. Alice's room on the third floor was just as lavish. The four-poster bed had white curtains, and the sage walls were adorned with paintings of the countryside.

As soon as she was alone, Alice unlaced her boots and slipped them off with a satisfied sigh. The maid came soon after to help her dress for bed. The service was more than Alice had ever experienced: the maid, her dress starched so stiffly it could almost stand on its own, also brushed Alice's hair and turned down her bedcovers before stoking the small fire. She left with a crisp "good night," Alice's outfit for the next day tucked securely under her arm to be pressed.

Alice slept soundly until the same maid returned the next morning, bringing Alice's freshly-pressed clothes and a tray of coffee. Alice took her time getting ready before heading to the dining room to meet the others for breakfast.

Everyone, Alice noticed, looked refreshed after a good night's sleep, except for Roland. Dark circles under his eyes betrayed his weariness, and his shoulders slumped.

"Did you have to do more repairs last night?"

Alice asked.

"No. I'm just worried that it won't work properly."

"I was thinking about that, Roland," Dr. Smith said. "Why don't we do a sort of dress rehearsal this evening? We can tweak the machine as needed without an audience watching."

Roland nodded. "I'll stop by the Ellis Theatre to ask if we can get in tonight. If the machine works, we can just leave it there until we return for the public demonstration."

The Ellis Theatre was the first stop for the group, who had piled into a carriage to see the sights of Washington, D.C. Alice waited while Roland went inside to enquire about testing the Ghost Machine there, and she knew the answer had been in the affirmative when Roland returned with a smile on his face. His relief made him much more relaxed as the carriage toured them past great mansions, monuments, and the White House.

Alice gladly took it all in, amazed at the grandeur of the mansions that lined the streets. Atlanta had some fine homes, but nothing like the places in Washington. Diplomats, politicians, and influential families certainly lived more richly than their counterparts in Atlanta.

On the return journey following dinner at a small inn, even Alice was tired of admiring Federal architecture and debating the price of the artwork inside the finest mansions.

Everyone retreated to their rooms for the afternoon, and Alice sat down at the small desk in hers to write letters. She sent one to Mama and another to Emma. They were very different in tone. To Mama, Alice spoke of the beauty of Washington and the morning's tour. To Emma, Alice expounded on their furious repair work on board the airship and of Jacob's unwelcome presence in the party.

With the letters sealed and addressed, Alice lay

down to nap briefly before supper. Traveling, it seemed, was more tiring than summoning ghosts.

Supper was a grand affair, and the dining room was filled with elegant people. Alice, for the first time, really felt her country roots as she looked at the women around her. Their ramrod straight backs, expensive dresses, and fine airs were no match for her proper but simple upbringing. Even with her new dresses cut in the latest styles, Alice felt her inferiority.

Surprisingly, it was Jacob who gave her comfort.

Alice didn't know if he had noticed her self-conscious glances at the other women or not, but as they were eating, he leaned over and said quietly, "Most of these high-class women are absolutely miserable, you know."

"Is that so?" Alice asked, sarcasm in her voice.

"It is. You're fortunate, Alice. You will never have to conform so strictly as these women do, and you can actually be yourself. None of these women have personality, except for what they're told they can have."

Alice frowned and looked at the women again. This time, she realized how similar they all looked, and how little they smiled or genuinely laughed.

"I'm sure they are all very accomplished," Alice suggested.

Jacob laughed. "So are you. But your accomplishments go beyond painting landscapes and playing a few songs on the piano."

Jacob raised his glass and clinked it against Alice's. "To being true to yourself," he said. As he took a sip, he winked at Alice.

Alice blushed, but at least she felt more comfortable among such elegant company.

Alice felt much more in her element at the Ellis Theatre, the Ghost Machine situated in the middle of the stage, and Roland, again, fussing over it and hunting for overlooked damage.

The theatre was spacious and elegant, with red

velvet covering the chairs and gilt carvings lining the walls. The gold shimmered in the reflection of the gas lamps, while the back corners of the auditorium were swathed in shadow.

Roland had ridden on the wagon that delivered the Ghost Machine. After the incident in Raleigh, he was being extra cautious. The theatre had no shows that evening, so the party was allowed entry as soon as they arrived.

The theatre's caretaker was a man whose time in the Army had aged him greatly. Though he couldn't be much older than Alice's father, he seemed withered and tired. A patch covered his right eye, and his thinning hair was gray and unkempt.

He had introduced himself as Captain Reginald Rogers, and Alice wondered if he expected all of them to address him as "Captain."

Roland paused long enough in his adjustments to allow Reginald to give them an overview of the theatre. "That there," he said, sweeping his arm toward one of the private boxes, "is where..."

Alice gasped. "President Lincoln, of course! Is it his ghost that haunts the theatre?"

Reginald narrowed his one eye at Alice. "Our glorious President didn't die here. He was shot at Ford's Theatre. As I was saying, up there is where our current President enjoys taking in the shows produced here."

"Oh," Alice said, thinking it might be better if she didn't speak to the caretaker for the remainder of the night.

Reginald waved his arm. "Come with me," he said.

The tour he took them on comprised not the auditorium, but the backstage area. It was the first time Alice had ever seen that side of a theatre. "So many ropes and pulleys," she commented to Dr. Smith.

"It takes a lot of work to put on a good show," he replied.

"Well, the theatre in Fairburn seems small and dismal compared to this place. I'm sure I should love to see a show here."

"I'll settle for seeing a ghost here," Roland said.

Reginald overheard the conversation and stopped. "You will. He won't like you, though. He doesn't like men in his theatre."

"What's his story?" Roland asked.

Before he would answer, Reginald insisted on escorting everyone back into the auditorium. Once the four scientists were seated in the plush velvet chairs on the front row, Reginald stood before them.

"The Ellis Theatre opened in December of 1871. The first show here was a production of *Hamlet*. The show was so plagued by tragedy that some people began to think the theatre was cursed." Reginald paused and looked around him dramatically. Alice had to stifle a laugh at the sight of the weathered man doing his own bit of acting.

"The boy playing Laertes contracted scarlet fever and died two days before the show was to open," Reginald continued. "Then, on opening night, the stage manager tripped over a prop backstage and broke his ankle. He insisted that the crew simply wrap his ankle in bandages, promising to go to the hospital after the final curtain.

"Things went fine until our last show of the run. The house was packed; good reviews meant that the theatre was sold out for every show. Apparently, there was a design flaw in the stairs leading to the balcony. They had held up since opening night, but it was finally too much. The stairs collapsed while people were leaving the balcony after the show. Three people died, and many more were injured."

"So there have been three deaths here?" Roland asked. "Maybe we should put the Ghost Machine near the balcony stairs."

"That was just the first show," Reginald said, clearly annoyed at having been interrupted. "Talks of a curse started after that, and a year later a stagehand was standing in the wrong place. A sandbag—a counterbalance to a scrim—came down during a set change and hit him in the head. We thought he had just been knocked unconscious, but he never woke up.

"And then there's the actor." By the tone of his voice, it was apparent that Reginald had saved the best story for last. "Silas Murphy."

Alice found herself leaning forward in her seat to hear the caretaker's voice, which had dropped so low it was nearly a whisper.

"He was playing Romeo, and by all accounts he was a bit of a Romeo in real life, too. The ladies all clucked about how handsome he was, and every night he had a different lady coming to visit him in his dressing room. He'd receive dozens of roses from admirers, and even the director thought he was God's gift to the stage.

"During a Saturday matinee, Silas put more heart into Romeo's death scene than anyone had ever witnessed. It seemed so real, as if he were truly dying of a broken heart. When the curtain closed, though, and the actors began to line up for the curtain call, Silas didn't get up. A heart attack, most people said, but some of us think it was more. Maybe one of those ladies got jealous and decided he didn't deserve to go on living. At any rate, the audience cheered like mad and demanded that Silas take his curtain call. The cast couldn't conceal their shock, and soon everyone in the house knew what had happened. Ever since then, strange things have been happening at this theatre."

"Like what?" Roland prompted.

"Females complain that they feel like they're being watched. Actresses especially feel it when they're alone in their dressing room. The leading actors have it worse. Their costume pieces will go missing, only to turn up in odd locations. A few of the actors have been scratched and pushed by the ghost."

"He sounds like a real charmer," drawled Jacob,

yawning into one hand.

"Some folks think he's angry about being murdered," Reginald said. "Others think he's just jealous about having other leading men taking all the glory and admiration."

"Well, there's only one way to find out, isn't there?" Roland stood and stretched. "Time to turn on the machine and find out if it still works. Dr. Smith, why don't you accompany me onto the stage?"

Dr. Smith rose, and Alice was left alone with Reginald and Jacob. She was still reluctant to talk to the former and loath to talk to the latter. Instead, she remained silent and turned her attention to the stage, where Roland was already winding the Ghost Machine. Reginald finally sat down a few seats away from Alice, as curious about the machine as the rest of them.

The velvet-covered drums were still building up speed when small sparks began to dot their surface. "Look," Roland called, "the dry winter air is making the machine work much more efficiently. Our energy output will be higher, too."

Curious, Alice rose for a better view. As she watched, the sparks increased along with the speed of the drums. From all of her past experiences, she knew it wouldn't be long before the ghost would appear underneath the Taylor's Cone. That was, Alice reminded herself, if the Ghost Machine were actually working properly.

Suddenly Alice felt a firm hand grab the right side of her waist. The touch was too intimate for a mere acquaintance, and she turned around with a cry of shock. "Mr. Masterson!" she said. "What are you doing?"

But Jacob was still in his seat, sitting on the opposite side of Alice. She no longer felt the hand on her waist, but its firmness lingered in her memory.

"What's going on?" Roland asked, again winding the machine to keep the drums turning.

"Someone just grabbed my waist."

Reginald barked out a laugh. "You just met the great actor, Silas Murphy. Told you he liked the ladies."

Alice's eyes widened and she rubbed at the spot where she'd felt the invisible hand. "Well, he's no gentleman, that's for sure."

"You and your narrow definition of a gentleman," Jacob interrupted.

Alice ignored Jacob and continued. "Why is he out here with us, instead of on stage beneath the machine?"

"I don't know," Roland answered. "Dr. Smith, keep the machine wound while I try to fix it."

Alice let out another cry as she felt the hand again, this time stroking her hair. "Please hurry," she called to Roland.

"If it likes you so much, why don't you lead it onto the stage?" Jacob suggested.

With a nod, Alice walked to the stairs leading up the right side of the stage. The flame of every gas lamp rose and grew in brightness as she passed, then returned to its original state once she had gone by.

"He's following you," Reginald said.

Alice bit her lip to keep it from trembling. Seeing ghosts appear in the machine was one thing, but having one flirt with her like this was frightening. Even the ghost of the builder that she'd seen in her own room in Atlanta hadn't intruded physically.

As she lifted her skirts to ascend the stairs, Alice felt the ghost's hand under her elbow, steadying her as she climbed onto the stage.

Everyone waited for the ghost to appear under the machine, but still there were only the sparks of the drums to see. Roland was running his hands over each part, and finally he gave a triumphant "Yes!"

At everyone's expectant looks, he continued. "You see, this wire leading into the Taylor's Cone is frayed right where it connects. It's so deep inside the cone that we didn't notice it in the dark of the cargo hold." Roland pulled a pair of pliers from his coat pocket and reached inside the cone. "Just a push that way, and we've got it."

Roland's eyes went expectantly to the machine, but still no ghost appeared. "I don't understand. The machine is fixed. Everything is the same as it was before the accident."

"Maybe..." Alice began.

"Yes?"

"According to Reginald, Silas is already very active here. Maybe he doesn't need the Ghost Machine to appear. He already draws enough energy from, well, the building or the actors, or something. And if he'd rather be over here with me, then why should he bother to appear under the machine?"

"Perhaps you're right. Most ghosts need the energy, and want to utilize it to communicate."

Alice frowned. "Maybe we're just not going about this the right way." She turned to her right. The ghost, for all she knew, could be in an entirely different room by this time, but she suspected he was still nearby. If the goosebumps on her right arm were any indication, he was standing very close to her. "Mr. Murphy," Alice said, her voice taking on a flirtatious tone, "this is the Ghost Machine. You can use the energy it generates to manifest. I know you're there because you touched me, but I really want to see you. All you have to do is come stand right here." Alice gestured to the space beneath the Taylor's Cone. "Please, Mr. Murphy."

Alice glanced at Roland and saw his odd expression. Was that jealousy? Over a ghost? Roland straightened up and averted his eyes under Alice's gaze.

"Mr. Murphy, think about it," Alice continued, turning back to the empty air. "This is your chance to be on stage again. Tomorrow night this theatre will be full, and they are all coming to see you. You're the lead actor, and this is our dress rehearsal."

As if he was finally swayed by her words, faint lights began to gleam beneath the Taylor's Cone.

When the ghost of Silas Murphy finally manifested, his gaze was locked on Alice's own wide eyes. The actor was a small man, but he had handsome features and thick waves of dark blonde hair. His jacket, short pants, and hose were obviously his costume from *Romeo and Juliet*. Silas had a small, self-confident smile, and to Alice it was clear why he was so popular with ladies during his lifetime.

"Well, he looks gallant," Jacob called dryly from his front-row seat.

"He looks very handsome," Alice said, so quietly that even Roland couldn't make out her words. She couldn't tear her eyes away from the specter that had so recently been flirting with her. No man had ever had the audacity to stroke Alice's hair or to touch her so boldly. Even though the behavior was shocking, it still gave Alice a thrill. Surely Roland would never be so forward.

But, Alice thought, Jacob would. That realization took some of the glamour out of Silas's attentions to her, but she still remained captivated by the flirtatious ghost.

"You're very handsome," Alice said, surprised at her own boldness. Somehow, speaking to a ghost so blatantly seemed more acceptable than addressing a living person in such a way.

Silas merely nodded, and Alice didn't know if he winked at her or if the light making up his image simply flickered.

"We understand that you were very popular with women who came to see you perform."

Again, a nod from Silas.

"But that you don't like men very much. Why are you so mean to them?"

Silas shrugged, as if his behavior were no big deal.

"Do you not like other men starring in the leading roles?" Alice persisted.

Slias's smile turned to a grimace in affirmation.

Roland finally interrupted the odd tête-à-tête. "Silas, as Alice mentioned before, this is a sort of dress rehearsal for tomorrow night's, ah, show," he said.

Silas turned away from Alice for the first time and looked at Roland with interest. Roland took it as his cue to continue. "You're the lead in the show. The audience would love to see you again, to have another chance to see you on stage, performing for them."

Roland paused. "Will you do this for us?" he asked anxiously.

Silas turned again to Alice, and he grinned. Alice thought he looked like a lion readying for a kill. Whatever thoughts were prompting that smile, Alice didn't know, but Silas turned back to Roland and nodded emphatically.

"Thank you," Roland said.

"Thank you so much," Alice echoed.

His agreement with the scientists made, Dr. Smith allowed the machine to wind down, and Silas disappeared.

The caretaker's laugh cracked through the theatre. "Excellent! You're going to give them quite a show tomorrow," he said. "Never in my years here has anyone actually seen the ghost of Silas Murphy. We'll have a sell-out crowd tomorrow."

"We certainly appreciate your help tonight, Mr. Rogers," Roland said.

"Captain," corrected the caretaker.

Roland merely nodded in agreement before throwing the great white sheet over the Ghost Machine. Once the cover was in place, he patted the machine and looked at it as a proud father would his son.

"Come on," Alice said. "It'll still be here tomorrow."

"And so will your new friend," Roland said. "The two of you had quite the connection, didn't you?"

"Well, I'm the only female present, so it only makes sense that he would focus his attention on me," Alice said, the blood rising in her cheeks.

Roland's voice was quiet when he spoke next, so that only Alice could hear him. "I thought I might have to be jealous of Jacob, but certainly not a ghost!" Alice laughed at the joke, but underneath Roland's teasing tone there had been a note of sincerity. Was he really worried about Jacob? While Jacob liked to imply that he was interested in Alice, he surely didn't mean any of it. Alice always assumed he was simply trying to get a rise out of Roland.

The party bid farewell to Captain Reginald Rogers in the lobby. As Alice turned toward the door, she felt a man's hand on her arm, holding her back. She knew it must be Silas since everyone else was standing in front of her. As they filed outside, she hung back, the hand still firmly on her arm.

Reginald held the door, and he turned to Alice with a curious look. "Coming, Miss?" The brow over his one good eye was raised, as if he knew there was more going on than he could see.

The hand released Alice at that moment, and she answered, "Yes, I'm coming." Before she could take her first step, though, she suddenly felt cold air against the right side of her neck. A small, gentle touch followed, like unseen lips pressed against her pale throat. Alice gasped and fled from the building, this last bit of flirtation too much for her sensibilities.

Jacob and Roland both noticed Alice's wide eyes and hurried step as she joined them on the sidewalk. Dr. Smith was already climbing into the carriage as Jacob leered over Alice. "Saying goodbye to your new beau?" he asked. "I'm jealous, Alice. Especially since you already said he's no gentleman, and I know how particular you are about finding yourself one of those."

"More like he was saying goodbye to me, and I

still say he's no gentleman." Alice walked past him and followed Dr. Smith into the carriage, where she sat and began to rub her neck absentmindedly.

"What happened?" Roland asked, settling in across from her.

Alice glanced at Jacob, who was obviously ready to continue his teasing. "Nothing," Alice said, her clipped tone bringing the subject to a close.

They spent the ride to the hotel discussing the night's surprising success. Silas Murphy's ghost seemed quite willing, and if he really did cooperate for the demonstration, then they would have a very satisfied audience.

Back at the hotel, Alice said goodnight to the gentlemen, who were going to the lounge on the ground floor to smoke. Jacob and Dr. Smith promptly went inside the lounge, but Roland lingered, calling Alice's name after she had begun ascending the stairs to her room.

Roland glanced behind him to make sure they were alone. "What did happen as we were leaving the theatre?" he asked.

"Oh, it's silly."

"Obviously it's not silly to you. You looked quite shocked when you came out the door."

Alice's voice came out as a whisper, and she realized she felt embarrassed by her words. "He kissed me," she said, putting her hand to her throat. "Here."

Roland's eyes widened, and his first few attempts at a reply failed. Finally he just said, "Oh."

"It made me very uncomfortable."

"Because he kissed you, or because he's a ghost?"

Alice thought she could detect a hint of jealousy in Roland's tone. Could he really be jealous over a ghost? No, Alice reminded herself for what felt like the hundredth time, Roland loves his science, not me. He never looks at me the way he looks at the Ghost Machine. "I don't know," she answered honestly.

"I've never been…" Alice stopped abruptly, appalled that the words "I've never been kissed before" had been about to come out of her mouth.

Roland, though, seemed to understand. He looked at her with a mixture of sympathy and humor. "You've never been kissed by a ghost before, of course," he said.

Alice smiled in gratitude, but was afraid to say more. "I'd better get some sleep. I'm tired after such an active demonstration tonight. I could swear Silas was using my energy, not the machine's. Good night."

As she walked up the stairs, Alice wondered if Roland was watching her go, looking at her the way he had looked at his invention earlier. As much as she wanted to turn around, she kept her eyes fixed in front of her, but her hand strayed up to the tiny music box hanging around her neck.

Chapter 21

"There is absolutely no possibility of it," Jacob was saying as Alice entered the dining room for breakfast the next morning.

"I think you're wrong," countered Roland.

"What are they arguing about?" Alice asked Dr. Smith as she sat down.

"Whether or not tonight's demonstration will be as active as last night's."

"It will be more active," Alice said firmly, loud enough to get the attention of both Roland and Jacob.

"Impossible," Jacob said.

"Not impossible," Alice responded. "Silas is fond of women. If he responded so well to having one woman to flirt with last night, just think what he'll do when there's a whole theatre full of them!"

Roland smirked. "Thank you, Alice. I knew you'd see my view of it," he said, looking pointedly at Jacob.

Jacob simply shook his head. "You two are dangerous together. One day, Alice, you'll be on my side. It's a much better view from over here."

As they ate a meal of toast and poached eggs, Alice wondered just what Silas might do in the presence of so many adoring female fans. Certainly the attention would not be centered on herself as it had been.

If only Roland paid those kinds of attentions to me, Alice thought.

Alice glanced at Roland, already deep in thought about the upcoming demonstration, and sighed inwardly. She had, once again, fallen asleep with her music box necklace lying open on her pillow.

Roland wanted to go to the theatre to check on the Ghost Machine, worried that something may have happened to it during the night. His paranoia since the incident at Raleigh was apparent, and Jacob agreed to accompany him, keeping up a constant stream of teasing as he went.

Dr. Smith and Alice chose to go for a walk, turning up the street on which the hotel sat and walking all the way to the Capitol building. It was a cold morning, and the sun was hidden behind a thick sheet of gray clouds. Alice was wrapped snugly in a new coat and her hands were deep inside a fur-lined muff, but still the cold found its way in.

Alice asked Dr. Smith constant questions about his work as a scientist, and the gentleman was only too happy to entertain her with stories of experiments gone awry, accolades for theoretical inventions that might never actually exist, and the abject horror with which his family viewed his choice of profession.

"They thought I was making a huge mistake," he explained. "They wanted me to be a medical doctor, where I could have really made a difference in the world."

"You are making a difference, in a way that benefits not just one patient at a time, but everyone."

"Spoken like a true New Scientist, Miss Alice." Dr. Smith hesitated, then continued. "You and Roland make a good pair, you know. Your hearts are both in the right place, and your intellects complement each other."

"Thank you."

"Jacob likes to make himself out to be the hero of

the story, but Roland is the better man."

That observation, while certainly true in Alice's eyes, was surprising since it was unsolicited. "I agree. You don't have to worry about Jacob's supposed charms working on me."

"I am glad to hear it," said Dr. Smith. "And it's not his charms that worry me; it's his money."

"What do you mean?"

"I mean Jacob comes from a very wealthy family. The Highcroft family is wealthy, too, but it is nothing to the Masterson fortune. If you married him, you'd be able to build every elaborate, expensive invention you could dream up."

Alice was surprised at Dr. Smith's casual mention of marriage. "I assure you I'm not marrying him. Jacob can't even convince me to be his assistant."

Dr. Smith smiled. "Very well, dear. Ah, look! We have reached Capitol Hill."

Alice looked up, finally pulling her curious gaze from her companion, and saw the dome of the Capitol building looming before her. It was the grandest building she had ever seen, and she stood still for a moment, taking in the perfect lines of columns and the rising spire atop the dome.

There was a flash of white directly in front of Alice's eyes. "It's snowing," she announced. "We only get snow once a year or so in Fairburn, and never very much."

"Then you're in for a treat, I daresay," replied Dr. Smith. "Though by the time we've reached New York, you'll be quite tired of snow and of slogging through wet streets."

Alice and Dr. Smith made a circuit of Capitol Hill, taking in the building from each vantage point. By the time they returned to their starting spot, it was snowing harder. Alice turned her face to the sky, loving the feel of the soft flakes landing on her cheeks. Still, she had to admit she was too cold to stay out any longer. Her toes felt numb inside her thin leather boots.

Dinner was already being served by the time Alice and Dr. Smith entered the dining room, and they found Roland and Jacob eating heartily. Roland was smiling, so Alice knew that all was well at the theatre.

"The Washington, D.C., chapter of the AAD Men will be in attendance tonight," Roland announced as Alice settled in and gratefully wrapped her hands around a hot cup of tea.

"Let's hope I warm up before then, or I'll be the ghost they see tonight," Alice said, but then she returned Roland's smile. "I'm very happy for your success."

"Remember, it's your success, too."

"If that's true, then Alice ought to be up on stage with you tonight. Let her share in the glory," Jacob said.

"Oh, no," said Alice. "I'd rather sit in the audience, I assure you."

"Suit yourself, but I'm not sure Silas would approve of that plan."

"I'm not about to make plans based on a ghost."

"But the two of you are already on such intimate terms! Roland and I are both still waiting for the chance to kiss you."

Alice gasped and turned to Roland, her expression holding accusation.

Roland held up his hands. "I'm sorry. He pried it out of me on the return trip."

"I'm so persuasive, aren't I?" Jacob said, laughing at Alice's embarrassment and Roland's exposure.

Alice shook her head. "I'll be perfectly happy in the audience this evening, and I assure you that I won't be sitting with either you or the ghost."

Roland, at least, looked sheepish for the remainder of dinner, and he apologized to Alice again before they separated to their rooms. "It's all right," she told Roland. "He is your friend, so I should expect you to share things with him. I just hate giving him more to tease me about."

"He does enjoy getting the two of us stirred up. He's already found my weakness and exploits it as often as possible."

"Your weakness?" Alice asked. "New Science is your only weakness, if you have any at all."

Roland raised his eyebrows. "There's more to me than science," he said.

"Of course there is," Alice said sincerely, reaching out to touch Roland's arm. Roland reached up to cover her hand with his own, but as he did so his expression changed to one of surprise.

"Your hand is like ice."

"I'm chilled to the bone after my walk with Dr. Smith this morning. I'm going to burrow under the covers with a hot water bottle, and maybe I'll thaw out while I nap."

"Sleep well, then," Roland said, releasing Alice's hand.

Once she was in her own room and buried under three blankets, Alice's thoughts strayed back to her conversation with Roland. What weakness had he been referring to? Was she his weakness? Jacob seemed to always make suggestive comments about her, but she wasn't sure if that was because she was Roland's weakness, or because he was hers. Jacob, obviously, had caught on very early to Alice's partiality for Roland.

Whatever the answer was, Jacob's behavior obviously extended to both Alice and Roland. She wasn't sure how long she would be able to tolerate it before she finally said something unkind in response. Mama had taught her to be proper at all times, but polite words didn't seem to make an impact on a man like Jacob Masterson.

Alice warmed up slowly, and as she did she drifted into a deep sleep. When she woke, it took Alice a moment to realize it was still Thursday. The sky outside her narrow window was very dark for such an hour, and the maid lit several lamps before stoking the fire.

Alice selected a dark burgundy ensemble with black needlework on the collar and cuffs. The bodice fit close to her body in the front, and there was a small bustle in the back covered by the drawn-up overskirt. Alice admired her reflection in the mirror, thinking how well the dress complemented her slender body and disappointed that it would be hidden beneath a heavy black cloak when she was outdoors.

The dress was equally popular with both Jacob and Roland. Jacob, in typical fashion for him, whistled when Alice met them in the lobby. Alice merely narrowed her eyes at his crude behavior, but she gave Roland a heartfelt "thank you" when he told her that she looked beautiful.

Alice smiled through all of supper.

Outside, the snow still fell gently, and it was slowly accumulating in little-used doorways and on windowsills. The wet streets shone in the light of the gas lamps, and the carriage ride through the dim streets felt like the perfect prelude to a demonstration of the Ghost Machine.

The carriage pulled up in front of the Ellis Theatre exactly sixty minutes before the scheduled demonstration, and all four of its occupants were surprised to see that people were already arriving.

Inside, the first two rows of the theatre were nearly full, and there was an excited twitter that ran through the growing crowd as Roland walked down the aisle. Roland, for his part, looked confident and self-assured, though his rumpled hair told Alice that he'd been running nervous fingers through it.

Captain Reginald Rogers met the foursome at the front of the stage, but he expressed little surprise at the early arrivals. "Could be that word got out about the successful 'dress rehearsal' last night," he said, winking his one eye. "Everyone wants a close view, though I daresay several ladies here want the *complete* experience."

Alice tried to smile politely at the caretaker's humor, but it looked like more of a grimace. She wasn't sure what kind of woman would want a ghost to touch her so intimately. To her eyes, the women present so far were all very sophisticated and genteel. Jacob was already straying toward one group of young women, his most charming smile fixed on his face.

Dr. Smith and Alice followed Roland backstage. The thick red velvet curtain hung down at the front of the stage, hiding the Ghost Machine from the audience. From her vantage point, Alice could see that someone—probably Reginald—had added several silk curtains to the area behind the machine, probably to make the stage look less bare.

"Dr. Smith, you'll assist me in keeping the machine cranked," Roland said. "Alice, you are welcome to stay on the stage with us. Jacob was right about you deserving the accolades."

Alice held up her hands. "Thank you, but no. I'm quite content to sit in the audience." Alice paused, then added, "As long as I'm not sitting next to Mr. Masterson."

Roland laughed. "You were serious about that?"

"Certainly."

With the machine ready to go, there was little else to do. Alice stayed backstage a short while longer, but the sounds of the incoming crowd prompted her to go find a seat before they were all gone. She wished Roland luck, then made her way back into the house. The best seats were, indeed, mostly gone, and Alice sat down on the far side of the seventh row. She saw Jacob at the front, sitting with a group of ladies and appearing to flirt with every single one of them at once.

Watching Jacob was actually entertaining when his focus wasn't on herself or her sister, and Alice was so absorbed in his antics that she didn't realize a gentleman had approached her until he spoke.

"Hello, Alice."

Alice recognized the voice in an instant, even before she turned her head to see the speaker. "Ian!" she said, rising hastily.

The two faced each other awkwardly, unsure how to greet each other. Finally, Ian took Alice's hand and kissed it gracefully.

"What are you doing in Washington?" Alice asked, when she had recovered from her surprise enough to think clearly.

"I got a job with a law firm here. One of the partners fought in the war with Father, and I joined the firm just a month ago."

"I'm surprised Mama didn't write to tell me."

"Perhaps she wanted it to be a surprise. She wrote to tell me of your visit here."

"You look very well," Alice said, changing the subject. Her compliment was sincere: Ian was dressed as finely as the rest of the upper class people Alice had seen since her arrival, and his demeanor looked less young and soft as it had just four months before.

"As do you, Alice. Your new life agrees with you."

"I am very happy."

"Your mother said that you enjoy Atlanta a great deal."

"I do. The Highcrofts are the nicest family, and I just adore the children." Alice paused, a question on her lips.

Before she could find the courage to ask it, though, Ian spoke again. "Won't you come and sit with us? I'd very much like to introduce you to my colleagues."

"Of course," Alice said. She allowed Ian to lead her back a few rows, where there were two empty seats along the center aisle. Two gentlemen rose at their approach, and Ian introduced them as other lawyers.

After some polite pleasantries, Alice and Ian sat down. Alice decided to ask her question before she lost the nerve again. "Why would a proper man like you attend a New Science demonstration?" She smiled as she spoke, but the words brought back the pang of Ian's betrayal during their short engagement.

"Oh, Alice," Ian said, "all the best society enjoys New Science. The most interesting conversations at social engagements are ones that revolve around the newest inventions, and whether or not they're foolhardy ideas."

"You've certainly changed your tone."

"I'm not saying I want to be a scientist myself, just that I can appreciate its merits."

"Oh." Alice wasn't sure how to respond to Ian's change of heart. Why couldn't he have felt that way last summer? Because, Alice answered herself, New Science wasn't acceptable in the little town of Fairburn. Here in Washington, though, everyone realized its worth and the subject was welcomed with delight. Here, New Science was fashionable, and Ian had always been a fashionable man.

"Your mother tells me that the scientist you're traveling with is quite successful," Ian ventured, clearly aware of Alice's discomfort.

"Oh, yes," she answered. "Roland's Ghost Machine is quite amazing. It took a while to perfect it, though. He tested it once in his study, and the ghost showed up in my bedroom! I didn't even know about the machine at the time, so you can imagine my surprise when I saw the ghost."

"You must enjoy living under the same roof as a real New Scientist."

Something about the tone of Ian's voice made Alice suspect that he might be either a little jealous or a little disapproving. Alice was, after all, traveling with a man who was even more steeped in New Science than she was. Ian was clever enough to know that Alice must be drawn to Roland because of their shared interest.

"It's nice having someone to discuss science with," Alice answered cautiously. "Though between the Exposition, demonstrations of the Ghost Machine, and his other scientific engagements, he was gone from home quite a bit. And, of course, my time was mostly given to the children."

Ian nodded, apparently satisfied with Alice's answer. They continued to talk, moving on to subjects like the snow and the impressive grandeur of Washington. Now that they had passed the subject of New Science, the conversation flowed much more easily, and Alice soon felt as if they had been separated for four days rather than four months.

The gas lamps lining the walls of the house were dimmed, signaling that it was time for the demonstration to begin. Alice glanced behind her and saw that every seat was filled. From the murmurs she heard above her, she suspected that the balcony was equally crowded.

The red curtain rose, and the Ghost Machine sat silently before the audience. Roland was the first to walk on stage, and applause began immediately at his appearance. After welcoming everyone and introducing himself, Roland began to tell the tragic story of Silas Murphy. Alice had to giggle at Roland's own bit of dramatic flair, but the audience hung on every word he spoke. Feminine exclamations of "Oh, my!" trickled through the theatre when Roland mentioned Silas's tendency to chase after women.

With the story complete, Dr. Smith walked onstage. Roland began to crank the Ghost Machine, then he turned the task over to Dr. Smith and returned to the front of the stage.

"Silas Murphy showed himself to us last night," Roland began. "He appeared right here on the stage, beneath the Ghost Machine. He promised us that he would do the same for all of you tonight in this, his latest role."

Roland paused for dramatic effect and turned expectantly to the machine, but there wasn't even the faintest flicker of light beneath the Taylor's Cone.

"Silas," Roland continued, now addressing the ghost himself, "your fans are anxious to see you again. They beg you for one more performance. Come stand beneath the Ghost Machine and let them cheer for you, as they once did."

Still, there was no response from the ghost.

Roland cleared his throat self-consciously and turned to the machine. A quick glance showed that the sparks were flying and all was in order. When he turned to the audience again, his eyes were bright with a new idea.

"Ladies and gentlemen, as you know, Silas Murphy was fond of the ladies," he said. "It seems he needs a leading lady to come onstage first. Miss Alice Meriwether, would you please join us?"

Alice blushed and heard Ian's exclamation of surprise. As she reluctantly rose, every head turned to her and followed each step she took to the stage. Most people simply looked curious, but several ladies appeared to be quite envious. Alice noticed Jacob laughing out loud, enjoying Alice's embarrassment to the utmost.

Alice climbed the stairs to the stage carefully, conscious of all the eyes on her. She stopped not next to Roland, but next to the machine.

"May I present my very talented and lovely assistant, Miss Alice Meriwether," Roland announced. The audience clapped politely—the single loud whistle Alice heard probably came from Jacob's lips—while Alice felt the blood rush to her cheeks.

"Silas," she called, too softly for the audience to hear, "last night you promised to give your audience a show. Will you please come onstage?"

The ghost answered with a firm squeeze on Alice's left shoulder. She jumped at the touch.

"What is it?" Roland asked.

"Silas just put his hand on my shoulder," Alice said, raising her voice so the audience could hear. She felt like a performer in a sideshow, but she knew that good showmanship helped Roland sell tickets to his demonstrations.

Alice gave another start as she felt another hand on her opposite shoulder. "And now his other hand is on me," she said. "One hand on each shoulder. Either he's standing directly behind me or directly in front of me."

A wave of anxious laughter spread through the theatre.

Silas's closeness made the hair on Alice's arms stand up. She got her answer as to where the ghost was standing in the next instant: her face became very cold and she felt a touch against her forehead. After Silas's farewell to her the evening before, she knew it was his lips pressed against her skin. She cried out and pulled away. "Silas, please!" she whispered, horrified at his forward behavior. And in front of so many people, no less!

Alice had pulled free of the ghost's embrace, but in the next instant his hands were on her again, this time gripping her waist. Her face became cold again and she knew Silas's impetuousness wouldn't stop. The crowd had fallen silent, not sure how to react to the look of fear and awkwardness on Alice's face. Even Roland took a step toward her, his brow furrowed.

"Silas, please," Alice said again. "They came here to see you. And I know you want to perform for them."

The cold air pulled away from her face, but the hands were still firm on Alice's waist. Her voice dropped to a whisper that not even Roland could hear. "Do this for me, and you can kiss me afterwards." She paused, then continued, "Just not on stage in front of everyone, if you please." The idea of being kissed by a ghost wasn't nearly as horrifying as being kissed by a ghost in front of hundreds of people.

Apparently satisfied, Silas released Alice and soon after began to manifest beneath the Ghost Machine. Alice breathed a sigh of relief and stepped away, allowing Roland to narrate the events to the audience.

Silas was the most animated ghost Alice had ever seen, smiling and waving grandly at the crowd. The audience still adored him as much as they had when he was alive, and soon the scattered cheers turned into a standing ovation. Someone had even brought a bouquet of flowers, which was tossed onstage. Silas bowed again and again, basking in the adoration.

Alice stood to the side, temporarily forgotten. She considered trying to creep back to her seat, but knew Silas might be unhappy if she did that now. At least the audience's eyes were no longer on her.

Dr. Smith caught her attention as he wound the machine. "What happened there?" he said. "You had such a look on your face, and you jumped as if someone had pushed you."

"Silas happened. He's certainly the boldest person—er, ghost—I've ever met. He kept trying to kiss me."

Dr. Smith laughed heartily. "No harm in that, though I can see why it was unfavorable to you."

Alice lowered her voice, barely audible over Roland's boisterous monologue. "I had to promise to kiss him later. Otherwise I don't think he would have relented."

Dr. Smith laughed again, his eyes shining with mirth. "Roland and Jacob are about to become very jealous men. It will teach the two of them to stop claiming rights to you."

The last statement confused Alice. Had Roland and Jacob been arguing about her? Surely Jacob had given up his nonsense about her becoming his assistant.

With such thoughts running through her mind, the

demonstration seemed to drag on interminably. The beginning of the evening had been exciting—between running into Ian and Silas's forward manners—but now that Silas was safely under the machine, Alice was at liberty to let her mind wander.

The audience, on the other hand, was still enthralled by the former leading actor. Roland had called another woman onstage, this time an actress who had once played Juliet. She and Silas were currently re-enacting the balcony scene from *Romeo and Juliet*. Silas couldn't make any sounds, but his facial expressions and dramatic gestures more than made up for his silence. Several people in the audience recited the lines in synch to Silas's lips.

Alice's mind was still engaged on the hinted strife between Roland and Jacob when she heard the former calling her name. Roland was beckoning her to stand by the Ghost Machine.

Alice complied, stepping into place. "Why? What do you need me for?" Alice asked.

Roland nodded at Silas, and Alice suddenly understood. The ghost had been gesturing to her, silently pleading for her to come forward. Now that she was closer, Silas crooked one finger and implored Alice to come even closer.

Sensing her hesitation, Roland addressed the audience. "She hesitates, as would any of us, but ghosts can't hurt us, and she has nothing to fear."

The words did nothing to soothe Alice. She clearly remembered Roland's burned hand, the result of an angry ghost who pushed him across a room one night. Besides, it wasn't bodily harm that she feared with Silas.

Alice leaned forward, her breath beginning to come in great gasps. Her heart began to beat faster as she grew more nervous.

Soon Alice's head was underneath the Taylor's Cone. She could feel the few stray hairs around her forehead beginning to lift away from her face, the static electricity giving them a life of their own. The air around Silas was ice cold, but beads of sweat were forming on Alice's brow.

For a long moment, nothing happened. Silas stood still, just inches from Alice's face, and gazed at her with a smug confidence. Finally, almost tentatively, he reached one hand forward and touched her face.

Alice had always pictured specters moving through people, but Silas's hand was firm on her cheek. Of course, she reminded herself, he had been able to touch her even before materializing.

One corner of Silas's mouth turned up in a smile. His eyes, once transparent, seemed to become corporeal. They were blue, Alice realized for the first time, dark and deep.

Alice realized that Silas's hand was still holding her face. Without warning, Silas's other hand shot out and grabbed her waist. He pulled her to him, her entire body suddenly underneath the Ghost Machine.

The static electricity around her crackled in her ears, and she felt the ghost's coldness through her dress. His body was pressed against hers, and she tried to turn her head as his face came closer. Silas's hand was too strong, though, and he held her face tight as his lips met hers.

Alice's entire body stiffened in both shock and embarrassment. Knowing that the entire audience was watching such impropriety was more horrifying than the ghost's boldness.

The kiss seemed to last for hours. Alice tried to pull away but Silas had strong arms, even in death.

Dr. Smith stopped turning the drums of the Ghost Machine in his shock. The machine wound down and the electricity faded to just a few stray sparks, yet still Silas stood beneath the machine with Alice in his arms.

Finally, after what felt like an eternity, Silas broke the kiss and looked at Alice with amusement.

He winked at her and gave her waist one final squeeze, and then he was gone.

Alice stood for a moment, frozen, and then she took a giant leap backwards to get away from the Ghost Machine, nearly tripping on her skirt in her haste. A roar filled her ears, and she turned to see the audience on their feet, cheering and applauding the demonstration.

"Miss Alice Meriwether," Roland said, sweeping his arm toward her. "And Silas Murphy, the great actor who can still bring down the house!"

The clamor grew at the mention of Silas.

The curtain closed in front of them, and Alice breathed a sigh of relief that it was over. Before she could walk off stage, though, the curtain opened again, and Roland bowed deeply to the crowd.

Roland took three more curtain calls before the din subsided. As soon as the curtain closed for the final time, Roland turned to Alice. His broad smile was gone, replaced by a look of concern. "Are you all right?" he asked.

Alice just nodded, her hand wiping at her mouth. Roland reached forward and took both her hands in his own. "You're freezing, even colder than you were after your walk in the snow."

"I am freezing right down to my toes," Alice answered, recovered enough to speak, "but probably red to the roots of my hair. I have never been so embarrassed in all my life. Such behavior, and from a ghost, no less!"

Roland smiled and gently squeezed Alice's hands. "You have no reason to be embarrassed."

"Though I suspect more than one gentleman feels very jealous," said Dr. Smith, joining them.

Roland gave a sidelong glance to Dr. Smith, but he kept his attention on Alice. He did not release her hands until the three of them turned to walk off the stage.

Jacob was already there, and Alice wondered if

he had stopped laughing from the time she was called onstage until now. Several of the ladies he had been sitting with hovered behind him, giggling in accordance with his laughter.

"Bravo, Miss Alice," Jacob jeered. "But from you, Roland, I expected more. You should have challenged the ghost to a duel after what he did to Alice. I must say, you don't put up a fight for a woman's affections."

"He's just a ghost," Roland said stiffly.

"A ghost who, I daresay, has shared more intimacy with your assistant than any living man."

"Who are your friends, Mr. Masterson?" Alice interrupted, anxious to change the subject. Roland's face had been growing more angry with every word that Jacob spoke. If the two of them really had been fighting over her, then she didn't want to see any of it.

Jacob turned to introduce the ladies behind him, but already Alice's attention had strayed elsewhere. Ian had come backstage to see her.

Ian ignored everyone else, making a beeline for Alice. "Was that part of the plan?" he asked.

"I assure you, it was not. I would never have allowed such a thing." Alice had, of course, promised Silas a kiss, but only after the show when no one could see it. And it was something she would never admit to Ian.

"I'm glad to hear it. I thought maybe you put on this show at every demonstration." Ian sounded much like he had when he had lectured Alice about her drawings.

"Certainly not."

Ian relaxed, satisfied of Alice's innocence in the matter. It was only then that the two of them realized every eye was watching their exchange.

"Oh, ah, Roland Highcroft, may I introduce Ian Forbes?" Alice said.

The two men shook hands. "I greatly enjoyed your demonstration this evening, Mr. Highcroft. I'd like to learn more about your plans for the machine."

Roland smiled. "Certainly. And how do you know Alice?"

"I'm her fiancé."

The shock was palpable. Roland opened his mouth to respond, but couldn't find any words. Alice herself was angry. "Former fiancé," she said, her tone firm.

"Yes, of course," Ian answered dryly.

"Well, this is quite a twist. You could have told us, you know." Jacob looked even angrier than Alice, and his anger was directed at her.

"I don't see how it's any of your concern," Alice answered. "Ian and I were once engaged. Now we are not."

"Is this true?" Jacob turned to Ian, his lips set in a thin line.

"Yes. I proposed, but Alice chose to break the engagement two days later. We had some differences of opinion at the time." Ian turned to Alice, one eyebrow raised. "Now, though, it seems we are quite of the same mind about things."

So Ian had also realized that the one thing that had stood between them was no longer an obstacle. Alice wasn't sure she could ever trust Ian again, though, after he had told her secrets to her parents. Not only that, but his idea of a happy life—with her sitting at home tending to their children—was far from her own views.

"This is a fine turn of events," Jacob said. Without bidding farewell to anyone, he turned and swept out of the room, his new female companions hurrying in his wake.

"My, he didn't take that very well at all, did he?" Dr. Smith said.

"What's he upset about?" Aliced asked.

"My dear, you are far too humble." It was all Dr. Smith would say on the subject.

"Perhaps you'd join me so we can discuss your

venture?" Ian's attention had returned to Roland. "There's a club my colleagues and I belong to just a short way from here. I imagine you're ready for a drink."

"Certainly," Roland said. "Dr. Smith, will you see to it that Alice gets back to the hotel safely? I trust that Jacob can find his own way when he's ready."

Dr. Smith nodded his acquiescence. Ian wanted to linger to inspect the Ghost Machine, but first he offered to escort Alice to the carriage. He took her arm just as he used to do. It had always felt comforting, but now Alice thought it felt possessive. Alice was acutely aware of Roland's presence. What would he think of Ian's easy familiarity with her?

Ian handed Alice into the carriage with his usual grace. "How long will you remain in Washington?" he asked, leaning through the open door.

"About two more days, and then we travel to New York."

"I certainly hope to see you again before you leave."

"Of course. I'd like to hear more about your new life here."

Ian smiled. "Good night, Alice." He shut the door, and the carriage rattled as it moved forward.

"You are a popular young lady," Dr. Smith noted.

"With everyone except the one who counts." Alice had said it quietly to herself, and she gasped when Dr. Smith replied.

"Many men have a hard time showing their affection. Take heart; it's not as dire as it seems."

Alice looked at Dr. Smith gratefully, and when he next inquired how she knew Ian, the full story came flooding out of her. It was the first time she had ever related the entire tale to anyone, and her voice shook as she described Ian's behavior toward her.

Dr. Smith patted Alice gently on the hand. "If he is so appalled by New Science, how did he come to be here tonight?"

"Because it's fashionable here. Ian has always prided himself on being a fashionable gentleman."

Dr. Smith uttered a contemptuous "humph" and fell silent. Neither of them spoke for the remainder of the carriage ride, and Alice was solemn as she ascended to her room. She felt again all the horror and sadness that she had felt when Mama had announced that her drawings were all destroyed. However kind Ian might be to her now, and no matter how supportive, nothing could ever erase those feelings from her memory.

Chapter 22

Jacob was grumpy at breakfast the next morning. He sat with his arm propping up his head, and his eyes drooped. Alice felt little better, still melancholy after the memories that had been stirred up the night before.

Roland was quiet, as well, a thoughtful look on his face.

Only Dr. Smith seemed in his usual spirits, but he eventually fell silent after attempts at conversation failed. When another guest wished them all a good morning, Jacob groaned. "He speaks too loudly," he said.

"Only to your ears. I expect whiskey amplifies sound," Roland said.

"That it does."

"How was your night?" Alice asked.

Roland nodded absently. "Good. It was good."

Roland was to be engaged in meetings with local AAD Men all day. Some wished to invest in his venture, and others wanted to share ideas. A reporter from the American Science Journal was also planning to interview Roland. He had been at the demonstration the previous night and hoped to publish pictures of Silas Murphy.

Roland and Dr. Smith left for their meetings after

breakfast. Jacob had been planning to attend with them, but he begged off so he could return to bed.

With nothing else to do, Alice returned to her room and wrote a letter to her mother. Mama knew that she and Ian were going to see each other and would surely be expecting a letter detailing the reunion. Alice did write that they met at the demonstration, casually mentioning Ian's newfound interest in New Science, but she left out any mention of her actual involvement on stage. Whether Mama would hear about it from Ian, Alice didn't know, but she hoped not. Mama had come around enough to let her travel with Roland, based largely on Mrs. Highcroft's glowing praise of the scientist, and Alice didn't want Mama having second thoughts. Knowing Ian now approved of New Science would help her cause; knowing Alice had been humiliated onstage by a ghost would not.

Once she dropped the letter off at the front desk of the hotel, Alice borrowed a book from the small library on the first floor and returned to her room.

Two hours later, Alice was lost in the pages of *The Mysteries of Udolpho* when a knock startled her back to reality. A porter was at the door, relaying a message that a Mr. Forbes was waiting for her downstairs. Surprised that Ian would pay a visit in the middle of the day, Alice went down to meet him after tidying up her hair and adding a fresh dusting of powder to her cheeks.

Ian was dressed very smartly, his black overcoat open to reveal a dark gray wool suit. His blonde hair, Alice noticed, still curled softly at the nape of his neck, but it was shorter than it had been in Fairburn. He greeted Alice with a small bow.

"This is a pleasant surprise," Alice said. "I assumed you would be at the law firm."

"Even lawyers have to eat dinner," Ian said. "If you aren't otherwise engaged, I'd like to take you to one of my favorite dining rooms."

"Oh, certainly," Alice said, feeling self-conscious at the idea of dining alone with Ian. She reasoned with herself that it might be quite common here in Washington, where what was "fashionable" was obviously less restrictive than it had been in Fairburn. If she could go to the Expo with Roland in Atlanta, Alice figured that it was acceptable to go to dinner with Ian in Washington.

Ian had hired a small carriage, which was waiting for them out front. It took them to a small restaurant on a wide green park, and Ian narrated the sites as they drove. The route overlapped very little with what she had already seen, and Alice enjoyed touring even more of the big city.

Alice and Ian made light conversation as they ate. She enjoyed hearing about Ian's work and how much he enjoyed living in the country's capital, and he promised to take a detour on the return trip so Alice could see the building where he worked.

It wasn't until they were in the carriage, on their way back, that the conversation took a serious turn.

"What I did to you wasn't right," Ian said abruptly.

"You mean at home?"

"Yes. You entrusted me with your secrets, with your deepest love for something, and I did all I could to destroy it." Ian's tone was repentant. "It was my place to guide you, to help you be a respected, proper woman, but I went about it in the wrong way. I'm sorry."

"I appreciate the apology," Alice said. "I owe you one, as well. I'm not proud of my behavior toward you. If I have any regrets, it's how I shouted at you."

Ian smiled tentatively. "Then we can still be friends?"

"Of course. But you know, Ian, even if you had gone about things differently, the fact still remains that you would have tried to prevent me from studying New Science."

"I would have."

"I'm glad you approve of it now, and that we can speak on the subject without contention, but just imagine if things had not happened as they did," Alice said, her boldness rising now that she had received an apology from Ian. "You would not be working at this firm here, and I would be absolutely miserable without my science."

"We do seem to have found happiness without each other," Ian conceded.

Alice leaned over and put her hand on Ian's arm. "Ian, I wish you every happiness, and I hope you find a wife who you don't need to change in order for you to love her."

Ian's eyes widened, but he nodded; Alice's message was clear. He leaned over and kissed her on the cheek, the action surprising both Alice and himself.

"Mr. Highcroft is a good man from a good family," he said suddenly.

"Yes."

"And he's quite an accomplished scientist."

"Yes." Alice narrowed her eyes, unsure what Ian was trying to say.

"This Ghost Machine is going to be exceedingly popular. Already people are asking him to build a second one that can remain at the Ellis. Someone would have to provide funding, and Mr. Highcroft would have to teach someone to use it, but still, there is great potential for making money from the machine."

Alice paused, realizing that Ian had switched from talking about love to talking about business. She had hoped, at the mention of Roland, that Ian might say the two of them had discussed her the night before. Maybe Roland had indicated a preference for her or jealousy that she and Ian were once engaged.

Or maybe they had just discussed business.

Finally, realizing that Ian was still waiting for an

answer, Alice agreed. "The Ghost Machine was wildly popular in Atlanta, too. People will pay more money to see a real ghost than they'll pay to see a medium."

"Especially with you exposing mediums as frauds." Ian smiled. The uncomfortable, but perhaps inevitable, exchange over, they fell into easy conversation once again.

Alice was surprised to find Roland and Dr. Smith waiting anxiously in the lobby when she returned. "Alice, we've been so worried!" Roland exclaimed before catching sight of Ian. "Oh, I see," he finished quietly.

"Ian took me to dinner," Alice supplied, feeling suddenly guilty. "I didn't think to tell anyone where I was going because I thought you'd be out all day."

"We were supposed to be, but we finished early," Dr. Smith said. "We're glad to see you've had some company today."

"Yes, of course," added Roland, finally acknowledging Ian's presence. "Thank you for keeping Alice entertained. We can't have her getting too bored on this tour."

Ian excused himself soon after since he was needed that afternoon at the firm. Alice walked him to the curb outside, where a gentle snow had begun falling again.

"I hope we see you before we leave for New York," she said. "If not, it's been a pleasure to see you again."

"It has been good to see a familiar face. And I'm glad that, well, that we're able to part on good terms with each other."

"We're able to part as good friends," Alice amended. She shook hands with Ian and waved as his carriage pulled away. It really had been good to see him, and she was glad that she could again feel comfortable with him. She really wouldn't have been happy as his wife, but at least now she knew he wasn't as mean as she'd once believed.

Alice kept waving until Ian's carriage turned the corner and was out of sight. She turned back to the hotel and was surprised to see Roland standing a short distance behind her.

"Following me to make sure I don't get lost?" she asked.

Roland's response was supposed to be humorous, but his voice was flat. "No, just making sure you don't take off with Ian and leave me alone with the fellows."

"No chance of that. I'm afraid it's going to be your duty to entertain me the rest of today."

"That I can do. Phineas Phelps, the leader of the Washington, D.C., chapter of the AAD Men, is hosting a dinner in our honor tonight."

"Your honor, you mean," Alice said. "You are far too humble, you know."

"I spoke correctly. All four of us are to be the guests of honor."

Alice's pleasure at the thought only lasted from the sidewalk to the lobby. As they walked inside, they saw Jacob charging toward them, waving a paper in his hand. Dr. Smith was hurrying after Jacob, imploring him to stop, but Jacob continued to stalk forward. Thinking there had been some misunderstanding between him and Roland, Alice stepped to the side to let the gentlemen speak to each other. She was surprised when Jacob rounded on her, his visage twisted with fury.

"Of all the ridiculous letters I've ever received!" he shouted, his cheeks turning a deep red.

"Mr. Masterson, would you please calm down?" Alice took a step backward, afraid of Jacob's closeness.

"I will not calm down!"

Now other people in the lobby were turning to look. Jacob's shouting was creating a scene, and Alice felt embarrassed to be at the center of it. Dr. Smith was tugging uselessly at Jacob's jacket, and Roland moved to wedge himself in between Alice and Jacob.

"Don't bother trying to protect her from me now. There's no point." Jacob sneered at Roland, his tone indignant.

"Perhaps we could discuss this like civilized people, hmm?" Dr. Smith said.

Finally, Jacob stopped shouting. He straightened his jacket and smoothed his hair, but his face remained a portrait of anger. His words were still biting, but at least his tone was lower when he spoke next.

"You've ruined it for me, Roland."

"I don't understand."

"You've tarnished my name, and now Mr. Meriwether refuses his consent."

"What?" The words came from Alice and Roland in tandem.

Jacob sighed, looking at them both as if they were stupid children. "I wrote to Mr. Meriwether to ask for Alice's hand. His reply came today. Not only does he refuse his consent, but he states his reasons for doing so. Apparently, my name has reached his ears before, and he has not liked what he heard. I can think of no other person who would speak ill of me other than you."

"Jacob, we have been friends for many long years." Roland held up shaking hands. Whether they shook from anger, hurt feelings, or fear of a physical attack from Jacob, Alice didn't know. "Why would I ever speak ill of you?"

"Because you want Alice, and you'll do anything you must to keep her."

"I would never betray a friend." Roland's tone was firm.

"But you have. You'll get no more payments from me on my investment. You and your silly machine can rot. Don't bother trying to talk me back into it, either. I'll be on the next airship back to Atlanta."

Jacob rounded on Alice. "I feel sorry for you. You could have married me and been rich and happy.

You never would have wanted for anything. Though, I guess, you can always go running back to your dear fiancé. You'll spend the rest of your life regretting the fact that you lost the privilege of marrying a New Scientist."

Jacob stormed off, stomping up the stairs to return to his room. Alice stood with her mouth agape, still not entirely sure what had transpired. Dr. Smith tutted to himself and looked around the lobby at the people who were pretending not to watch.

"That was unexpected," Roland said simply.

"He'll come to his senses later," Dr. Smith said. "No use in talking to him when he's in this state. Come, let's go into the dining room and have some tea."

Once the three of them were seated, Alice spoke her first words. "I don't understand. Why would Jacob ask my father for my hand? He never indicated a serious romantic attachment to me."

"Because, my dear, Jacob has been listening to your sister," Dr. Smith said, as if that summed up the entire situation.

"He flirted with her when she was in Atlanta," Alice said, "and Emma accidently told me that they'd been writing letters to each other. I half expected him to make her an offer."

"Why marry her when he could have you, who can assist him in his scientific pursuits? You have all the beauty of your sister, but far more intelligence and just the same amount of money."

"Money? What does that matter when he's so rich?" Alice asked.

"My dear Miss Alice," Dr. Smith said, patting her hand, "the richer a man is, the more he wants, and Jacob is a very selfish creature. Your sister told him that the Meriwethers are the richest family in Fairburn. To him, you were the perfect bride."

"Except for the fact that I don't like him," Alice said. "Nor, do I think, does he really like me. He only ever talked to me to tease. Did you know he'd written to my father, Dr. Smith?"

"I had no idea he'd taken that step, though I knew he was considering it. He must have written it when we were still in Atlanta, or else it would have never arrived here so soon."

Roland was still silent, a frown on his face. Alice turned to him with sudden sympathy. "And I've ruined your tour! Without Jacob's money, what will we do?"

"I'm not worried about that," Roland answered. "I've spoken to several men here who want to invest. I'm more disturbed by Jacob's accusations against me. I would never write such a letter, even if those were my true feelings."

"Apparently someone did write such a letter. I am very curious who it may have been," said Dr. Smith. "Someone who, obviously, cared very much about keeping you safe, Alice."

"It was Mrs. Highcroft. I'd wager on it," Alice said. "She didn't trust him, either. She probably noticed Emma's preference for him and wrote to warn Mama. Roland, your sister-in-law was already dear to me, but now I think she must be a saint."

"I just hope that saint's actions don't mar my reputation in Atlanta. Jacob may slander me before he's had time to come to his senses."

"It's your word against Jacob's," Alice said. "Further, you'll have the AAD Men to support you."

"True. I'll draft a letter to them right away to warn them of the hurricane that's approaching." Roland stood, his tea only half-drunk. "I'll try talking to Jacob later, once he's calmed down, but it may be futile. And, frankly, I'm not sure I want him on this tour anymore." Roland looked pointedly at Alice before taking his leave.

When it was just her and Dr. Smith, Alice looked at him kindly. "Now I understand your words about marriage earlier. Thank you."

Dr. Smith chuckled. "You're most welcome,

though I must say, I never had any idea it would play out like this. I think Jacob was inspired at the theatre last night. Such drama!"

"Indeed. And now if you'll excuse me, I have my own letters to write."

Alice spent the remainder of the afternoon drafting three letters. One was to her father, asking for details of Jacob's letter to him. The second was to her sister Emma, warning her in case Jacob should renew his flirtations with her once he returned to Atlanta. He knew now that marrying either of the sisters was out of the question, but that wouldn't stop him from attaching Emma to him again. He was always a flirt, and Alice suspected that he could be a vengeful flirt.

The third letter was addressed to Mrs. Highcroft. Alice glossed over Jacob's confrontation, but pointedly asked if she had been the one to warn Mr. Meriwether. If so, Alice assured Mrs. Highcroft of her heartiest thanks for the intervention.

When the letters were finished, Alice sat down in front of her vanity and stared at herself in the mirror. How could so many others have suspected what was coming, when Alice herself never saw it? Even Dr. Smith had offered a warning about the perils of marrying a man like Jacob. She hadn't understood it at the time, though she was grateful for the fatherly advice.

Alice's thoughts also lingered on Jacob's accusation that Roland had written the mysterious letter to her parents. She desperately wanted to know Roland's feelings in the entire matter, but knew she would never have the pluck to ask him outright.

Alice sighed and put her head in her hands. Science was so much simpler than men!

Chapter 23

Alice put on one of her two finest gowns for the AAD Men dinner that evening. It was made of a rich green wool, so it was warm as well as fashionable. The snow had stopped, but it still lingered on the ground, turning slowly into gray slush.

The party was scheduled to meet in the lobby at six o'clock, and Alice half expected to find Jacob among them. Surely he would come to his senses or confess that it had all been an elaborate joke. After all, Alice could hardly believe her bad luck: first Ian proposed, resulting in an engagement that lasted only two days, and then the man she most despised in the world asked for her hand. Two suitors in only four months, and neither of them at all suited to Alice.

Jacob was not waiting downstairs, and Roland sounded resigned when he said that all attempts to talk to his former friend had failed. He wouldn't listen to any logical argument and insisted on believing that Roland had been the one to warn the Meriwethers about him.

"He's leaving on the early morning flight tomorrow," Roland said. "There is nothing more we can do."

Alice felt immense relief that Jacob would no

longer be traveling with them, but she still felt sorry for Roland, who had the biggest burden to bear. He had been wrongly accused by a friend, and now he had to find new investors so the tour could continue to New York.

He'd also had the shock of learning his friend had been making plans to marry Alice.

When the coachman came in and announced that their carriage was waiting, Alice sighed and shook her head as if she were trying to fling out any more thoughts of Jacob. She didn't want to ruin tonight's party by rehashing her afternoon over and over again. Tonight was a celebration, and Alice was determined to enjoy it.

The AAD Men had their own private club about four blocks from the White House. The front door was inconspicuous, and when Roland knocked, the man who opened it sized them up for a long while before speaking.

"And why should you and your party gain entry?" the man, who was wearing a butler's uniform, asked.

"Because we believe that science is the key to our future and that invention is the highest accomplishment of man," Roland recited.

"Then welcome. You may come in."

Roland's answer must have been some kind of secret passcode, Alice thought. It seemed a little ridiculous, and she wondered if all of the local AAD Men had to repeat that phrase every time they came to the club.

The door opened onto a long hallway. The walls were covered in a dark gray, flocked paper and the few gas lamps hanging from the ceiling were so dim that everything took on a spooky look. The party deposited their coats on racks hanging at the end of the hallway and stepped through another door, which was painted bright red and covered in elaborate brass scrollwork that intertwined with three giant locks. Thankfully, the door was not locked, and Alice let out a surprised,

"Oh!" as she entered the next room.

The ceiling was two stories high, and dark wainscoting lined the bottom of the walls. Between the wainscoting and the ceiling, the walls were packed with framed photographs and little shelves holding various contraptions. Every photograph—some of people, others of inventions—had a small, typewritten card posted below it, describing the inventor or his invention. The things on the shelves were mostly made of brass and copper. The purpose of some was apparent: a squat machine built around a bellows was obviously for automated fire stoking. Others were a mystery to Alice.

Overstuffed, mismatched chairs were situated in groupings all around the room. At the center stood a huge marble statue of a scientist wearing a lab coat and holding aloft common New Science tools. A plaque screwed to the base read, "The Spirit of Invention."

The room was already filling with AAD Men. Most of the men were standing, and a strange, slow movement at the height of their knees caught Alice's eye.

Tiny wooden tables were moving throughout the crowd! Drinks sat on top, each nestled in a divot in the wood, and a series of cogs and wires filled the space below the tabletop. At the bottom, four wheels made the machine glide forward. If the table ran into a person or a wall, it backed up about a foot and continued in a different direction. As Alice watched, one of the tables slowed to a halt. One of the AAD Men reached down and wound the machinery, the cogs came back to life, and the table continued on its way.

Alice had been so distracted by the automated tables that she hadn't looked above her. At a nudge from Roland, she lifted her eyes to the great chandelier, which hung down perilously close to the head of the statue.

A rod stuck out perpendicularly from the top of

the chandelier, and a mechanical figure with wings hung from the end of it. The figure was about a quarter of the size of a real person, and the wings stretched about four feet across. The framework was all brass, but the wings were made of a pale cream silk. The rod spun, sending the figure on a never-ending flight around the chandelier.

"Do you see how it works?" Roland asked.

Alice squinted to look at the contraption. "The chandelier has a wire running from each gas candle to a point in the middle, but I can't imagine how it powers the flyer."

"The wires are heated by the flames, and they in turn heat air that's fed into a chamber inside the chandelier. The warm air rises, spinning a fan that then spins the cogs of the flyer."

"How clever! He doesn't have a practical purpose, but it is amusing," Alice said.

Roland laughed at Alice's judgment. "Some think the Ghost Machine has no practical purpose, either. Besides, some inventions are just meant to entertain. We can't be serious all the time."

"We shan't be serious at all tonight, if I can help it," Alice answered.

Roland was welcomed as a visiting celebrity. He made his way slowly around the room, shaking hands with every man they passed. Looking around, Alice realized that she was the only woman present. Even the staff—who only had to pour the drinks and perch them on the automated tables—was all male.

That made Alice an instant celebrity, too. Every man wanted to know what she had accomplished as a scientist. Alice told them she was merely Roland's assistant, until he overheard her. "She is more than that," he corrected, beaming at Alice proudly. "It was her idea to use the Taylor's Cone on the machine. Without her, I'd probably still be hiding in my study, cursing the machine and myself."

By the time they had made a full circuit of the

room, word had spread that Alice's ingenuity had been integral in the Ghost Machine's success. That made her even more popular, and at any moment she had at least three men vying for her attention. Their eagerness to hear her stories made Alice shy; most of the men surrounding her were young and unmarried, and more than a few hinted that they would like a new assistant. Reminded of Jacob and his teasing, Alice fought to maintain her composure while she complied to their requests for stories.

A bell rang loudly, and the butler appeared to announce that supper was ready. A path immediately cleared for Alice, Roland, and Dr. Smith, and the three of them led the way through a set of double doors on one side of the room.

The dining room was less cluttered than the sitting room had been but still every bit as impressive. A small stage stood at one end of the long room, and an organ sat on it, playing away of its own accord.

Alice had heard of player pianos, but she had never seen one, nor had she ever heard of a player organ. A low vibrating hum emanating from below the stage gave away the presence of a steam engine.

The three of them sat at the head table, and they were joined by two other gentlemen, whom Roland introduced as Phineas Phelps and Francis Gordon: the president and vice-president of the Washington, D.C., AAD Men.

"I see that the fourth member of your party is missing," Phineas said conversationally. "Surely he's not still ill following his, ah, overindulgence last night."

"Jacob has decided to return to Atlanta," Roland said carefully. He ran a hand through his hair, and Alice realized that they had never discussed what they would tell people who asked about his absence.

"I'm afraid it's all my fault, Mr. Phelps. As it turns out, Jacob attended our tour because he was hoping to win me over to be his assistant." Alice put emphasis on the last word. "I refused him enough times that he finally believed me."

Francis laughed. "I have always said that having women in science is a bad idea. Though, from what Roland tells us, you can more than hold your own with many of the AAD Men."

Alice dropped her eyes to the table. "Oh, no. I don't have the education that they do."

"She's very clever," Roland said. "If she had gone to school to learn New Science, I daresay she would be the one taking an invention on tour, rather than me."

Alice directed a grateful smile at Roland. "If I had listened to Mrs. Crowfoot's advice, that's exactly what I would have done."

"You know the Crowfoots?" Phineas asked. The casual mention had piqued his curiosity.

Roland, Alice, and Dr. Smith all answered in the affirmative.

"Ah, of course you do, Roland. The two of you would have met at the Exposition there in Atlanta. But you met him as well, did you, Miss Meriwether? And how did you like him?"

"He is an imposing character, though I must say I like him a great deal more than his wife."

The entire table erupted in laughter at Alice's candid answer. She was glad when the soup arrived soon after, and the attention shifted away from her. The automated tables were being used again, and the bowls of tomato soup came perilously close to slopping over every time one of the tables ran into a chair or, worse, an AAD Man.

Waiters came out to serve the soup. Alice would have been happy to get her bowl off the table herself, and wondered why they bothered hiring real waiters when the tables did such a good job of delivering things on their own.

When Alice saw a waiter anxiously wiping at one AAD Man's sleeve, which was splattered with soup,

Alice understood why.

Alice listened to the conversation with interest as they ate. The gentlemen talked much about the politics of New Science, mentioning names she had only heard once or twice. She felt too uninformed to participate in the discussion but was grateful for the chance to listen in.

Phineas Phelps stood to deliver a toast in honor of Roland, Alice, and Dr. Smith as soon as the main course was cleared. Phineas was a wide man, the buttons of his black wool coat straining against his girth. He wore a number of medals and pins on his lapel: one signified him as the president of the Washington chapter of AAD Men, but Alice couldn't guess what the others meant.

Alice stood along with Roland and Dr. Smith while the audience clapped politely for them. All this attention! From being onstage at the demonstration to being honored at this dinner, Alice felt that she'd been stared at quite enough for a lifetime. She wondered how Roland dealt with it, considering the amount of attention he'd received since the Ghost Machine debuted.

For the first time since they had arrived in Washington, D.C., Alice took a long look at Roland. He smiled widely, and waved at his fellow AAD Men with the easy manners of a man who had become accustomed to so much attention.

As happy as Alice was for Roland, she couldn't help but reflect that the two of them hadn't shared any of those delightful private moments since arriving in Washington. Roland was always too engaged with other activities, too busy visiting other scientists, or too worried about his machine. Alice missed joking with Roland; the quiet moments when they spoke not as a scientist and his assistant, but as a man and a woman. Roland's few attempts at flirting always made her blush, but she wished he would make her blush every day. Instead, it was all business—all science—

for Roland.

Everyone lingered after supper had been cleared from the tables. Roland got up and approached several of the AAD Men. Whatever they discussed, Alice knew Roland was unhappy with the results by the way his shoulders slumped.

They were all in the carriage to return to the hotel before Alice could ask Roland why he seemed worried. Roland shrugged and sighed. "All those gentlemen who wished to invest were sincere, but they don't have the money that Jacob did. Even if I combined the money they wish to invest, it will never cover our trip to New York."

"Don't despair, Roland. I can write to the University and ask if they'd be able to give us some more," Dr. Smith said.

"Ian wants to invest." The words left Alice's mouth before she could stop them.

Roland's head snapped up. "I am sure he does. We spoke about it last night after the demonstration."

"This is your," Dr. Smith hesitated, "acquaintance from Fairburn?"

"Yes."

"How much money would he want to invest?"

"I don't know. Roland? You spoke to him in more detail than I did."

"More than the AAD Men I met with tonight. I'll pay him a visit tomorrow." Roland sounded like approaching Ian was the last resort for him. Alice wondered if it was simply because of his former relationship with her, or if there was more to Roland's hesitance.

"Does he have a good reputation here in Washington?" she asked.

"As far as I know," Roland answered. "I know he hasn't been here long, but he's already become a patron to a scientist who's building an experimental flying machine. I would have thought you'd know his reputation better than me."

Alice waved her hand dismissively. "Not me; I didn't even know he was in this city until I saw him at the demonstration."

"I would have thought, given your relationship with him…" Roland stopped mid-sentence, and even Dr. Smith looked uncomfortable at the subject he'd introduced.

"Ian's family and mine are friends. He and I will never be more than that to each other." Alice's tone was firm.

"But he said that—"

"Yes, we were engaged for two days. It was what our families wanted, and I had hoped it would be what I wanted, too," Alice interrupted. "I told him about my love for New Science, and he promptly told my father. He, of course, told Mama, and she ordered all of my designs and drawings burned as a result. Tell me, Roland, could you ever marry someone who betrayed you like that?"

"He did that?"

"Yes."

"I'm sorry. If you'd rather I didn't speak to him about investing, I can find the money elsewhere."

"No, he's the best option," Alice said. "Besides, I believe he feels some remorse for what he did to me. I think his purpose in taking me to dinner was to formally apologize. Finally."

Roland nodded but didn't answer, and Alice felt compelled to fill the silence. "He speaks highly of you. He was impressed with the demonstration and felt you were a man of good character when he met you."

"I am glad to hear it."

Little else was said on the remainder of the ride. Roland parted with a solemn "good night," and Alice was left feeling strangely lonely.

Chapter 24

The next time Alice saw Roland, he was in much better spirits. By the time she came down to breakfast, he had already left to meet with Ian. Roland finally returned to the hotel just before dinner, and his satisfied smile told Alice he had been successful.

"He's investing exactly what Jacob still owes us," Roland said as they sat down at what had become "their" table in the dining room. "And he's only asking for the standard share of profits."

"Congratulations!" Alice reached over and brushed at wet drops clinging to Roland's jacket. "Snowing again?"

"Yes, and if it doesn't stop coming down like this, we'll be hard pressed to leave for New York in the morning."

The remainder of the day was a busy one. Now that they had the money they needed for the tour, Roland and Dr. Smith were anxious to continue to New York. Alice spent her afternoon packing her trunk and writing letters to let everyone know of her impending departure.

Their last supper in Washington was a simple one, taken again in the hotel dining room. Alice realized with some surprise that she hadn't left the

confines of the hotel all day. She had been so caught
up in packing that she had missed her last chance to do
some sightseeing or to even pay Ian a visit. Judging by
the snow still piling up outside, though, it wouldn't
have been a pleasant day at all for being outdoors.

Alice woke before dawn the next day. She was
bleary-eyed as she pulled on her traveling outfit and
packed the last few items into her trunk. The porter
arrived just as she shut the lid and secured the two
latches.

Downstairs, a cup of coffee perked Alice up a
little, but it was still far too early for her taste. The air
outside, at least, swiftly woke her up. The snow had
stopped, but the wind blew so violently that flakes
were still swirling through the air. It bit through
Alice's winter coat, and she hurried to take refuge in
the carriage. By the time she, Dr. Smith, and Roland
arrived at the airship port, Alice's nose and cheeks had
gone numb. She gasped when she finally caught a
glimpse of herself in a mirror inside the terminal: her
cheeks were bright red, an almost comic contrast to the
rest of her pale skin.

Alice found a seat in front of a wide fireplace and
warmed herself while the gentlemen saw to the tickets.
Alice turned around with interest at every male voice
she heard. She kept expecting Ian to show up to see
them off. Not for her, but to give final well wishes to
this venture he was funding.

Alice couldn't blame him for staying in a warm
bed on a cold morning like this, though. She would
have liked nothing more than to be in her hotel bed,
with a warming pan filled with fresh coals under the
covers and a cup of coffee in her hands.

Thankfully, the airship was well heated. It was
the same model as the ship they had flown on from
Atlanta. In the winter months, the exhaust of the steam
engine was routed through copper pipes that fed
through the passenger compartment. The steam heated
the pipes and warmed the air.

Watching the sunrise proved to be a worthy compensation for getting up so early. As the ship began to rise over Washington, D.C., the gray light on the edge of the horizon turned to a dark blue, and then to a crystal blue tinged with orange. The snow-covered ground below shone with the early morning light, and Alice had to shield her eyes from its brightness.

The flight to New York City took only ten hours, so the sun hadn't yet set when the city came into view. Alice had thought Washington, D.C., was big, but New York seemed to be an endless sprawl of buildings and neatly-laid streets. Even Roland was amply impressed by the sight: he leaned over Alice so he could stare out the window, too. His face was so close to hers that she could smell his faint cologne, and she could clearly see the stubble on his cheeks. Apparently Roland hadn't bothered to shave, probably deciding it was better to get five more minutes of sleep.

Dr. Smith was amused by the two of them, saying that they looked like children trying to glimpse Santa Claus on Christmas Eve. "If you peer any further out the window, I'm afraid you'll tumble right through the glass," he laughed.

The airship drifted down over Central Park and glided into the port on the park's east side. The imposing marble building had a high ceiling, grand staircases leading to each dock, and a giant clock that watched over all the people bustling through the terminal. The place was ablaze with a multitude of gas lamps and chandeliers.

No snow was falling, but the streets were wet from a recent shower. The hems of ladies' gowns had soaked up the damp, and men had tromped dirty snow inside on their shoes. Clockwork mops, supported on wheeled tripods, swept the marble floors routinely, as people skillfully dodged their violent side-to-side motions.

Roland and Alice kept their faces pressed to the windows of the carriage, too. Block after block rolled by as each made exclamations.

"So many dining rooms!" said Roland. "How shall we ever choose where to eat supper?"

"Look at the gowns in that window!" Alice dreamed of going home as the most fashionable woman in Atlanta.

Through it all, Dr. Smith continued to laugh heartily at their wonder. "I'm glad to be here with you," he said. "It forces me to look at my own city in a new light. I had forgotten how impressive it can be."

Their lodgings were just as impressive. A patron of the University had offered up his townhome for the visiting scientists, and it was very finely decorated. Heavy burgundy drapes barred the cold that seeped through the floor-to-ceiling windows, and the thick carpets had a scrollwork design. Mahogany wainscoting, marble fireplaces, and family portraits that looked at least a hundred years old made the place both formidable and elegant.

The owner of the home wasn't there, but his housekeeper was, and she greeted them warmly. She explained that her employer, a Mr. McGovern, was staying with his family at their country home north of the city.

Alice's eyes widened. "How very rich they must be!" she told Roland in an undertone.

Roland was given the master suite, and Alice was put in a smaller, but still elegant, guest bedroom. She had time to acquaint herself with the lavender-trimmed room before the housekeeper knocked on her door and invited her down to supper.

Alice had taken so many meals with Roland and Dr. Smith that they were beginning to feel like family. The first meals on their tour had been a little awkward as everyone tried to make conversation. As their comfort level grew, though, they had become easier. There might not be as much conversation as there once was, but it was more heartfelt and much more enjoyable.

"It seems you won't have to go through the difficult task of choosing a public dining room after all," said Dr. Smith. "I hadn't realized that Mr. McGovern's generous offer included meals."

"I trust we'll be able to meet him and extend our thanks during our stay here?" Roland asked.

"Certainly, certainly."

All three were weary after the day's early start and long journey, and the rest of the meal was taken in near silence. When she was finished, Alice sat back and closed her eyes briefly. The warm fire, crackling happily at one end of the dining room, and her full stomach made her sleepy.

"Alice has the right idea. I think it would do all of us well to go to bed early." Dr. Smith stood up. "I'll see both of you tomorrow. The carriage will be here to pick you up at ten o'clock, and I'll meet you at the University."

"Do you mean you're leaving?" Alice asked.

"Yes, I haven't seen my own home in many weeks. It's not as fine as this house, but I do look forward to returning there."

"I very nearly forgot that you live here," Alice said. "I must be more tired than I thought."

Dr. Smith took his leave, and Alice was left alone with Roland. He gestured to her to follow him, retreating into the study. He sat down on a leather chair, allowing Alice to have the settee, which looked much more comfortable.

Roland leaned his head back and looked at the ceiling; his face was drawn. The excitement he'd had earlier had been overcome by weariness. "Do you miss home?" he said, still staring upward.

"No," Alice said simply.

"You don't miss Fairburn at all? Your mother, your sister?"

"Fairburn? Oh, certainly not. When you said 'home,' I saw Atlanta in my mind. Isn't that odd? I pictured my room in your brother's home, not my room in Fairburn."

"But you don't miss even that?"

"I suppose I miss your family, particularly the children. They are dear things. But you were my best friend in Atlanta, so I don't feel that I've left so much behind."

Roland finally rolled his head forward and looked at Alice. "I'm glad you feel that way," he said.

"Are you homesick?"

"Yes and no. I only miss my study and being able to work on projects in there for hours. I am much happier in my study than I am on a stage."

Alice couldn't help a smile. "And here I thought you loved the notoriety. You seem so comfortable in front of a crowd."

"It's not so difficult once you get used to it, but it's not what I love."

"It's your study that you love, then."

"Working, inventing, discovering new ways to do things. I love that," Roland said.

"I cannot argue with that."

"Do you resent me for not having other pursuits?" Roland asked suddenly.

"I beg your pardon?" Alice couldn't imagine what had prompted the question, nor what it might mean.

"Many men of my upbringing are well-rounded. They play polo, they can sing along when a lady accompanies them on the piano, they join benevolent societies. I was just wondering if you resent my single-mindedness."

"Of course I don't. After all, New Science is really my only pursuit. I mean, I can play and draw and such, but they don't bring me the joy that science does. Besides," Alice continued, "it is not my place to resent it. As long as you behave as a gentleman, I have no right to complain."

"But what if you did have the right?" Roland was looking at Alice earnestly now, his cheeks pale but his eyes bright.

"I don't understand." Actually, Alice thought she did understand, but she could hardly believe her fortune was that good.

"What if your happiness depended on how I live my own life?"

Alice felt a thrill tingle through her body, from her toes all the way up to her scalp. Her breath felt short, and she unconsciously brought a hand to her breast, covering her heart as if it might burst through her corset.

The next words she said might determine her happiness forever. Roland was waiting breathlessly for her answer; the tension in the silent room was nearly palpable. If Alice gave the right answer to his question, perhaps Roland would propose to her then and there. Perhaps he would confess that he really did love her, that his distractedness with the Ghost Machine had been the only thing to prevent his saying anything earlier.

Part of Alice wanted to jump up and proclaim her love for him. She very nearly did so, sliding to the edge of the settee so that her knees almost brushed Roland's. But the calmer, still rational side of Alice's mind knew better. It was very likely that Roland still thought of her as no more than his assistant, and that his intentions were merely platonic.

Alice opened her mouth to speak but no words came. She was too torn between giving her true answer or reciting a polite yet guarded response. Finally, she chose an answer that fell somewhere between the two battling sides of her mind.

"It is your happiness that I care about," she began. Alice took a deep breath and was about to continue when there was a loud knock on the door.

Alice and Roland both jumped. Alice had been so absorbed in the exchange that she had entirely forgotten there was a whole world around them. They both stood up quickly, as if they were children caught doing something naughty.

Roland moved to answer the door, with Alice on his heels. It was Dr. Smith, coming back to hand over one of Alice's hat boxes. The coachman had overlooked it when they first arrived.

When the door was again closed, Alice turned to Roland. Before she could speak, Roland gave her a quick nod. His cheeks were flushed, and he looked away, as if in embarrassment. "Good night, Alice. I'll see you at breakfast. Sleep well."

He turned on his heel and marched upstairs, leaving Alice alone in the hallway. She shook her head sadly, wondering how long it would take before she really knew Roland's mind.

Chapter 25

The next morning was bright and sunny. The winter sky was a deeper blue than it was in Atlanta, and every patch of ice and snow twinkled with sunlight. Alice arose and dressed in a hurry; she was anxious to meet Roland at breakfast in hopes that their conversation of the night before might continue.

Alice was encouraged when Roland greeted her warmly, but once they were both seated at the table, their conversation revolved around the upcoming day's activities.

Aside from a few long, searching looks that Alice glimpsed out of the corner of her eye, Roland behaved as if their conversation in the study had never even started, let alone been cut off abruptly.

There was one marked difference in Roland's behavior once they climbed into the carriage. After he handed her in, Roland settled in next to Alice instead of taking the empty bench across from her. Roland sat so closely that his shoulder and arm rested against Alice's. When she shifted her feet, she found their legs nearly touching, as well.

As the carriage pulled onto the street, Roland leaned over Alice to point out the window. "Look, there's Central Park. We couldn't see it so well last night."

"It's lovely. Do you think we'll have time to take a walk through it while we're here?" Alice was very conscious of how close Roland's face suddenly was to her own, but he settled back into his seat just as she mustered the courage to face him.

"We'll make time, even if we leave our audiences to run the Ghost Machine themselves."

When the carriage finally pulled up to the New Science Studies building on the campus of New York University, Roland and Alice were both laughing. Each was trying to outdo the other in teasing. Alice kept accusing Roland of being excessively fond of adoring audiences, and Roland surmised that Alice only came on the tour because she had known it would mean a new wardrobe.

Dr. Smith was waiting for them when they alighted, and Alice was surprised to see a small cluster of men and women just behind him. All of them had obviously been waiting anxiously for Roland.

After wishing Dr. Smith a good morning, Roland turned hesitantly to the others. Three men instantly stepped forward, pulling out small notebooks and pencils as they did so. Three reporters here to greet Roland! Alice smiled, thinking to herself that for a man who didn't crave attention, Roland certainly handled it with grace.

Roland answered the rapid-fire questions of the reporters, and after a few intense moments, they stepped back to let a photographer capture the moment. The photographer turned to Alice and inquired if she was Roland's wife. He needed to know so he could record who was in the photograph, he told her. Alice smiled in spite of herself, even as she corrected the photographer.

Others in the crowd now came forward to shake hands with Roland. They were mostly male and identified themselves as students and professors of New Science.

Of the few women present, one of them stepped up to Alice. She was perhaps two years older than Alice, and her clothes were the height of fashion, but Alice detected a shrewdness in the woman's smiling face. "You're Mr. Highcroft's assistant, are you not?" she asked.

Alice confirmed it, and the woman put out a suede-gloved hand to shake with Alice. "I'm Bernadette Foley. I just became a scientist's assistant myself. I wonder if you'd like me to give you a tour of the campus this morning?"

Dr. Smith, overhearing the invitation, turned to the newcomer. "How kind of you. Alice, we'll be dealing with a lot of administrative things this morning. A tour would be a lot more interesting for you. We can meet you back at this spot at one o'clock."

Alice graciously accepted Miss Foley's invitation, but inwardly she was hesitant to leave Roland's side.

Still, after Dr. Smith's encouragement and not wanting to seem impolite, Alice felt obligated to comply. Alice turned to Roland, tugging gently on his sleeve to pull him out of earshot of the students who stood eagerly in front of him. "One of the girls here is going to give me a tour. Miss Foley has promised we'll be back here at one to meet you for dinner," Alice said. She hoped that Roland would respond that it was impossible, that he needed his assistant this morning. Instead, he was as enthusiastic about the proposal as Dr. Smith had been.

Resigned, Alice put on her most polite face for Miss Foley. It wasn't the girl's fault, after all. She was being kind enough to entertain Alice, and as long as she was going, Alice hoped they'd get to view some of the students' inventions.

When Alice said as much to Miss Foley, she smiled primly and glanced keenly at Alice. "Oh, we'll be seeing so much more than that," she said. Alice tried to pry Miss Foley for details, but she refused to say any more for fear of "spoiling the surprise."

Alice had expected Miss Foley to lead her right inside the New Science Studies building, so she was surprised when they skirted the building and continued down the brick walkway behind it.

Miss Foley made conversation during their walk, but instead of telling Alice about the University, she asked Alice all about the journey so far. She was especially interested in Alice's account of the demonstration in Washington, D.C.

"I understand the machine's success is due in part to your expertise," she said.

"Mr. Highcroft gives me more credit than he should. I only made some suggestions," Alice said. She was surprised that Roland's glowing praise of her skills had already traveled to New York.

"You sell yourself short, I'm sure. You must be a keen observer if you found fault with such a great machine." Miss Foley gave Alice an odd look as she spoke, almost as though she were issuing a challenge.

Suspecting that Miss Foley might share the same sentiment as Mrs. Crowfoot, she asked, "Are you a member of the League of Women Scientists, by chance?"

"No. Should I be? I have just become a scientist's assistant and am still learning my way."

Alice shook her head. "I am not a member. If you join, they'll encourage you to be your own scientist, rather than serving as someone's assistant."

"I see."

"Who is it that you assist? A professor here at the University?"

"No, he works just off campus. We're close to his laboratory now. I thought I'd take you there first." Miss Foley gestured vaguely ahead, and Alice realized that they had nearly reached the edge of the campus. The brick walkway ended at a wide street, and the neatly-manicured lawns and grandiose marble buildings gave way to narrow, dank townhomes packed closely together along muddy streets.

Alice pulled her coat tightly around her body as they crossed the street. She did it not so much because of the cold—their brisk pace and the sunshine were keeping her warm enough—but because she felt like she needed some barrier between herself and the grimy buildings.

Miss Foley led the way down several streets, which got progressively narrower. Her fur-lined coat and silk boots were so out of place that it was almost comical. Eventually, Miss Foley turned and walked down the steps to a door that sat below ground level.

"His laboratory is in the basement of his townhome here," Miss Foley said, almost apologetically. She knocked sharply on the door three times, and soon after it creaked open. Dim light fell out into the shadowed stairwell, framing a hunched man with goggles perched on his balding head.

"Ah! Miss Foley and Miss Meriwether, welcome!" The scientist opened his door wide to let them in, his voice as cracked and old as the houses surrounding them. Alice noticed that his white lab coat was stained with dark, almost black splotches. If she thought Roland usually looked messy when he was working, then this scientist was downright filthy. She nearly recoiled as he gave her a bow that brought his head far too close to hers. "I am Dr. Mathis."

"A pleasure, Dr. Mathis," Alice said, as politely as she could. She was ushered inside and shown to a low wooden bench along one wall of the basement laboratory. "I'm sorry we don't have finer seating, Miss Meriwether," said Miss Foley. "Since this is a lab, we are not used to entertaining company."

"Of course," Alice said, gathering her skirts up so they wouldn't skim the dirty stone floor. She felt uncomfortable in the dim place, though it was more than the dirt and grime that were affecting her. There was something in the overly polite manners of Miss Foley and the discomfiting smile of Dr. Mathis that put her on her guard. "I hadn't expected to find myself in a lab this morning. I had understood that we were touring the campus."

"Well, there will be time for that later, my dear," the scientist answered. "But first, we have some business to attend to." He leaned back against a high table, which was littered with beakers, cogs, and what looked to be old pieces of scrap metal.

"I understand you were quite instrumental in the success of the Ghost Machine," he began. It was virtually the same thing Miss Foley had said to her, and Alice tilted her head in polite acknowledgment while wondering where they had gotten their information.

"I am in need of similar assistance," continued Dr. Mathis. "A patron of mine has requested a very similar device, and I am hoping you can help me build it. We must devise a way to make ghosts appear, but with as little mechanical equipment as possible. It must be elegantly staged, and less obviously scientific. Perhaps disguised as a lamp or covered with an embroidered screen. Your room and board will be covered while we perfect the machine, and of course we can pay you handsomely."

As shocked as she was at the proposal, Alice immediately thought that there was certainly no way a scientist living in such a squalid townhouse could pay "handsomely." More importantly, though, she knew she had to refuse. How could she ever work for another scientist, especially for one who was building another Ghost Machine? That would be disloyal to Roland, and she was quite surprised that Dr. Mathis would even make the suggestion. Surely he saw the impropriety of it!

"I thank you for the honor of asking me to work with you," Alice answered carefully. "However, I am currently engaged as Mr. Highcroft's assistant, and I assure you I have no inclination to leave his employment."

Alice expected an equally kind response, so she was surprised when Dr. Mathis answered with a frank, "That is unacceptable."

"I beg your pardon?"

"Your services are necessary to me. I doubt I will be able to complete this project without your input, and I've been given only six weeks to complete it, so we must get started immediately."

"You have Miss Foley here as an assistant," said Alice. "Surely she will be beneficial."

"She has done her job in bringing you here. Miss Foley is pleasant enough to look at, but she doesn't have your mind." Alice saw Miss Foley's eyes narrow at the insult to her, but Dr. Mathis continued. "You are known to be the key to making the Ghost Machine work."

"Perhaps your patron should have approached Mr. Highcroft about building one," Alice answered, deciding to be as frank with him as he was with her.

"Mr. Highcroft cannot be involved in this project. You, however, are integral to it. I am prepared to pay you one thousand dollars for your services over the next six weeks."

One thousand dollars! The sum was far more than Alice could have imagined, though it was not nearly enough to tempt her to betray Roland.

Seeing Alice's reluctance, Dr. Mathis tried another tack. "This machine is for a celebrated medium who needs the latest paranormal technology if she is to continue her success. Madame Beauregard is famous for her abilities, and you would be wise to align yourself with such an influential woman."

At the mention of Madame Beauregard, Alice actually snorted in laughter. Of course a woman like Madame Beauregard would want a Ghost Machine! She was already using New Science to fake her séances, so it made sense that she would use science to make real ghosts appear. Alice recalled that Dr. Mathis had said this machine would need a subtle design.

Madame Beauregard would, surely, never admit to using a Ghost Machine. She would simply point to her own talents as the reason ghosts began appearing for her paying guests, and her fame—and income—would grow accordingly. Alice took a moment to compose herself before responding, "I assure you, Madame Beauregard and I are already acquainted, and she will not want my help on this project. She does not care for me or my forward manners, sir."

"She wants help from anyone who can make this machine possible. If you and she are not on good terms, then you need never meet her. Miss Meriwether, I am offering you a significant sum of money. With one thousand, you can easily go on to build your own lab and be free not only of me, but of Mr. Highcroft. You will be an independent woman and so much more than a mere assistant."

"Your money cannot entice me from my present situation," Alice replied, more firmly this time. "I am very sorry, but it is impossible for me to work for you."

A different male voice suddenly spoke up. "If you can't be enticed by money, then perhaps you can be enticed by Roland's losing everything."

Chapter 26

Alice's head whipped around to where the voice was coming from, behind a tall cabinet in one corner of the laboratory. Even before she saw the form that stepped out to meet her, she knew from the voice that it was Jacob Masterson.

"Mr. Masterson, what on earth are you doing here?"

"Trying my best to ruin the man I thought was my friend."

"He was your friend, and still would be if you didn't jump to such ridiculous conclusions."

"He purposely ruined my name so he could have you all to himself. It's bad enough that his invention is getting all the notice, but then I had to put up with him wanting you, too. At least he could have been honest about it!"

Alice shook her head. "Roland was very hurt by your accusations. He never wrote any letter to my parents. Someone clearly did, but I assure you it wasn't Roland. Perhaps it was someone more interested in protecting my sister Emma."

"And I suspect you're just taking his side. Maybe you won't be so inclined to help him when he loses the remainder of his funding. I know your fiancé," Jacob spat the word out as if it were vulgar, "will withdraw his funding if he suspects inappropriate behavior between yourself and Roland."

Alice gasped. She knew Jacob was selfish, but this was even more than she had expected him to be capable of. Not only would he get Ian to withdraw his funding, but he would ruin both hers and Roland's reputations in the process! All of this, Alice realized, over a letter that Roland didn't even write.

"So, you hired Dr. Mathis to build a rival Ghost Machine," Alice conjectured.

"Yes. I knew if I approached you and asked for the help myself, you wouldn't hesitate to say no. I didn't realize you'd be so difficult to convince, especially with so much money available. I should have known the only way to your heart was through Roland's ruin."

Alice frowned, still trying to piece everything together. "And Madame Beauregard?"

Jacob shrugged. "I needed someone with enough fame who could overshadow Roland and his stupid invention. If she could seem to summon ghosts without need of a special device, then Roland's invention wouldn't be nearly as sensational."

Alice stood, feeling her anger rise. "Mr. Masterson, you are the most ridiculous man I ever met!" At this, Jacob reared back, shocked by her honest opinion. "Even if you had gotten my father's consent, you would have never gotten mine. As for Roland's funding, I assure you he is quite safe with his benefactor. Ian knows I would never behave in such a way. Even if he did think it possible, we've had Dr. Smith with us to act as my chaperone."

Jacob's face grew redder as Alice spoke, and his chest was heaving. Alice expected an outburst and steeled herself for the onslaught, but Jacob merely pointed a shaking arm at the door. "Get out," he said, his voice barely audible.

Alice needed no further invitation. She swept past

Dr. Mathis and Miss Foley, who both looked confused and scared, and was up the steps and back on the street within seconds. Alice walked as quickly as she could back toward the campus, hoping her memory of the route was correct.

She rounded a corner and saw the brick tower of the New Science Studies building just a few blocks away. Alice was so busy looking up at that guidepost that she didn't notice the man in front of her until she ran into him.

"Alice! Are you all right?" Alice brought her eyes down to meet Roland's blue ones, just inches away from hers. When she collided with him, his arms had instinctively gone around her waist to steady her. Though she was clearly still firmly balanced, Roland's arms didn't move.

"Yes, I'm fine. But it was Mr. Masterson, and he's so mean, and he set this whole thing up with Miss Foley and Dr. Mathis, and he wants to ruin you!" The words tumbled from Alice's mouth just before she felt tears running down her cheeks.

Roland's expression was grim, but his voice was sympathetic. "I know. A professor asked where you were, and when I said you were in the care of Miss Foley, he mentioned that she was acquainted with my former investor. I suspected something odd was going on and immediately got directions to where I might be able to find you."

Alice quickly explained Jacob's plan and her intended role in it. "When I refused, Mr. Masterson threatened to make claims against our reputations, hoping it would get Ian to withdraw his funding," she concluded.

"And what did you say to that?" Roland's face seemed even closer to Alice's now, and she felt her breath catch before she could answer.

"I assured him that Dr. Smith would stand in our defense, if it came to that. I think he finally realized that you have too many friends to be vulnerable to his schemes. He was very angry."

Roland grimaced. "I've no doubt. I don't think we've heard the last of him, either."

"All over a letter you never even wrote."

"Yes, but at least I don't have to worry about him trying to steal you away from me anymore." Without waiting for a response from Alice, Roland tightened his grip on her waist and kissed her. Surprised, Alice stiffened for a moment before she recovered her senses and returned the kiss.

Finally, Roland pulled back, and Alice was once again looking into his eyes. "I don't just want an assistant, Alice. Today, when I heard you might be meeting with Jacob, it was more than jealousy that I felt. I was afraid for you, knowing how angry he is with both of us. As I was walking here I realized I couldn't bear the idea of any harm coming to you. I also realized that with two men trying to marry you already, I had better make my own affections known before someone else came along and claimed you."

Alice's wide smile was the only answer that Roland needed to know she returned his feelings, but she still said, "No one else could have claimed me, but I was beginning to think you'd never realize it."

After so many months of feeling that Roland either didn't care for her or just didn't know how to tell her, here he was actually confessing his affection! Alice laughed with joy, and soon Roland joined in, the dreary scene around them momentarily forgotten.

Roland linked Alice's arm through his, and they walked back to the University slowly, completely absorbed in their conversation. They smiled at each other and spoke with enthusiasm, covering every topic of interest to them except New Science.

About the Author

Beth Dolgner started writing short stories at a young age, and having a journalism teacher for a dad certainly set her on the right track. After she graduated from Florida Atlantic University with her degree in Communications, Beth began working as a freelance writer, journalist and public relations representative.

"Georgia Spirits and Specters," Beth's first book, debuted in the spring of 2009 and was followed by "Everyday Voodoo" in 2010. "Ghost of a Threat," Beth's first novel, debuted in October of 2011 and is the first in the Betty Boo, Ghost Hunter Series.

In her free time, Beth enjoys traveling, sewing and riding motorcycles. She and her husband Ed live in Atlanta, Georgia, with their five cats. Beth is online at www.BethDolgner.com.

Made in the USA
Lexington, KY
18 October 2012